A Final Thread: A Christian Suspense Novel

Book 3 in the Dangerous Redemption Collection

Robert Goluba

Evertouch Publishing

Edited by Laurel Garver

Cover Design by Stephen Novak

Contents

Dangerous Redemption Collection

Each book in the Dangerous Redemption Collection can be read as a standalone story, but for those that prefer the series experience, I recommend reading in the following order:

- Absolute Command, the prequel to Inviting Danger.

- Inviting Danger, Book 1

- Last Second Chance, Book 2

- A Final Thread, Book 3

Email Notification List

If you want to receive updates about new releases, discounts and promotions, and exclusive stories, sign up for my email notifications at: https://robertgoluba.com/newsletter/

OR

Text **NEW** to **(844) 465-7100** to receive a text notification of each new book I release. Nothing else. Ever.

Chapter 1

Alex Garza rose from his desk chair, stretched, and walked to the windows of his new corner office. The streetlights illuminated his solitary vehicle in the parking lot. Yet another Saturday, he'd worked into the dark and missed dinner. He turned back to his desk, powered off his laptop and adjusted the pictures of his family he recently added to his desk.

His lips curved upward at the five faces smiling back at him. It was a picture from their vacation to San Diego last summer, and Alex beamed at the sight of his family. The setting sun turned the surface of the ocean into a mosaic of red, orange, and purple, which highlighted the glow in his wife Allison's eyes. Olivia, Gaby, and Daniel sat patiently and smiled wide at the camera after a stealthy bribe from Allison of ice cream from their favorite shop on the pier.

Alex turned to the adjacent frame with a similar image from thirty-five years ago. It was one of the few times Papa took time off from work to treat his family to a week in Cancun. Alex and his two brothers still had sand on their faces, and their hair flapped in the wind when the friendly stranger snapped the picture. His father's powerful eyes still captivated Alex to this day.

"Check out this office, Papa," Alex said to the picture as he picked it up and rotated in his chair. "Not as big as yours, but I'm getting closer." He set down the frame gently and snatched his keys from the top drawer.

Alex directed his black Volvo XC90 luxury SUV to his home twenty minutes away in North Scottsdale. The visitor parking pass from Florence State Prison sat in the passenger seat, reminding him of his failure that morning.

It seemed like a week had passed, but seven hours earlier Alex had attempted to enter the prison to attend a worship service for the inmates. His older brother Mateo led the service through a non-profit organization they started together a decade earlier. They formed Education Stars Behind Bars or ESBB to help inmates prepare themselves for success before they were released back into society. Although the brothers started ESBB together, it had been years since Alex crossed through the multiple layers of security to attend an ESBB event inside a prison. He thought he could accomplish it today and drove seventy-five minutes to attend the service, but the tightness in his chest only worsened at the sight of the high fences lined with razor wire. Alex tried to convince himself that he was ready to enter the prison while in the visitor parking lot, but when his head began to throb, he started his vehicle and drove to his office instead.

Alex pulled from his office parking lot and started for home. He tapped a button on his steering wheel and commanded the pleasant female voice to call Mateo.

"How was the service?" Alex asked.

"It was amazing. Four men gave their lives to Christ today. I wish you would have been there to see it."

"I'm sorry. I thought I could, but I felt a panic attack coming on in the parking lot. I had to get out of there. I'm grateful for your leadership at ESBB, and I want to be a part of things as much as I am able."

"I understand. I appreciate that you tried. It means a lot to all of us."

"Let's both focus on each of our strengths from now on. I'll raise as much money as possible this year."

"I don't doubt that," Mateo replied with a chuckle.

As Alex neared his home, the streets lined with palm trees in the median transitioned to a narrow road resting under thirsty branches of palo verde and mesquite trees. The engine's roar grew louder in the cabin as it climbed higher into the foothills of the McDowell Mountains. Alex looked in his rear-view mirror and noted the city lights' twinkle growing on the horizon behind him, a vista that he never ceased to admire. This view was a key motivation behind the missed dinners with Allison and long business trips earlier in his career. After he descended through a dry wash in the road, the familiar view of the terra cotta tile roof with beige stucco surrounding his six-bedroom single-story home appeared in his headlights.

Alex arrived and found every light on inside the house with the TV playing in an empty family room. He continued his journey to the adjacent kitchen and found Allison leaning over the island in the kitchen, scrolling through her phone. The pendant lights deepened the red of her strawberry blonde hair. She didn't greet him or even glance in his direction.

Alex noticed the empty dishes in the sink and his shoulders slumped. "Sorry I'm late. I got caught up on something at work."

Allison shook her head and tapped on her phone for a few seconds. "You'll have to make yourself something. We have leftovers in the fridge."

The cool response sent Alex to the refrigerator. He pulled open both stainless steel doors and noticed a bowl of beef stew on one shelf and a half of the sausage loop that he grilled two nights ago.

This wasn't the dinner Alex was hoping for after another long week. His stressful day needed a better ending than his meager options in the fridge.

"I have a better idea."

Alex took several steps toward the long hallway near the kitchen. "Daniel, Gaby, and Olivia come into the kitchen!"

Seconds later, his youngest child Daniel and middle child, Gaby, trotted down the hallway and into the kitchen.

"Dad!" they cried as they gave their father a group hug.

"Do you want to go out for gelato?"

"Yes!" They responded in stereo.

Allison frowned. "It's kind of late to be heading out for ice cream."

Alex looked at his watch. "It's open until nine, so if we leave now we can still make it. Everyone grab your shoes and meet at my car in two minutes. Oh, and Gaby, could you tell your sister?"

"Try texting her," Gaby replied.

Alex typed *salted caramel gelato? Leaving in 1 min* into his phone and hit send. Three minutes later, Olivia joined the rest of the family in the kitchen.

The Garza family closed down the neighborhood gelato shop. Everyone except Allison chose two scoops of their favorite frozen treat and took their cones to the outdoor tables while the owner locked the door and turned off the neon sign.

"I want to own my own gelato shop," Daniel said after taking a long lick of his frozen dessert.

"Why's that? So you can eat gelato every night?" Alex teased.

"Well, not just for that. I want to own a business. I want to own a hundred gelato shops."

Alex felt a warm sensation in his chest and it was impossible not to smile. He leaned over and put his hand on Daniel's shoulder. "I bet you'll own a thousand."

Daniel flashed a quick grin and resumed the destruction of the bottom scoop.

"Gaby, what about you? What do you want to do when you grow up?"

Gaby looked to the sky and then smiled. "I want to be a lawyer."

"A lawyer? That's exciting. Do you want to be a prosecutor and put bad guys in jail?"

Gaby's smiled disappeared. "No, I want to help people stay out of jail like you and Tio Mateo."

For a second, Alex felt like he might tear up, but he regained his composure. He stood and moved behind his middle child and kissed the top of her head. "I love that idea."

Alex sat back down and turned to Olivia. "How about you? You only have a couple more years in high school. What do you want to do?"

Olivia picked at her cone with her fingers and shrugged her shoulders.

"You don't know or you don't want to tell us?" Alex asked.

"I don't know."

"Is there anything that you think you'd be good at or would find rewarding to do for a career?"

"I don't know. I really don't think about stuff like that right now."

Alex tilted his head, "You are going to have to pick a college in a little over a year so you should start to think about—"

"She said she doesn't know right now," Allison interrupted. "Let's not rake her over the coals for it."

"I'm not trying to rake her over the coals. Olivia is very smart and can do anything she wants with her life, so I don't think it's a bad idea for her to think about what she wants to do."

"I know that may come naturally for you, but Olivia isn't ready yet. I didn't have any idea what I wanted to do while I was in high school. She still has plenty of time to figure it out."

Alex put his arms up in surrender. "Fine, I won't put any more pressure on her. I just want what's best for the kids."

The only sounds from the table were the crunching of their cones until Daniel started naming all the flavors he would make in his gelato shops.

When they arrived back home a few minutes before ten, Alex sent everyone to the back yard with a promise of a surprise. He popped into the garage and pulled out the box he'd been saving for their New Year's celebration.

Minutes later, Alex arrived on his back patio with Allison and all three kids waiting for him in the balmy Arizona air. They stood on the stone patio and waited for their father to reveal why they were standing outside.

Alex held up a large box of fireworks. "I don't think we properly celebrated my new promotion. Mateo purchased a ton of fireworks during his last trip when he drove to see Mama and gave these to us."

Daniel and Gaby jumped and clapped for the looming light show. Olivia and Allison did not share their enthusiasm.

"You're going to upset the neighbors. They might call the police on us this time," Allison said.

Olivia moaned, "Really, Dad? This is so embarrassing."

"This is embarrassing?" Alex asked. "So screaming for your mommy to protect you from baby dinosaurs when you saw a little lizard in the yard was cool?"

Olivia rushed over and slapped Alex gently on his arm, "I was four, Dad. It was the first lizard I saw in our yard. I didn't know it was harmless."

Alex laughed, continuing to remove the packaging and assemble the fireworks display.

He clicked the lighter flint and ignited the wick for a chain of fireworks. Moments later, an explosion of bright red and green burst eighty yards above them and cascaded into their yard. The explosive display of colors continued with more red, green, white, and blue bursts. Alex turned from the sky and scanned his family as they basked in the glow of each explosive display of color. A reflection of light appeared in their eyes just above the smiles on their faces.

Alex didn't care about angry neighbors or the police. He wrapped an arm around both Allison and Olivia, and for a moment, neither of them shrugged it off as bright colors flowered in the air. A wide smile formed and held on Alex's face until the sky turned black again.

Chapter 2

Alex arrived five minutes early for his meeting with Dennis Park, the Executive Director of the Scottsdale branch of Emerson Churchill Consulting and Alex's new direct supervisor. At ten o'clock, the door opened and Mr. Park welcomed Alex into his office.

He shook Alex's hand and pointed to a round table with four chairs in the corner of the colossal space overlooking the urban mountain peaks.

Mr. Park was four years younger than Alex and was on an enviable trajectory to a senior position in the New York City corporate office. The Stanford Business School graduate and eldest son of Korean immigrants was on the fast track to the top at Emerson Churchill.

"I'm sorry it took so long for us to meet in person. I was in New York for the last two weeks, first for a partners meeting and then last week for a budget and planning session for next year."

Alex smiled. "I know you're very busy, so I'm happy that we can meet today."

"So, Alejandro, how are you getting settled into your new role?"

"Please call me Alex."

"As you wish. Alex, how was your first month as senior director of business development?"

"It's been both challenging and exciting. I'm eager to bring in some new clients."

"That's good to hear. We need to increase our client base and revenue at a much higher rate than we have in the past. Last week the partners were clear that they have high expectations for the

Scottsdale office, and your contribution will be instrumental to our success."

Mr. Park leaned toward Alex.

"Do you know what makes Emerson Churchill unique to our clients?"

Alex cleared his throat and gripped the arms of his chair tighter. "We focus on tax, IT, HR, and strategic management for small to medium-sized companies so their owners and leaders can focus on growing their business."

"Exactly! Unlike most of our competitors, we become a partner to smaller companies so we can grow with them for years to come. That's why we created the new position you are in today. The senior director of business development will engage the business community and foster new relationships that grow into Emerson Churchill clients."

Alex nodded. "I look forward to building strong relationships with the business community."

Mr. Park rose and walked around the table. Alex stood when he extended his hand for another handshake.

"It will take a significant investment of your time in the community, but I know you are up to the task. That's why we selected you for this new position."

The seriousness in Mr. Park's eyes caught Alex by surprise, but he was able to recover.

"I look forward to it."

The meeting ended, and Alex returned to his office. Although it was half the size of Mr. Park's office, it had an optimal view of Camelback Mountain beyond the parking lot. Alex stood in front of his black leather office chair and let gravity pull him into his seat. He locked his fingers behind his neck and enjoyed the view from his window.

He was on the path to becoming a partner, a word that still tickled Alex's ears after three decades. When Alex was seven, Papa's brother, Tio Miguel moved to Chicago to work for a large accounting firm. A year later, Tio Miguel hosted an enormous party when he was promoted to partner and Papa bought plane tickets for everyone to attend the celebration. It was Alex's first time on a plane and his first time seeing snow, but that's not what made the trip so memorable. He could feel the pride radiating from Papa when he heard the news from Tio Miguel. Papa walked around the house for days saying, "Miguel is a partner now. I can't wait to see him." Alex longed to get that same reaction from Papa. He assumed becoming a partner was the key to admiration and love from his father. Now Alex was closer than ever to knowing.

Alex would never forget the day that Papa's success as an executive for a concrete company changed his life forever. His father returned from work to their modest home in Santa Catarina, Mexico, a suburb of Monterrey in Northeast Mexico, where Alex and his big brothers Mateo and Edgar enjoyed playing with dozens of cousins and having noisy, joyful gatherings with extended family nearly every week. Antonio assembled his wife and three boys in the kitchen filled with the familiar aroma of fresh ground chilies and simmering pork.

They sat in chairs and stared quietly at their father standing before them. Alex rubbed his thumb nervously along the rough mortar and pestle that has been a fixture on their table since he was born. That was when Papa announced he was getting promoted. Everyone clapped at first, but Antonio did not smile. Alex didn't hear his next words as much as he felt them.

"We have to move to the United States. We will live in Phoenix, Arizona."

A wide range of emotions washed over Alex. Fear was first to appear. He has lived nowhere but Santa Catarina, and outside of a few vacations in South Padre Island in Texas and their single visit to Tio Miguel in Chicago, Alex had limited knowledge of the United States. He was happy living in Mexico, having Mama's sisters and their children right in the neighborhood, and being free to roam from Tía Maria's to Tía Victoria's to Tía Linda's, stuffing his pockets with sweet and spicy Pulparinda candy along the way.

Excitement was the next emotion to emerge. Alex had seen TV shows with people living in America like *Beverly Hills 90210*, *Friends*, and *Saved by the Bell*. He'd heard about other families from his neighborhood moving north to the land of opportunity. He dreamed about all the exciting things he could do in a new country like wear designer brand clothes from the mall, see all the best music groups in concert, and buy a red sports car after he got a job. The United States was a shiny object in the distance, and Alex wanted to get closer.

The first impression of the United States was positive for Alex. His family moved into a house in Phoenix with a swimming pool and a bedroom for everyone. He noticed dozens of other boys and girls outside enjoying the impeccable February weather in the Valley of the Sun. After exploring his neighborhood, Alex was pleased to find a grocery store, convenience store, and a gas station within walking distance where everyone spoke Spanish, which helped Alex feel more comfortable. He loved his fruity candy and trying to speak English to purchase his lemon- and lime-flavored treats was a source of anxiety for young Alex. Once he resolved his candy-related concern, Alex settled into his new house in a land a thousand miles northwest of his old home.

The Garza family took advantage of their new residency in Arizona. They enjoyed Jeep tours amid the red rocks of Sedona, went hiking in the Grand Canyon, and floated down the Salt River in old tractor inner tubes.

Although Alex missed his family and his friends back in Santa Catarina, he was happy they moved to Phoenix. It brought him closer to Mateo and Edgar as they stuck together to explore their way around this unknown world.

Edgar hung out with his younger brothers more than most teenagers. He'd take them for a bike ride to the edge of the desert to show them how to find lizards and scorpions under rocks. He taught them how to negotiate for extra candy with the clerk at the convenience store, and Edgar spent countless hours teaching Alex how to hold a bat and catch a baseball.

Ping.

A text notification appeared on Alex's phone. He leaned over the phone on his desk and saw it was from Allison.

Call me. We need to talk.

Alex dialed Allison.

"Guess who I just got a call from?" Allison asked when she answered the phone. He could tell by her tone that she was annoyed.

"Who?"

"Mrs. Steele, Olivia's biology teacher."

A teacher had never called home before, but Alex sensed it was not good news. "What did she say?"

"Olivia failed a test and had the opportunity to retake it to raise her grade. Olivia said she would come in to retake the test during lunch but then never showed up. Mrs. Steele said that was out of character for Olivia and wanted to know if everything was okay at home to cause such a dramatic change."

"What? Olivia always gets good grades. That's not like her to just blow off a test," Alex said.

"I know. I told Mrs. Steele I wasn't aware of anything at home or with friends, but I'm not sure that is completely true."

"Is something wrong that I don't know about?"

"No, but I'm not so sure about those two new girls she's hanging out with. She seems to really like them, but Olivia has been acting different since she met them."

Alex didn't want to consider that Olivia could choose to hang around girls that are a poor influence. That was a sensitive topic for him, and he'd rather avoid it now until he had more information. "Olivia's sixteen and a sophomore now, so she's changing a lot every year. We need to find out why she failed that biology test."

He hung up and spun around in his chair until his back was to his desk. Alex looked straight at the side of the mountain outside the window, but saw nothing.

The call prompted a scene from three decades ago to appear to Alex. He and Mateo were sitting with fourteen-year-old Edgar on the banks of one of the Central Arizona Project canals. They threw rocks at the carp and shared what they wanted to do once they grew up. Alex couldn't remember the exact details of the conversation but remembered they all had big dreams for their educations, careers, and families of their own. Many of those youthful dreams had come true for Alex and Mateo, but not Edgar.

Alex shook off the images of teen Edgar and turned back to his computer. He had to find local business networking events. Forty minutes later, he'd identified a half dozen business mixers in the Phoenix metro area that he planned to attend.

Chapter 3

For the next two weeks, Alex left his office at six and drove to a restaurant, bank, or other small business to meet local business leaders and owners. He enjoyed representing Emerson Churchill while he outlined the benefits his firm could deliver to each company, but it wasn't the same as when he spoke on behalf of Education Stars. Alex still got excited to share the mission and vision that he co-created with Mateo to turn every inmate into a new person ready to benefit society. Typically, Alex received substantial donations by the end of each event, which validated his efforts. Networking for Emerson Churchill had less immediate results and required more tedious follow-up, a chore for a go-getter who expected instant results.

At the end of the two weeks, Alex had a handful of strong leads and a more extensive list of prospects. During that time, his networking efforts were successful, but he had to do it all over again week after week. Now he knew what Mr. Park meant when he said the new position would require a significant time investment. Alex arrived home after nine each night after leaving fourteen hours earlier.

Is this sustainable?

The mere thought of doing anything to deviate from his path to partner at Emerson Churchill snapped Alex back into attack mode.

"Just a little short-term pain for a big long-term gain," Alex said to himself as he drove home down the dark freeway after his final meeting of the week. "Just a small price to pay today for future success."

The next Saturday, Alex slept in and was meandering to the back patio with a cup of coffee when his phone buzzed.

"Hey, Papa," Alex answered.

"Hi, Alex. Are you at the office right now?"

"No, I'm having coffee on my back patio. It's Saturday."

"Oh, okay," Papa responded. The call was silent for several seconds.

"Did you see the truck I bought? I posted it on social media and noticed that neither you or Mateo liked or commented on it."

"I've been very busy the past few weeks so I haven't opened up any of the social media apps on my phone."

"But you said you're enjoying your coffee after ten on a Saturday," Papa quipped.

Alex sighed. Nothing was good enough for Papa. "I already put in almost seventy hours so I wanted a minute or two to relax."

"That's great, Alex. Be sure to show your kids how important it is to work hard if you want them to amount to anything in life. My kids all got to see how hard I worked and I think that motivated you and Mateo to work hard, so be sure to model it for your kids. By the way, how are my grandkids doing?"

Alex shared the usual highlight reel of the accomplishments of Daniel, Gaby, and Olivia. The good grades, club ribbons, and sports trophies. Papa loved to hear all the good news, but when Alex talked about the unusual behavior from Olivia, Papa cut him off and ended the call. This was typical of Papa. He always was a hard worker and achieved success in his career because of his efforts, but he didn't like to discuss any of the actual stuff that accompanied the highlight reel in life. Papa was the same way growing up, and Alex's older brother Edgar did not have the same success in school, sports, and life as Alex and Mateo. He saw his father sweep problems he didn't want to deal with under the rug versus fixing them. Alex still thought about the missed opportunities to help Edgar.

Two years after the Garzas moved to Phoenix, storm clouds gathered over their lives. Mateo and Alex developed a good grasp of their new language, and they primarily spoke English with friends and at home with their father. Edgar and their mother, Ana, preferred to speak Spanish. This affected the success of the Garza boys at school. Mateo and Alex achieved good grades while Edgar struggled. At first, it was just his grades, but then Edgar got reprimanded for disciplinary problems. Ana would drive to the high school, nod at the vice-principal and take Edgar home for another suspension. Antonio was rarely around to help Ana with problems at school or with Edgar. He worked long hours and traveled extensively with his new position in the United States. Alex saw the fear and sadness in his mother's eyes every time she had to pick up Edgar from school.

During that school year, Alex started fourth grade, Mateo sixth, and Edgar high school. Alex and Mateo joined sports teams at their schools, while Edgar got involved with a group of young men with little parental supervision and even less hope for the future.

Alex noticed the sudden change in his brother. His once approachable and patient sibling grew distant and angry. Alex had seen the other boys hanging around the convenience store and gas station in the past and knew they were trouble. Two of them were permanently expelled from school for breaking the nose and jaw of a classmate when they attacked him for bumping into them before school, plus several local shop owners banned all of them for shoplifting. Now Edgar was part of that group and that concerned Alex.

"Edgar is acting differently now that he's hanging out with those new guys. Do you think we should tell Papa?" Alex asked Mateo.

"No, don't bother Papa with that stuff. Edgar is a teenager now, and they rebel against the rules. It's part of growing up," Mateo replied.

"Are you sure?"

"Yes, I'm sure," Mateo answered with the calm confidence Alex needed to hear.

Not long after Edgar turned fifteen, he had his first encounter with the police. The owner caught him shoplifting with his friends at the convenience store near their home. Because of his age, Edgar got off with a warning. Alex wasn't so lucky. The store owner knew he was Edgar's brother and stopped giving him extra candy.

Alex was sure his parents would take more interest in Edgar's antics and intervene after the police brought him home, but nothing changed. Antonio continued to work long hours while Ana spent hours on WhatsApp talking to her mama and sisters back in Santa Catarina.

Edgar continued to drift away from his family, and his sixteenth birthday marked a higher level of defiance. He was suspended twice from school and once ran away from home for five nights. Antonio and Ana fought about Edgar while Alex and Mateo continued to thrive in school and sports.

Once Edgar turned seventeen, he was barely recognizable. Alex thought he looked similar to the young men who always stood outside the convenience store Edgar once warned him about. The confused boys in the bodies of grown men lived for the moment with no concern for the future. Baggy pants, tattoos, and crooked hats were the uniform of Edgar's new team.

Despair grew in Alex. It was apparent to him that Edgar had chosen to take the wrong path, and without intervention, he'd never find his way back. He waited for his parents to do something, but they did nothing to alter Edgar's path. Neither did Alex.

Alex blamed two things for Edgar's demise. First, he faulted the lack of specialized educational opportunities for a young man in Edgar's position; hands-on courses in trades would have enabled him to feel accomplished despite his poor English. Alex also blamed his father. He felt that his father should have seen the signs that Edgar was veering off the right path and got him back on track. Instead, Papa did nothing and blamed Ana for Edgar's behavior.

Alex also blamed one other person—himself.

Chapter 4

The cool nights in October arrived, but Alex could not enjoy them. He was still working late almost every night while attending business networking and social events. On a Tuesday night, Alex took part in a business event in Chandler, Arizona, a bustling suburb southeast of Phoenix where Mateo lived.

One hour into the event, Alex wasn't feeling the energy to pitch Emerson Churchill to potential clients. He was physically and mentally exhausted. He texted Mateo.

I'm leaving an event a few miles from you. Will you be around if I stop by?

Mateo responded that he just put four juicy ribeye steaks on the grill and would save some for Alex.

Mateo's wife Daniella greeted Alex at the door. They exchanged kisses on each cheek.

"It is so nice to see you, Alex. What brings you down to Chandler?"

"I had a business networking event over at a resort nearby. It wasn't the right target customer for me, so I thought I'd visit you instead."

"I'm glad you could stop by. Mateo is in the back with the boys."

Alex and Mateo exchanged hugs. Alex pulled up a chair from the outdoor dining table and Mateo tended the grill.

"Alex, you look tired."

"Good to see you too, Mateo."

"I don't mean it that way, but I haven't seen bags under your eyes like that before."

"I haven't felt this tired in a long time. This new position has me running a hundred miles an hour, and that doesn't include everything at home and fundraising for ESBB."

Mateo held up a bottle of water. "You want something to drink?"

"Nah, I'm good."

"You know what you need to do?" Mateo asked while he pointed his tongs at Alex. "You need to slow down and find balance. Life's a marathon and not a sprint."

Alex suspected Mateo was right. He was missing moments with his wife and kids that he'd never get back, but Alex didn't know any other way. Papa taught him to charge ahead to achieve your goals if you wanted to win in life and Alex wasn't sure how to find balance.

He put his hands in his pockets and turned his attention to his two nephews while they kicked a soccer ball back and forth in the backyard.

"They get bigger every time I see them. I can't believe Ricardo is going to graduate from junior high this year."

Mateo looked through the smoke billowing from the grill at his two sons. He stood straight and stiff as a proud buck watching over his offspring.

"Yeah, I can't believe I'll have a kid in high school. I'm feeling old."

"That's because you are old."

Mateo shook his head, "I just had to wait a little longer to find the perfect wife."

"So that's your excuse for all those weekends without a date?" Alex asked.

Mateo threw the towel resting on his shoulder and they both laughed.

Steaks sizzled on the hot grates as Mateo flipped each ribeye. The sound of the two young boys hanging out together took Alex back to his youth. His first couple of years in Arizona were some of the best in his life. Alex, Mateo, and Edgar always hung out together. Alex cherished his time with his brothers more than anything else.

"We sure had some good times growing up here," Alex blurted while watching his nephews.

Mateo closed the lid of the grill and looked at the boys. "We sure did."

A sheepish grin appeared on Alex's face. "I remember that time that Edgar caught a bull snake and told you it was a rattlesnake. I've never seen you run so fast. I laughed so hard my belly hurt."

"How was I supposed to know the difference? I wasn't about to walk up and investigate it. I hate snakes."

"Did you wet yourself?" Alex asked.

"Did I what?"

"Did you pee your pants? Edgar said you did."

"No, I didn't pee my pants. I ran all the way home and locked the door. For the rest of the summer, I jumped two feet high anytime I saw something that resembled a snake. I almost lost it over a small section of hose in the backyard one day."

The two brothers laughed until it got quiet again.

"It's too bad Edgar isn't here to enjoy this," Alex whispered.

"Don't go there. You've got to stop blaming Papa and yourself for Edgar. He made those choices himself. Neither of you forced him to do anything."

Alex looked down and shook his head. "Papa could have pushed harder to get citizenship for all of us while Edgar was still in high school. The new opportunities from US Citizenship helped you and me get into college, so maybe that would've changed Edgar."

"You know Papa went as fast as the process allowed. He couldn't control that."

"I know. I just wish I could've done more."

"Do more? You've worked with me to create one of the biggest charities in the state to help inmates. You give the Edgar Garza Scholarship to one inmate a year that turns their life around. I don't know many people that have done more to honor the legacy of their fallen brother."

Those words penetrated Alex deep in his gut. For a moment, he considered pulling back from his commitment to Education Stars Behind Bars but knew now that he couldn't. He'd worked hard with Mateo to help get ESBB where it was today. It was his bond with Mateo and a way to honor Edgar.

Alex and Mateo started Education Stars Behind Bars six months after another inmate killed Edgar inside San Quentin prison in California. It was Edgar's third stint in prison for various drug-related charges, and instead of rehabilitating in prison, Edgar just became a better criminal. Alex and Mateo believed that Edgar might have chosen a different path had one been available, so they created Education Stars Behind Bars to provide the skills to help inmates secure good jobs after leaving prison. ESBB provided educational courses on finance, management, and leadership with spiritual healing so inmates could thrive once they re-entered society.

"Thanks. I needed to hear that," Alex replied. He looked toward the ground and muttered, "Now I just need to find balance."

"What's that?" Mateo asked as he spun around from the grill back to Alex.

"How can I find balance between ESBB and Emerson Churchill? I think it would help if I could convince Mr. Park that my time with ESBB is good for the community. I'm not sure what I could tell him, so I was hoping you had some of your patented wisdom I could share with him."

Mateo pointed his tongs at Alex, "You know flattery will get you everywhere with me." The patio was quiet as Mateo looked up at the smoke ascending into the dark sky.

"The key is…"

Alex watched patiently as Mateo worked out the suggestion in his head.

"The key is to get Emerson Churchill to become a corporate sponsor of ESBB. That would help you cut back on multiple fundraising events for ESBB, which would give you back hundreds of hours a year. That would be a good start to finding balance."

Alex considered the suggestion and nodded, "I can see how that would help, but how do I pitch investing in a sponsorship of ESBB to my boss?"

"What about the Arizona Business Angels Awards banquet I emailed you about this morning?"

"What about it?"

"Didn't you get my email that Education Stars Behind Bars is a finalist for an award?"

"No, I planned to read it when I got home tonight. What type of award?"

"We are one of three finalists in their Non-Profit of the Year category in their new Adult Education and Rehabilitation category. The business community hosts the event on the second Saturday in November, and we're given a table at the banquet. I can't go, so you should go with Allison and invite your boss. He'll not only see how the business and non-profit communities complement each other, but he may even see ESBB win an award."

"That's perfect. I'll invite Mr. Park. It would be great if ESBB wins while he is there to see it," Alex replied.

"It's just an honor to be one of the three finalists."

Alex stood up and gave Mateo a hug. "I'm going to head back now."

"I'm just about to pull the steaks off the grill. You sure you want to leave?"

"I don't want to, but I need to. I haven't been home for dinner in two weeks. Balance, remember?"

Chapter 5

A lex strolled into the kitchen thirty-five minutes later and found his family seated around the table. Nobody acknowledged his effort to make it home for dinner. The kids were debating whether a fictional superhero could beat a fighter jet in a race and Allison offered a quick "Hi, honey," when he sat down.

"How was everyone's day?" Alex asked as he sliced into his pork chop.

"I had lunch with Rebecca. It was great catching up after all these years," Allison replied.

Alex tried to flash a confirming smile, but he knew his furrowed brows gave him away. "I'm sorry, who's Rebecca?"

Allison put down her fork and tilted her head, "My old neighbor from Boston that I've been friends with since the sixth grade. I told you that Rebecca and her husband Steve moved to Phoenix a month ago, but we just got together for the first time today."

"Oh yeah, Rebecca. How's she doing?"

Allison did not respond. Instead, she gave her full attention to her asparagus so Alex turned his attention to his kids.

"How about any of you? Doing anything exciting at school?"

Gaby jumped up and started toward her bedroom, "My science project! Come with me and I'll show you."

Alex followed Gaby to her room. She stopped at a large tri-fold poster board on her desk and unfolded it to expose a question stenciled at the top of the middle poster. It said: *Can Different Materials Help Reduce the Heat Island in Phoenix?*

It had aerial images, pie charts, and bar graphs that put any of Alex's presentations at Emerson Churchill to shame.

"Wow, Gaby, this looks amazing!"

Gaby bounced from one chart to another as she explained her hypothesis, testing methods, and conclusion.

"At the rate Phoenix is going right now, if they don't do something soon nighttime temperatures will be intolerable. It's not only about comfort, but it puts pressure on the utility companies to generate more energy during what is normally an off-peak time. Plus, water evaporation and agriculture are negatively impacted. That's why I tested all these different materials to find one that can help with the heat island problem."

Alex stood in front of the display with his hands on his hips. His spunky daughter who was hosting play tea parties a few years ago now sounded like an experienced scientist. She sounded more like an adult for the first time in her life.

He pulled Gaby into his arms and told her the project was amazing while he gave her a tight hug. Alex wanted to show Gaby how proud he was of her. He also wanted to hang on to his youngest daughter a little longer. The poster board showed more than a solution to an important environmental problem. It was a stark reminder that his kids were growing up fast and Alex was missing too much of it.

Minutes later, Alex and Gaby arrived back at the dinner table and finished their meal. Alex helped clear the table and took the empty plates to Allison at the sink rinsing the dishes before putting them in the dishwasher.

"Did you see the project Gaby did for the science fair?" he asked.

"Yeah, she has been working on it since the summer. She took the temperature of all those different building materials in the corner of the yard twice a day."

Alex nodded, although he wasn't sure he ever saw Gaby work on her project.

"I can tell she put a ton of work into it. I wish I would have had more time to help her."

Ping.

Alex pulled out his phone. It was a text from Mateo asking what he thought about the email on the Business Angels Awards.

"You can help Daniel with the Halloween decorations that are due tomorrow," Allison said as she closed the dishwasher. "I think he still has a few pumpkins he needs to cut out and paint."

"Sorry, I can't help tonight. I've got to respond to this. Maybe another night."

Alex hurried to his home office so he could concentrate on the email. He read the email Mateo sent on the Arizona Business Angels Awards twice. He clicked the link and learned that the event was a celebration of the impact that both businesses and non-profit organizations make on the community. Alex couldn't think of a better way to showcase Education Stars Behind Bars to his boss. He spent the next hour fine-tuning his plan to pitch Mr. Park on attending the banquet.

The event was in less than three weeks, so Alex had to invite Mr. Park soon. Alex submitted an invitation to Mr. Park's assistant Lisa for a meeting on Thursday afternoon at three.

This would be the last domino to fall for Alex to achieve the balance he sought; with Emerson Churchill's corporate sponsorship, he could finally pull back from ESBB and give his meager free time to his family. He stood outside Mr. Park's office a few minutes before his meeting started. At precisely three o'clock, the door opened and Mr. Park invited Alex into his office. A ping sounded in Alex's pocket and he reached down and turned his phone to silent in one fluid motion before he sat down.

For the next sixty minutes, Alex updated Mr. Park on his progress with the business community and all the new leads he nurtured into prospective clients. He ended with an overview of the Arizona Business Angels' mission to promote the benefits of businesses and non-profit organizations working together. Last, Alex went for the close.

"Mr. Park, I'm on the board for an organization called Education Stars Behind Bars and the Arizona Business Angels has nominated them for an award at their annual banquet in two weeks. It would be an honor if you and your wife would join us at our table to celebrate this nomination."

Mr. Park smiled. "Thank you for the invitation. What does your organization do?"

Alex was hoping to avoid too much discussion of his past personal life but knew it would eventually come out, especially if Mr. Park attended the banquet. Alex shifted his weight in his chair.

"We provide specialized and individualized education to inmates who want to turn their lives around and live as productive citizens after the state releases them."

"How did you get involved with an organization like Education Stars?"

That was the question that Alex most hoped to avoid with Mr. Park. Alex had kept his personal life private his entire career at Emerson Churchill and preferred to keep it that way, but he was in too deep now. He shared his story about Edgar's struggles and his death that led Alex and Mateo to create ESBB.

Mr. Park nodded. "That sounds like a fine mission and a worthy cause, Alex. Let me discuss it with my wife and I'll give you an answer by the end of this week."

Alex spent the Saturday morning of the Arizona Business Angels Awards writing some emergency emails, then he turned his attention to trimming the shrubs and tidying up the yard. He took a break to enjoy lunch outside near the water feature's soothing sounds from the pool. After lunch, he cleaned the pool and went inside to get ready for the black-tie event.

He heard arguing in the kids' hallway, so he changed course from his bedroom on the other side of the house.

"I told my friends I would meet them out tonight," Olivia shouted.

"And I told you last week that we needed you to stay home and watch your brother and sister tonight," Allison responded.

"I don't need a babysitter," Gaby contested.

"Me either. I'm always stuck with the girls. It would be so much better if I had a brother," Daniel chirped.

Alex arrived as Olivia stomped down the hall and into her room. She stuck her head out and yelled, "you're ruining my life!" Then she slammed her door.

"Is everything alright?" Alex asked.

"Never better," Allison replied as she rushed down the hallway with a smile. "I need to get ready for tonight."

Alex stood in front of the mirror as he tightened his tie and buttoned his suit coat. At forty-four, he still had a thick head of dark brown hair and was in relatively good shape despite his growing potbelly from all his time in the office the past year. Alex smiled at the man in the mirror.

Moments later, Allison walked out of the closet. Alex stared, open-mouthed. Her ankle-length navy dress coordinated perfectly with high heel shoes the same color. The blue hues in the dress accentuated her strawberry blonde hair's redness as it touched her shoulders.

"Wow, just wow," Alex crooned. "I'll have the most beautiful lady in the room on my arm tonight."

"Thank you." Allison beamed.

Alex continued to admire his wife while she added the final touches of makeup. "We should get dressed up more often."

"That would be nice."

"When I make partner, we'll be going to fancy restaurants and charity events all the time. It's part of the job and I can't wait until it's part of our life."

Alex and Allison Garza arrived at the Chateau Luxe event center after the sun retreated behind the western mountain peaks. They turned their SUV over to the valet parking attendant, and Alex escorted Allison through the building and out to the back terrace. The polished travertine tile's expanse provided a 360-degree view of the North Phoenix valley as the white stone glistened under the string of lights.

"Let's go over by the railing so I can take some selfies with all this in the background," Alex suggested as he took Allison's hand. "I'll send them to Papa. This place may even impress him."

As the sky darkened under the moonless night, Alex looked at his watch. The event was scheduled to start in ten minutes, and Mr. Park and his wife were not there. Alex's heart raced.

He accepted the invitation, but maybe he changed his mind.

Alex checked his phone to see if there were any last-minute cancellations from Mr. Park.

"Is everything okay?" Allison asked.

"He should be here by now," Alex replied as he scanned the terrace for another familiar face.

The terrace attendant announced it was time for everyone to head to the ballroom so that the event could start. Alex smiled at Allison and took her hand, but inside he was a mess. Mr. Park needed to see how the business community supported ESBB.

Where was he?

Chapter 6

Alex and Allison weaved through the first batch of tables to one left of the main stage. Alex noticed two people were already sitting at their assigned table. It was ESBB marketing manager Kristen and her husband Mike. Alex flashed a half-smile, and he scanned the room one more time for Mr. Park. He felt his phone vibrate and quickly dug it out of his pocket.

Was Mr. Park lost? Arriving late?

His shoulders slumped when he finished reading the message. Something came up with an important client and Mr. Park could not attend the banquet.

Introductions followed and everyone took their seat. The event began, and they all bowed their heads for an invocation. Pastor Scott from Mountain Shadows Christian Church, Alex's church, led the ballroom in prayer. Once he finished and everybody's eyes were open, the staff served the food and the event began.

For the first hour, a speaker got the audience excited about how companies with a cause and a mission to make the world a better place enjoy greater financial success in the long term. This was the message Alex wanted Mr. Park to hear. But short of pulling out his phone and recording the event like it was one of Gaby's piano recitals, there was no good way to do so.

After the speaker finished, the presentation of the awards began.

Alex watched seven categories of nonprofit organizations get recognized before his category. Education Stars Behind Bars was part of the new category, adult education and rehabilitation.

The emcee announced the category name for the award Alex had been waiting to hear all night. They were next.

Alex closed his eyes and folded his hands underneath the table. He said a silent prayer thanking God for allowing him to be in this position and for the opportunity for ESBB to promote the impact it makes on the community.

The emcee described the category and how the nominees helped adults turn their lives around through education and similar means. Alex opened his eyes when he heard the emcee say, "and the winner is…"

Alex heard a name he had never heard before – RIHARP. Another program was the winner.

Alex's heart sank, but he clapped as eight people from a table nearby stood up and walked to the stage. One of those people was Pastor Scott from the invocation.

A man stepped forward, took possession of the award, and shook hands with the emcee. The man introduced himself as John Nickerson with his wife Stacy, and then he introduced Rey and Christina Mendoza to his right and then Rick and Felicity Powell further to his right and then Pastor Scot and his wife Kelly to his left. Mr. Nickerson shared the story of RIHARP or Residential Inmate Housing and Rehabilitation Program with the audience. He shared how Rey and Christina Mendoza were part of the first wave of families to take an inmate into their home and turn his life around.

He gestured toward Rey and Christina Mendoza, "Your RIHARP inmate, David Kimball, was convicted of murder, but after eighteen months in the guest room of the Mendozas' home, Mr. Kimball is out on parole and working at an oil pipeline equipment manufacturer near Houston."

Next, John Nickerson asked Rick and Felicity Powell to swap spots with the Mendozas. Once they were next to John, he shared how they were the first citizens in Texas to take on a RIHARP inmate and help him become better prepared for life outside of prison.

"Similar to Mr. Kimball, their inmate, James Edmunds, was convicted of murder. John leaned toward the microphone, "I'm proud to announce that Mr. Edmunds has been paroled and is a free man for the first time in twenty-two years. He's prepared to be a productive citizen in Texas because of the Powell family, and I expect great things from James."

The audience approved with applause.

"Thank you. Now Pastor Scott has an exciting announcement to make about RIHARP."

John backed away from the microphone, and Pastor Scott took his position near the mic. He cleared his throat. "If anyone is interested in learning more about RIHARP, we are holding an open house on the Mountain Shadows Church campus in Scottsdale at four o'clock tomorrow. RIHARP is launching a new program in Arizona that specifically works with teens in the justice system, and we are interested in businesses and individual partners that will help us launch this exciting new program."

This revelation knocked the air from Alex's lungs. It took several seconds to catch his breath as he processed all the information that unfolded on stage in the past ten minutes. Not only did ESBB lose to another organization after Alex was confident of a victory, but they lost to a program that was very similar to ESBB. RIHARP was also intriguing.

Alex was quiet during the drive home.

Allison broke the silence. "It's too bad your boss wasn't able to make it."

"I hoped I could get Mr. Park to see how great ESBB is for the community, and maybe get Emerson Churchill to be a corporate sponsor so I wouldn't have to fundraise so much on top of the extra work in my new position. But we lost, so maybe it's just as well he didn't see that."

It was Allison's turn to be quiet.

"The winners sounded like an interesting organization, though. Helping teenagers… it made me think of—"

"Edgar," Alex said.

"I was going to say Olivia. She seems… I don't know, a little adrift this year. When she was in peer tutoring last year, it seemed to give her more of a sense of purpose. I can understand why she might prefer costume design in the drama club, but she's not as happy as when she was helping other kids. I wonder…"

"Should we go to that informational meeting?" Alex asked. He glanced toward Allison, who was gaping at him. "Oh, never mind."

Allison touched his arm. "That's what I was going to say, honey. It's been ages since we've been on the same page about anything."

Alex smiled for the first time since they announced RIHARP as the winner of the award.

Chapter 7

Alex and Allison took their seats at a table inside a room where Daniel attended children's ministry. At precisely four o'clock, the double doors to the room shut, and the meeting began.

Pastor Scott walked to the front of the room and stood beside an empty chair. The people who joined him on the Arizona Business Angels award stage the night before, plus one unfamiliar face, occupied seven other chairs. He walked to the edge of the ten tables that contained people interested in learning more about RIHARP.

"If you attend Mountain Shadows church, you probably know that I moved here from Austin, Texas, fifteen months ago. One program I was proud to launch the year before I left Texas was the RIHARP program. I could see firsthand the effect it had on the inmates, our church, and our community. That's why I helped bring RIHARP to Arizona. Last night we won a prestigious award for our work nine months after placing our first inmate in Arizona with a host family. The award was an honor to receive, but we're not finished. I've assembled much of the team here that was responsible for the success of RIHARP in Texas so we can share more about it and tell you about a new program that we are launching right here in Arizona."

Pastor Scott sat down in the empty chair and then turned toward a fit man sitting in the chair next to him who was about Alex's height with a square jaw and a military-style high and tight haircut.

Pastor Scott gestured toward the man. "Rey Mendoza launched RIHARP in Texas. He also hosted an inmate and has led the Texas Department of Criminal Justice's efforts to place seventy-three additional inmates in homes in under two years. Because of his intimate knowledge of the program, I asked if he would be kind enough to come here and share the program details of RIHARP, and he agreed."

Pastor Scott passed the microphone to Rey.

"Ladies and gentlemen, RIHARP has been a significant change for inmate reform in Texas, and it's already showing promise here in Arizona. RIHARP stands for Residential Inmate Housing and Rehabilitation Program, and that's exactly what it does. RIHARP works with inmates that are serving medium to long-term sentences in state prisons and places them in residential homes to provide those inmates with a positive environment for optimal rehabilitation prior to their release.

"Now, that may sound like a scary proposition if it weren't for an ingenious invention by the man sitting right there." Rey turned and pointed to the tall blond man in wire-rimmed glasses. "John Nickerson invented a new technology called Sure Cuffs, which allows the host to house an inmate while maintaining a safe environment for the host individual or family."

Rey passed the microphone over to John. "Sure Cuffs is your baby, so why don't you share more about how it works?"

John feigned a look of shock but then flashed a smile. "Of course. The success of RIHARP hinges on the high degree of safety we provide host families with the most advanced technology in law enforcement today. It's called Sure Cuffs. Each inmate has tiny rice-sized transmitter chips inserted under the skin in ten key areas of their bodies, and we activate Sure Cuffs with an emergency keyword, GPS, sound, or the Sure Cuffs app."

John stood up and pointed to his wrists, elbows, knees, inner thighs, and hips as areas where they have chips implanted.

"Thanks to families like Rey and Christina during the beta test and Rick and Felicity Powell during our initial launch, we've improved Sure Cuffs to deliver optimal safety for the host families. We like to think we've thought of everything before it will happen in the home of a host family."

Now it was John's turn to pass the microphone. "Rick and Felicity, could you please share your experience with Sure Cuffs and your RIHARP inmate?"

Felicity took the microphone. "I'm not going to lie. We did it for the money."

Laughter filled the room.

"I'm only partially kidding, but we had some bumps in the beginning, and they were all smoothed out by the time our second inmate, James, was granted parole. One time I had to activate Sure Cuffs during a tense moment with an inmate, and it worked as advertised. After that, I felt confident that my family was always safe. Honey, what about you?"

Felicity handed the microphone to Rick.

"I have the same positive feedback on Sure Cuffs. It was hard at first to accept that a convicted felon was alone with someone in your family, but after I saw Sure Cuffs work, I felt completely safe with a RIHARP inmate on my property."

Rick held out the microphone for someone else to grab. Pastor Scott took the cue and took it from Rick.

"Now that you know a little more about RIHARP, I want to share more about the new program we are launching in Arizona. So far, they have limited RIHARP to adults who have served at least forty percent of their sentences, but because of the program's early success, we want to expand it. In the coming days, the state will open up applications for host families to take in a younger inmate or juvenile. One of the key benefits of RIHARP is the reduction in recidivism, and we want to bring that benefit to younger inmates to turn their lives around with plenty of time to live a long, productive life."

Pastor Scott walked down to the end chair and knelt beside the woman sitting in it. The pointy chin of the lady in her upper forties protruded from her mane of wavy chestnut hair.

"This is Anne Lewis, assistant director of inmate programs and rehabilitation at the Arizona Department of Corrections, Rehabilitation, and Reentry or ADCRR, and she has more information to share on this new program," Pastor Scott informed the audience.

Anne took the microphone and remained seated. "Good evening, everyone. As Pastor Scott mentioned, all of us at ADCRR are excited to launch the next generation of RIHARP here in Arizona. We are calling it RIHARP JR. The JR stands for juvenile reform since it will help our younger inmates with a program tailored for their specific needs. Next week, we will start accepting applications for the first wave of citizen hosts."

Mrs. Lewis continued to outline the RIHARP JR program's details when Alex felt an elbow in his side.

"This is interesting," Allison whispered.

Alex nodded. He agreed that it was interesting and hosting may be a distant possibility, but he was also a little disappointed.

Why wasn't a program like RIHARP JR available when Edgar needed it? Early intervention could have saved his life. Why didn't someone think of this sooner?

Despite the potential advantages of participating in RIHARP JR, Alex had his doubts.

How on earth would RIHARP work in the real world? I'd still have to put in long hours to become a partner at Emerson Churchill if I can't get them to become a corporate sponsor of ESBB and that will be a bigger challenge now that we lost the Business Angels award. Plus, I still need to fundraise so Mateo's family and all the others that depend on ESBB wouldn't suffer.

Was this whole idea just a self-serving pipe dream?

The meeting ended, and the panelists walked from table to table to answer questions from the audience. Christina Mendoza and Felicity Powell were the first to stop at the table occupied by Alex and Allison.

"How was it having an inmate convicted of a serious crime living in your house?" Allison asked.

Felicity responded first. "It wasn't easy. I prayed about it a lot, and once I decided it was something we were called to do, I committed to seeing it through to the end. It got easier once everyone got into a routine of having someone living in our house that was in something similar to house arrest. Now I'd consider James a friend."

Christina nodded and asked Allison and Alex a question. "Do y'all have any children at home?"

"Yes, we have three kids from age ten to sixteen," Allison answered.

"That was the hardest part for me, and we had an advantage because Rey used to be a corrections officer, so he knows how to deal with inmates. After several months, I learned to trust the Sure Cuffs technology, and that helped. I also set up physical and virtual boundaries for our inmate David, and that gave me the peace of mind I needed to allow our small children to live under the same roof. It took some time, but the kids also built a relationship with David. He's like an uncle to them now."

Christina and Felicity continued to share their experiences with RIHARP until Pastor Scott interrupted them.

"I'm sorry ladies and gentlemen, but the cleaning crew is heading home soon, and they need to get in here to clean this room for our children's ministry events this week. I'll have a link on our website to access all the information on RIHARP JR. Thanks again to all of you for coming."

Allison gave both Christina and Felicity a hug. They gave her their phone numbers so she could call with questions.

During the short drive back to their home, Allison turned to Alex.

"Well, what do you think?"

"I sure wish this existed when Edgar was a teenager."

"I feel like there's a big 'but' coming. What is it? You think this will trigger your anxiety?"

Alex felt a cold fury rise inside him. "I'm not *scared*, Allison. I'm *concerned* about the huge time-suck a troubled teenager would be when we're already too busy. We couldn't even let Daniel join the club baseball team. And right now… I'm so close to making partner I can taste it."

Allison turned away from him and sniffled. Then she whispered, "but what about us?"

Chapter 8

Allison or Alex didn't mention RIHARP JR for the next several days, but Alex got home for dinner every night, even if he retreated to his home office to work afterward. Among other projects, he was working hard to hone his pitch to Emerson Churchill to become a corporate sponsor of ESBB.

On Wednesday afternoon, Alex entered Mr. Park's office. He presented several slides on how Emerson Churchill would benefit from a partnership with Education Stars Behind Bars.

"We could promote how Emerson Churchill supports Education Stars because we both believe in customizing our programs to best suit our client's needs. Plus, we both stick with our clients long-term to grow alongside them as they achieve higher levels of success just like Education Stars does with our inmate students," Alex reminded Mr. Park as he closed his presentation.

"Your organization is very impressive, Alex. You've given me a lot to consider."

"Thank you, sir."

"I apologize again for missing the banquet, but I would like to see ESBB first hand before I could include it in my expense forecast to corporate finance. Are there other ESBB events coming up that I could attend?"

Alex swallowed hard. All the future events for the next several months were inside the prisons.

"Yes, we do have other events at ESBB that you can attend."

"Great, please give me a couple of weeks of advance notice on another ESBB event I can attend and I'll be there to observe first hand."

Alex wobbled back to his office like a boxer that took multiple body blows and a roundhouse punch to the jaw. He entered Mr. Park's office hoping to get support for ESBB to regain balance in his life, and he left with pressure to walk back into a prison with him. Alex sat down as the room spun.

How can I attend an ESBB event with Mr. Park and convince him to sponsor us if I have a panic attack? This plan may not only be bad for my anxiety but also a disaster for my career.

He lowered his face into his cupped hands and his body stiffened. His eyes closed tighter to block out all the light and escape his current reality. Images of Allison and her gentle touch and soothing voice filled his mind. Alex relaxed and soon he opened his eyes and finished his work.

Alex arrived home earlier than usual, and nobody else was inside. He heard noises out back, so he slid the sliding glass door open and found his family in the pool. Allison reclined in a lounge chair while all the kids and their friends jumped in and out of the water.

Allison looked shocked when she saw Alex heading toward her. "Hey, Honey, I didn't expect to see you home so early."

"Is this what you do all day when I'm at work?" Alex asked with a playful smile.

"The kids wanted to do something with their friends, so I heated the pool so they could hang out here."

Gaby noticed her father. "Hey, Dad, are you coming in?"

"Don't tempt me. I might jump in right now."

That caught the attention of Daniel and his friend, "Do it, Dad!"

Alex shook his head. "Nah, I don't want to jump in with these clothes on."

"Dad, I dare you to jump in now," Daniel shouted as he slapped the water with his Styrofoam noodle.

Gaby moved to the edge of the pool. "I double dare you."

Alex turned to Allison. "Sorry, they double dared me."

After he removed his shoes, Alex set his phone on a table and darted toward the pool. He jumped over Gaby and tackled Daniel in one motion as he entered the cool water. He turned to splash Olivia, but she moved to the opposite end of the pool with her friend.

For the next fifteen minutes, Alex picked up Daniel, Gaby and their friends and tossed them in the pool. After each monster splash, they all pleaded for their next turn, but eventually Alex had to move to the side of the pool to catch his breath.

He watched his entire family having fun, and his heart filled with joy. To get more of this, he would tackle his anxiety. He had to.

Chapter 9

T he clock embedded in the brick veneer above the doors to the conference room displayed a quarter past six. Alex was already fifteen minutes late for his meeting with Mateo and the board of ESBB, but the host of the event would not stop talking.

"The software stores the video in the cloud so you can direct any of your target customers around the world to view your sales presentation," the eager owner shared with Alex. "Plus, you can pull up any video you want with our smartphone app and show it to a potential client anytime or anywhere. It allows for amazing continuity of your sales message."

For a second Alex thought about giving the aggressive sales rep Mr. Park's contact info to pay him back for suggesting he bring him to a prison to see ESBB in action, but he didn't. Instead, he made his second attempt to leave.

"Thank you, Stuart, for the information and interesting overview of your company, but I have to get to another meeting."

"What kind of meeting starts at six-thirty at night?" Stuart asked.

"A board meeting for my non-profit organization, and it started at six."

"Oh, what's the name of your NPO? Do they need any video presentations in the cloud to attract donors? We offer a ten percent discount to non-profits."

Alex was out of words and excuses. He didn't want to be rude but was out of options.

"Have a good evening," Alex said as he moved toward the door and never looked back.

Fifteen minutes later, Alex pushed open the door to the conference room. "Sorry, I'm late. I was at a networking event and couldn't get out any sooner."

The four men and two women in the room stopped to greet Alex. They all exchanged handshakes, and the meeting resumed.

Two hours and fifteen minutes later, Mateo pounded his gavel. "I adjourn this meeting."

Small groups of conversations formed around the room as everyone said goodbye. While the other board members were leaving, Alex put his hand on Mateo's arm.

"Could you stay for a few more minutes? I have something interesting I want to share with you."

Mateo waved to the last board member to leave and sat back down at the board room table while Alex took the adjacent seat.

"What's going on?" Mateo asked.

"I pitched Mr. Park on the potential for Emerson Churchill to become a corporate sponsor of ESBB. He seemed impressed with what I shared and seemed interested in supporting ESBB. But before committing he first wants to see the program in action."

"That's great news, Alex. We have worship services all the time and if you really want to impress your boss, the Fourth Annual Education Stars Behind Bars All-Star Certificate Celebration is in April."

"I thought of that too, but that is months away," Alex whispered. The thought of going into the prison again made him shudder.

The room was silent as Alex scratched at a stain on the board room table.

"I think the certificate celebration is the perfect event, but I have a favor to ask before I invite Mr. Park."

"Sure, shoot. I'll help any way I can."

"I need to do a trial run to get my anxiety under control inside the prison. It's been a long time since I've tried it and I'd like to do it with you first."

"Are you sure?" Mateo asked as he leaned closer to Alex.

"Yeah, I'm sure. I want to take your advice about finding more balance and corporate sponsorship of ESBB by Emerson Churchill is a necessary step for me to get there. I need to do this."

Mateo stood and slapped Alex on his back. "Alright, I'll shoot you some dates and times for our next couple worship services and we'll do this together."

Over the next week, Alex slipped back into his routine of a full day in the office and a networking event after work. As exhaustion set in, RIHARP JR felt like it happened a year ago and was no longer a concern.

After a business mixer at a North Phoenix resort, Alex drove home and went straight to the couch. He kicked off his shoes, loosened his tie, and put his feet on the coffee table. He leaned his head back and closed his eyes.

A minute later, Alison arrived.

"Hi, Hon, did you get my text?"

Alex opened his eyes and sat up. "Yeah, yeah, I'll get to it."

Alison put her hands on her hips. "Alex, the list is growing. Olivia and her friends want to use the hot tub, but it won't heat up. You said you'd look at it two days ago."

Alex dropped his feet back to the floor and put his face into his cupped hands. "Can't you call somebody to look at it?"

"I would have, but you said you would do it. You're barely home anymore, so I thought you would want to help around the house a little."

"I do, but I'm exhausted."

Alex looked up to Allison, hoping to see a sympathetic expression, but when it wasn't there, he stood up.

"Let me change out of my work clothes, and I'll be right there."

Ten minutes later, Alex arrived at a maze of pipes and pumps. He turned on the flashlight on his phone and examined the situation.

"Ah, they didn't turn off the pool intake valve last time. No wonder it wouldn't heat up. They were pumping cold pool water into the spa."

Alex yelled into the house, "I fixed it. It should be warm in a few minutes."

Olivia and her new friends came traipsing out of the house. Four girls and two boys surrounded the spa. All the girls wore bath robes while the boys were still in their jeans and t-shirts. Alex was used to Olivia's old friends that would run around in just their swimsuits without a care in the world. This new group of friends felt more guarded, so Alex approached the teens to initiate some small talk.

"It's a perfect night for the spa," Alex observed out loud.

All the high schoolers looked down at the ground except Olivia. They shared quick glances at each other without looking up and one boy even chuckled. Alex felt like a stranger in his own backyard, so he went inside.

As soon as he closed the door behind him, Alex darted to his bedroom and looked out the window at all six kids whispering to each other in the spa. Olivia's new friends acted differently from all the other kids that spent time in their pool or spa. Perhaps Olivia's friends were nervous or just very shy.

Or were they being sneaky?

Alex continued to justify their behavior in his mind and was sure they'd open up once they got used to coming over. His gut sent a different message. It screamed that something wasn't right with Olivia's new friends.

Chapter 10

S ound waves reverberated off the concrete walls penetrating Alex's bones as the convicted murderer next to him clapped to the beat. Alex used his peripheral vision to scan the array of tattoos on the inmate's pale fleshy canvas to his left. On his right, a short but stout man with a square face and a scar across his forehead bumped into Alex's hip to the same rhythm. Alex inched forward to provide some distance between himself and the room full of men serving life sentences, but the bumping continued. Thick, colorless walls inched closer with each vibration from the bass.

I can't do this.

The first song ended, and Alex exhaled. It wasn't until then he realized that he was holding his breath for the last half of the song. Alex felt his chest tighten as he searched for the exit. The second song started, and once the first chords reached the man's ears with a cobweb tattoo, he grabbed Alex's hand raised it into the air with his. Alex stood on his tiptoes to reduce the four-inch gap between him and the inmate deep in worship.

At the start of the third song, the man dropped Alex's hand and raised both of his hands. Alex spun around and located the exit. A guard was standing in front of the only way to leave the room. Alex struggled to move his legs. He could feel his pulse exploding in his neck. He turned to Mateo behind him. No words were exchanged, but Alex's face shouted he was losing this fight and Mateo understood.

Mateo nodded and Alex scrambled toward the metal door. The corrections officer kept his eyes on Alex and placed one hand on the baton secured in its holster.

"I'd like to leave now," Alex whispered.

"The service just started. Are you sure?" The corrections officer asked.

Alex turned to observe sixty men in white prison uniforms with arms outstretched, all singing and swaying to a popular Christian music song. Mateo was in the middle of the pack, comfortable and engaged with the service. He was in his element.

Alex swung back to the officer and whispered, "Yes, I am ready." The door opened, and Alex passed through three more checkpoints before he returned to the freedom of the asphalt parking lot.

He could breathe again. The dry breeze reduced the perspiration on his forehead, and the heat released from around his collar. Alex's heart rate was almost normal again by the time he arrived at his SUV. Alex climbed inside and pulled the door shut. He pushed the button to start his engine and looked into the rear-view mirror. The brown eyes told him what he already knew. He should never have gone back inside that prison. Alex shook his head and put his vehicle in drive.

Forty minutes after Alex left the parking lot his phone rang. It was Mateo.

"Are you okay?" Mateo asked when Alex answered.

"I'm doing better now. I thought I could make it, but as soon as the music started I knew I had to get out of there."

"Have you ever thought about seeing somebody about your PTSD?" Mateo asked with the same calmness as if he asked Alex what he wanted for lunch. Alex caught his breath and responded.

"I don't have PTSD! I just get anxious in tight spaces. Prisons feel like a coffin to me."

"I'm not trying to offend you. I just know what we went through with Edgar was very traumatic. You were still young when you had to cross through security checkpoints to visit him in prison. That's hard on anybody. There's no shame in getting help to process it."

Alex couldn't remember crossing through the security checkpoints to visit Edgar until he was much older. He didn't have any traumatic memories of that period in his life, so a therapist probably couldn't help him.

"I appreciate the concern, but I'll be fine as soon as all this stress is behind me. Besides, I don't have enough time for all my existing responsibilities as it is, so adding another appointment with a counselor isn't going to happen now."

The call ended and Alex pulled into his garage fifteen minutes later. He told Allison about everything that happened over lunch. They agreed his current high levels of stress weren't helping his situation inside the prison walls.

After they finished talking about Alex's day, Allison shared the stressful schedule she was trying to juggle the next week.

"It's holiday crunch time again with the commercials. I have several full days scheduled to do makeup at the studio so I asked Rebecca to come over and play chauffeur for a couple of days to help," Allison shared as she pushed her empty plate into the middle of the table.

Alex lowered his brows and wrinkled his nose, "why would you have Rebecca come all the way over here to drive the kids around? I'll do it."

Allison reached across the table and patted Alex's hand, "I appreciate the offer, but you're working crazy hours and can't always break away from the office when you want to. Gaby and Daniel can't be late and Rebecca said she didn't mind. I'll return the favor after my busy holiday season is over."

Alex wanted to object but knew Allison was right. She couldn't rely on him to take his own kids to practices or recitals because he overly committed himself to Emerson Churchill.

"Okay, but if something comes up, just have Rebecca call me."

Next week, Allison pushed the button to close the garage door and drove to the studio while the sun was just sneaking up behind the McDowell Mountains. She knew today would be a long day and that it would be dark again before she completed her makeup work for the commercials.

Allison finished her work on three actors in the first commercial. It amazed her when the director called it a wrap and started filming the second commercial hours ahead of schedule.

Now that Rebecca will help take Gaby to piano lessons, I'm going to sneak down to the mall to look for a new Christmas dress.

It had been a while since Allison could shop alone and try on clothes without a kid or husband complaining that she was taking too long. Thoughts of coordinating outfits for their annual family picture at church and then matching PJs on Christmas morning gave Allison her second wind. They were on schedule to finish after lunch, and she was working as fast as possible to achieve it.

The bell rang, signaling that the second commercial finished early.

"Great job, everyone. You get half your day back now!" the director shouted to a happy audience.

Allison skipped lunch two hours earlier to apply makeup to the four actors in the second commercial. She was starving now and envisioned sitting outside along the canal, eating lunch before going inside the mall to shop. After she shut the door to her SUV, her phone pinged.

It was the vice-principal, Mr. Patterson, from Olivia's high school, and he wanted Allison to call him immediately.

Allison dialed the number and spoke to Mr. Patterson in under twenty seconds. He shared that Olivia skipped school and that he wanted Allison and Alex to meet with him after school to discuss the infraction. School would be out in thirty minutes, so shopping was off the table.

Allison texted Alex and told him to call her ASAP. Next, she turned her SUV around and stopped at a sub shop to get a quick sandwich before driving to the school. When she saw Alex did not respond, Allison sent another text.

It's urgent. Olivia is in trouble at school. We need to meet the vice principal after school. Meet me there and call me ASAP!

Allison watched all the students leave the building, and then she entered the administrative office. The receptionist told her to sit in a row of chairs outside vice-principal Patterson's office. Allison could see Mr. Patterson talking to Olivia. Her blood warmed up.

She rechecked her phone—no texts or calls. Now lava coursed through her veins. Olivia was in big trouble at school, and Alex left it all up to her to take care of it.

Mr. Patterson called Allison into his office. She took a seat next to Olivia, who sat with her gaze locked on the floor as he levied the charges against her. Fifteen minutes later, Allison and Olivia left the school and drove home.

The house was quiet when Alex arrived home a little before five. He found Allison putting laundry away in her closet.

"What happened with Olivia?"

"Why didn't you answer any of my texts?"

"I was in an important meeting with Mr. Park."

Allison's pale face turned a deep shade of red as her voice rose with every word. "That's why I can't even rely on you to take Gaby to lessons. You could at least reply so I know what's going on. I shouldn't be the only parent that has to do all this, but that seems to be the new norm around here."

Alex had no rebuttal. He lowered his head and whispered, "Sorry. I will reply next time."

"I'm not looking for an apology; I'm looking for a change. You're busy with work all the time now since they promoted you."

It was Alex's turn to raise his voice. "I know. That's why I'm working hard to find some balance. I need more time."

Allison stared deep into Alex's eyes. The redness in her face faded.

"What did he say about Olivia?" Alex asked.

Allison put a stack of clothes on top of her dresser. "The vice-principal said that Olivia and three other girls left at lunch and never came back. None of them had an excused absence. They all just took off and never returned to school."

"Where's Olivia now?"

"She's in her room. I told her she's lost her phone, and she's grounded for two weeks."

"Did she say why she did it?"

"Yeah, she told me a real whopper of a story. Something about one of her new friends having a headache, and they all went to the store to help her find medicine. They couldn't find what she wanted at the first store, so they tried another store. It took longer than they expected, and then they realized they were going to be late for the first class after lunch. That's when the driver of the car said she would not go back late and turned the car around toward the mall. Olivia said she was freaking out but said nothing to the other girls. She tried to make it sound like she was a hostage and against the whole thing."

"Do you believe her?"

"I want to, but Olivia has been acting strange ever since she started hanging out with those new girls this school year. When she had them over, they seemed… I don't know. I'm not sure they're the best influence on her."

Allison picked up her clothes and resumed putting them away.

Alex's mind raced back thirty years. That was the same thing that happened to Edgar. *Was I making the same mistake as Papa?*

Chapter 11

A lex texted Olivia.

Your mom and I want to talk to you. Come to the family room.

Two minutes later, Olivia shuffled into the family room and sat down. She looked like the little girl she once was a blink ago and at the same time, the grown woman she was destined to become. Her pouty lips and glistening brown eyes always softened Alex in the past, but not this time.

"Why did you skip school?" Alex barked.

"I already told Mom. I don't want to keep telling the same story over and over. I said I'm sorry. What more do you want from me?"

Alex tossed both hands into the air. "Olivia, I want to know why you thought it was okay to miss school. Why didn't you call the school or us to say something came up and you were going to miss a couple classes? That would have been the responsible thing to do."

Olivia rolled her eyes. "It was only two classes. I've missed more school to leave early for vacation or for a dentist appointment. It's not that a big deal."

The words hung in the room until Alex took in a deep breath and exhaled loudly. He stopped yelling and spoke slower.

"Olivia, we are trying to raise you so that you can have the best opportunities in life. If you work for a good company and just don't show up one day, it could get you in big trouble or even fired. It would be really hard to find or keep a good-paying job if you aren't reliable. Would you want that?"

Alex's softer tone with the opportunity to lower the temperature in the room offered a truce, but Olivia was not interested.

"I don't care about climbing the corporate ladder or working all the time to make more money like you do. I hope I never have a job like that."

The room went silent. Alex glared at Olivia, but did not, or could not, make a sound.

Allison jumped in to break the silence. "Olivia, you're grounded. Put your phone and keys in our bedroom. We'll let you know when you can get them back."

Olivia shuffled toward their bedroom with her phone in hand and turned back after several steps, "Am I in trouble because I said I don't want to have a job like Dad?"

"No, you're in trouble because you skipped school," Allison snapped.

"It's just that money isn't that important to me. I want a life."

Allison stood and pointed toward her bedroom. "Keys and phone in our room now!"

The last four words from Olivia stung the most. It wasn't just the rudeness but the pinpoint accuracy that bothered Alex the most. He prided himself that he was good at hiding from his family his fear of failure and total dedication to success at work. His sixteen-year-old daughter saw right through his charade. Alex wouldn't have been able to do the same at her age. He thought every father came home from work hours after dinner to spend a few minutes with his kids before his wife tucked them in for the night. Alex's current situation was eerily similar to Papa's. That wasn't the only similarity. The issues with Olivia were starting to feel familiar to Alex. He'd heard similar fights with Edgar and his parents. He had to do something different soon. He knew the ending to that movie and didn't want to spend a single second watching a sequel.

Alex left work early and drove to the Mountain Shadows Christian Church campus two miles from his home. He parked his SUV near the main worship building and ambled under the canopy of palo verde trees. The worship center was empty so Alex walked around the corner and located a sign with an arrow pointing to the Administrative Offices. A friendly woman in her sixties greeted Alex. She sent Pastor Scott an instant message that he had a guest waiting to see him.

A minute later, Pastor Scott arrived and the two men shook hands.

"Great to see you Alex, follow me."

Pastor Scott led Alex past several offices and cubicles until they reached a room with a half dozen round tables and a coffee machine.

"Welcome to my office. Want anything to drink?" Pastor Scott asked.

"Sure, I'll take a coffee. Black please."

A minute later, Pastor Scott arrived back at the table with steam emitting from two coffee mugs. Pastor Scott's mug said: ***All I Need Today Is A Little Bit of Coffee and A Whole Lot of Jesus.*** Alex turned his cup to see what catchy phrase they painted on his mug. It said: ***Until this Cup is Empty, Talk at Your Own Risk.*** He chuckled and turned his attention to Pastor Scott.

Pastor Scott leaned back and crossed one leg over the other. "You said that you had some questions for me in your message. How can I help?"

Alex exhaled. "I'm trying to do more with the non-profit organization, Education Stars Behind Bars, that I started with my brother, but I struggle with anxiety every time I pull into a prison parking lot. I used to enter prisons all the time to visit my older brother but over time it got harder and harder for me. Now I can barely breathe once they lock the security doors behind me. There is so much more ESBB can do, but it won't ever achieve its potential if I can't set foot into a prison. I'm hoping you can give me some guidance or tips that can help me."

Pastor Scott nodded as he listened carefully to Alex. Once Alex finished, Pastor Scott closed his hands as if praying and raised his index fingers to form a steeple. He tapped them against each other as he looked up and around the room. In an instant, Pastor Scott put both feet on the ground and scooted his chair in.

He leaned over the table toward Alex and said, "I am familiar with your organization and that's a wonderful prison ministry so I'd love to help you in any way I can."

"Thank you, Pastor," Alex replied.

"Anxiety can be tricky because it's often induced by a wide variety of reasons from abuse, trauma, grief, and other emotional scars. What I'm about to share is just a bandage and you may still need surgery from a professional therapist to address the root cause of your anxiety. Make sense?"

Alex nodded.

"Great. I'll share some mitigation tactics that seem to work best for me and some others that have asked for help. First, start journaling every night before you go to bed and write down whatever is on your mind. Don't worry about making everything grammatically correct or coherent sentences. This exercise is just to get out and onto paper all the thoughts overflowing in your head like a swollen river ready to break a dam. Unload as much as you can every night so you can start to let go of those thoughts and soon you should feel a physical and emotional release from all those stressors. Is that something you can do?"

Alex looked down at the table and then up at Pastor Scott. "Yes. I have a lot on my mind before I go to bed so sometimes it's hard to fall asleep. I can see how writing it down can help."

Pastor Scott took a sip of his coffee and continued, "Journaling every night and praying in silence every morning will help long term, but I have another tactic that may help when you feel an attack coming on. When you feel your chest tighten, close your eyes and focus on taking slow, measured breaths. Tune out everything else and concentrate on inhaling and exhaling, nothing else. Listen to the air enter and leave your lungs. Do that as long as you need until you start to feel some relief in your chest."

The suggestions from Pastor Scott gave Alex hope like the promise of a glass of cold water waiting inside on a hot day. It was potential relief for a problem that was starting to feel unsolvable to Alex.

"I will definitely try that next time I feel a panic attack coming on. I'm so glad I asked for help and I'm looking forward to implementing your suggestions," Alex replied with a smile.

He was ready to get started, so Alex pushed his chair away from the table, but Pastor Scott leaned back and crossed his legs again.

"Alex, what did you think about the information you heard at the RIHARP JR meeting we had here a couple weeks ago?"

"It was a great presentation and very informative."

"I'm curious why you and Allison came to the informational meeting when you are already involved in a prison ministry. Why'd you come?"

Alex shuffled in his seat. He wanted to give Pastor Scott a compelling answer but didn't have one. "Honestly, I'm not sure myself. I was intrigued with what I heard during the Business Angels event and I guess I just wanted to learn more about RIHARP JR."

Pastor Scott explained all the details of RIHARP JR and answered questions from Alex for the next twenty minutes.

"Thank you for answering all my questions. RIHARP JR sounds like a great program," Alex said.

"RIHARP JR is an excellent program, and the stipend is a nice bonus, but it's not for everyone. It's best for a family that is passionate about helping a teenager who has fallen off the right path get his or her life back on track before it's too late."

"That's one reason my brother and I started ESBB. My oldest brother Edgar got mixed up with the wrong crowd in high school and was in and out of jail the rest of his life. I think they could have done more when Edgar was young to help get his life back on track and it's been a passion of mine to help others avoid the same fate as Edgar. Although that's my passion, I also want to challenge my kids, who have not had to deal with adversity yet, to get out of their comfort zone and maybe even learn to show Jesus' grace and love to another kid who hasn't had the same advantages they've had."

"It sounds like your aware of the pros and cons of RIHARP JR so that you can make a sound decision. It also appears that you are at a crossroads. Jesus may have big plans for you and they may be even grander than you've been thinking."

Alex tilted his head and stared at Pastor Scott without responding. He hadn't considered a bigger plan than what he was currently facing, but he knew it was possible.

"You have a lot of tough decisions ahead of you, Alex, so let me pray for you." Pastor Scott bowed his head and closed his eyes.

Chapter 12

Alex left the meeting in a fog and moseyed into the empty worship center. He sat in a chair, looked up at the stage, and thought more about why he couldn't shake the feeling Jesus was calling him to take a RIHARP JR teenager into his home. Memories of Edgar flooded in, and Alex recalled the helplessness he felt with Edgar because nobody else would help him. His mind took him back to that fateful day when he tried to change Edgar.

Despair grew in Alex. It was clear that Edgar had chosen the wrong path, and without intervention, they would lose him in the substance abuse abyss. He waited for his parents to do something, but when they did nothing, Alex decided to talk to Edgar himself.

After lunch one Saturday afternoon, Alex slowly opened Edgar's bedroom door. The stench of body odor caught Alex by surprise, so he backed up to let his eyes adjust to the small slit of light penetrating the room. Edgar had placed cardboard over the lone window in the room to keep light and prying eyes out.

He noticed Edgar sit up in bed.

"What do you want, Alex?" he asked in Spanish.

"I want to talk to you."

"About what?"

"About you."

Edgar's tone softened. "Come in and shut the door behind you." He switched on a small lamp on the nightstand, rubbed his eyes, and swung his feet over the side of his bed. "Okay, I'm awake now. What do you want to talk about?"

Alex exhaled and raw emotion took over. "I miss you. I miss hanging out with you and doing stuff as a family."

Edgar smiled. "I'm still here, little man, but we all have to grow up. I'm a man now, so I have to take care of myself. You'll be here someday, too."

"Not like this."

Edgar's smile vanished. "What did you say?"

"I won't be getting in trouble and doing drugs. I wish you would stop hanging around those guys. They're bad news."

Edgar leaped from his bed with a veracity that Alex didn't know he still had in him. He grabbed Alex by the shirt and pushed him against the closet door. He pointed his index finger an inch from Alex's nose. "Don't you ever talk about my boys like that. They're my family now, and nobody messes with my family!"

Alex froze and did not respond.

Edgar let go of Alex's shirt and started pacing. "I don't do drugs, and I don't know what you have against those guys. They love me, man."

Alex found his voice. "We love you, too."

Edgar snapped his attention back to Alex. The rage was evident in his eyes. "Mama loves Mexico, and she's been homesick for her family back in Santa Catarina ever since we moved. Papa loves money and is always at work, so don't tell me about how much my family loves me."

Alex swallowed hard. "Me and Mateo still love you. You're our big brother."

Edgar stopped pacing and stared at Alex. His face softened and he shook his head. "I'm done talking. Close the door after you leave."

That was the last conversation Alex had with Edgar that wasn't through a secure phone and one-inch-thick clear Plexiglas inside a prison. Alex felt he could have done more for Edgar but didn't. He couldn't make that same mistake again.

The sound of a door closing in the worship center snapped Alex back to reality.

Could I help someone like Edgar? Can I help prevent another family from suffering the same pain I felt?

When Alex got home, he went directly to his home office. He leaned back in his leather chair and rocked gently as his eyes locked onto the ceiling. Minutes later, Allison passed his home office.

"Hey, Hon, you got a minute?" he called to his wife.

"Yeah, let me get this load out of the washer and the dryer started."

Moments later, Allison returned and leaned up against Alex's bookcase. "What's up?"

"I just got back from a meeting with Pastor Scott."

Allison raised her eyebrows and Alex filled her in on his meeting with their pastor. He confessed that he sought help with his anxiety with prisons so he could execute his plan for ESBB. Alex shared that Pastor Scott gave him some excellent suggestions, but then the conversation turned to RIHARP JR.

"He was curious about why we came to the informational meeting."

"What did you tell him?" Allison asked.

"I didn't have a good answer about why we attended the meeting, so we talked a little more about RIHAPR JR and he answered all of my questions. I am clear on the RIHARP JR program now, but my mind was murkier than ever when I left the meeting."

"How so?" Allison asked as she moved from the bookcase to the chair across from Alex's desk.

Alex inhaled deeply, looked down at his desk and then up at Allison. "I know this is going to seem crazy, but I can't shake the feeling that we should do it."

Allison tilted her head, "RIHARP JR?"

"Yeah. The stipend to host families is pretty generous and although we don't need it, the extra money could be very beneficial to ESBB. Maybe I could fundraise less and that would help me gain some sort of balance. Like I said, it's all still murky to me. What do you think?"

She stared at Alex expressionless but then nodded. "It's going to require us to change our lifestyle a lot, honey. But I think we can handle it. Every time I pray about it, I feel overwhelmed with the feeling that we should do it."

"Really?" Alex asked with wide eyes.

"I'm nervous about how it may affect the kids, but the positives outweigh my concerns. The possibility that we may have the opportunity to turn around a young man's life that needs help clinches it for me. I'm in."

A smile grew on Alex's face and quickly faded. "Should we ask the kids what they think?"

Allison shook her head. "No, I think we should tell them we've made this decision and share the reasons. This is an opportunity for them to learn and grow too."

"Okay."

"What is the next step?" Allison inquired.

"I need to let Pastor Scott know we are committed, and he'll get us in touch with someone at the Arizona Department of Juvenile Corrections. ADJC will get everything set up with RIHARP JR."

"Do you want to tell him now?" Allison asked.

"No, I need a minute."

"Okay, I'm going to get dinner started."

Allison left the room, and Alex paced in front of his desk. He walked over to the picture on the wall of his family. Allison and Alex were sitting on a rock ledge at the Grand Canyon with Olivia, Gaby, and Daniel standing next to them. He stared at it for over a minute, walked back to his desk, and fell back into his chair.

It was risky to upset the relative harmony Alex had worked hard to create for his family. A troubled teen could provide the unique perspective of someone who has had to struggle for the basics in life that none of his kids have ever faced beyond a quick brush with one at school or church. That same teen could also introduce chaos into Alex's family as Edgar did three decades earlier. Was now a time to play it safe or trust in the plan the Lord was placing upon him?

Alex exhaled and texted Pastor Scott.

I talked to Allison and we'll do it. Sign us up for RIHARP JR.

Chapter 13

A lex understood he was going to have even more pressure for his time with RIHARP JR so he crafted a plan to cut a few hours a week from his current schedule. Becoming a partner at Emerson Churchill was closer than ever so it wasn't the right time to pull back there, but he could reduce time spent fundraising for ESBB if he could convince Mr. Park to commit to a sponsorship of ESBB.

It was too early to pitch a full corporate sponsorship, Alex thought, but he recently created a new program called Sponsor-A-Star that would be a better fit. The Sponsor-A-Star allowed a business to commit a monthly donation to ESBB to help a single incarcerated student with a custom education plan. In return, the company would get regular updates on the ESBB student's progress and receive an invitation to the student's graduation ceremony at their prison. The prison graduation ceremony garnered good media attention so the business would get positive publicity for their sponsorship of a student putting in the hard work to turn their life around. Alex concluded that he'd invite Mr. Park to visit the training room at ESBB to see how the volunteer teachers craft the curricula for each student.

Alex scrolled through his online calendar at work for a date that worked for both himself and Mr. Park when his landline phone rang on his desk. He answered it after the second ring.

"Alex, where are the Christmas lists for the kids?" Papa asked as soon as he heard Alex's voice.

"Um, what?" Alex replied.

"I need the Christmas lists for the kids so Andrea has time to find them their favorite gifts. They know that Abuelo Garza always gives them the best gifts at Christmas, but it takes time and we are cutting it close this year."

Alex's phone buzzed on his desk. It was from an unknown local number.

"Papa, I have a call I need to take. I'll get you the list in a few days," Alex said as he hung up the landline and answered his cell phone.

"Hi, this is Linda Flowers from Arizona Department of Juvenile Corrections. I received a message that you are interested in the RIHARP JR program."

"Yes, we are."

"Thank you for your commitment to this exciting new program. I'll be your contact throughout the entire process."

Mrs. Flowers gathered information on the Garza family and their living arrangements for the next ten minutes.

"Mr. Garza, I will submit this information to the subcommittee for RIHARP JR assignments. They'll do a background check on your family and come for a site visit of your home in the next week. We'd like to have the entire family present when we visit your home. Does that work for you?"

"Yes, it does," Alex replied.

"Do you have questions for me before we submit your application?"

Alex cleared his throat. "Can I request a Hispanic male for our RIHARP assignment?"

The line was quiet for several seconds. Alex wondered if he crossed a line by asking for a specific ethnicity.

"Can I ask why you want a Hispanic person, Mr. Garza?"

Alex exhaled loudly into the phone. "My older brother was in and out of the prison system most of his adult life. Rival inmates murdered him in his cell a decade ago, and I've always wished I could have done more for him. I just thought that a Hispanic boy would allow me to help someone like my brother now in ways I wasn't able to help him then."

Alex tapped his fingers on his desk as he waited for her reply.

"As an African American woman and daughter of a man incarcerated for many years while I was young, I can understand your request. It's a key reason I choose to work at ADJC. However, I think that you'll find that all of our juvenile detainees seek to improve their lives and simply need someone to believe in them. I believe RIHARP JR will allow you to make the difference in a young man's life that you wish your brother would have had. I'll note your preference, but our policy for RIHARP JR assignments does not allow for special requests."

"I understand."

Alex left the office at six and drove straight home. He told Allison that he officially signed up for a RIHARP JR detainee. They agreed to tell the kids after dinner.

Once everyone took their plates over to the sink and put them in the dishwasher, Alex made his announcement. "Before you all go, your mom and I want to share something with you. Please have a seat at the kitchen table."

Everyone returned to their seats.

"You all know how Tio Mateo and I started Education Stars Behind Bars to help inmates after Tio Edgar died, right?"

Alex observed three heads nodding with looks of confusion on their faces.

"Well, we are taking a step forward to help younger people that are not yet in prison in a new mentorship program called RIHARP JR. Your mom and I have agreed to take part in this program."

The three Garza kids looked back at Alex with blank stares.

Allison jumped in. "What your father is trying to say is that we've invited a teenage boy to live with us as part of this program."

Daniel and Gaby smiled. "That's cool. It'll be like having an older brother."

Olivia jumped up, knocking her chair backward to the floor. "Who is he? When is he coming? How long will he stay here?"

"We don't know who he is yet. A group from the Arizona Department of Juvenile Corrections will soon visit us to verify our house and family are a good fit. Then they'll assign someone, and then he'll be here shortly after that," Allison shared in a calm voice.

"Why would we volunteer to have a juvenile delinquent live with us? Am I the only one concerned about our safety with a dangerous criminal living in our house?"

Alex stood and walked over to Olivia. "Honey, you need to give this a chance. I don't think it will be as bad as you think."

Olivia took several steps away from Alex and yelled, "You're crazy! He could stab us all in our sleep, or steal everything we own, or, or… do who knows what in the middle of the night to me and Gaby and Mom. It sucks that your brother made such a mess of his life, but that's no reason to punish us! I can't be here with a kid from juvie. I'm going to live with Tio Mateo and Tia Daniella. They'd never do this to their kids."

Alex started toward Olivia, and she bolted to her bedroom. Alex took two steps down the hallway until Allison stopped him. "Let her go. She needs to blow off some steam."

The remaining foursome discussed the RIHARP JR program at the kitchen table when Olivia stormed into the kitchen with a gym bag bursting with clothes. She grabbed her keys and started toward the garage door.

"Where are you going?" Alex asked with his voice rising.

"I'm going to Chandler like I said," Olivia choked with tears streaming down her cheeks.

"You can't drive upset like that. You haven't had your license that long. It's dangerous," Alex said.

"What do you care about my safety? You are inviting a criminal to live here."

Olivia let the door slam shut behind her.

Alex turned to Allison. "Should I go get her?"

"No, but let me talk to her and see if I can at least get her calmed down. It's a lot for a sixteen-year-old girl to process. Some time away from us right now might be a good thing."

Allison opened the door as soon as the security camera chime buzzed, indicating someone was entering or leaving their driveway.

"She's already gone," Alex announced.

Allison yanked her phone from her pocket and fumbled to open her home screen. "I can track her iPhone to make sure she goes to Mateo and Daniella's house. She's done the drive several times to babysit her cousins. As long as she goes there, I'm okay. But I should probably text Daniella and let her know what is going on."

Forty-five minutes later, Alex heard a ping on Allison's phone. "Is that Olivia?"

Allison checked her phone. "No, it's Daniella. She said that Olivia arrived, and she's calmed down. She's going to spend the night."

Alex paced in the living room while Allison sat on the couch. He started to speak several times and stopped.

"Are we making a big mistake?" Alex finally asked.

"I don't think so," Allison replied. "I think we're doing the right thing and sometimes doing the right thing requires making unpopular decisions. Olivia will be okay. It was a shock to her to hear the news, but she'll come around. She'll eventually see it's the right thing to do."

"I know, but what about what she said about putting our family in danger? What if this boy hurts us or is a negative influence on our kids?"

Allison looked through Alex at the blank wall behind him. A moment later, she shook her head. "Pastor Scott said the kids who qualify for the program don't have a history of violence. Plus, our boy will have that fancy tech to subdue him if he suddenly acts dangerously. Christina Mendoza had much younger kids around a convicted murderer, and they were okay. Besides, there are three Garza kids and only one from juvie. Our kids are going to influence him, not the other way around."

"I hope you're right," Alex whispered.

Allison chuckled. "Besides, how menacing can a sixteen- or seventeen-year-old boy be?"

Alex thought back to some of Edgar's friends in high school and shuddered. "Pretty bad, actually."

Chapter 14

One week after the blowout with Olivia, ADJC arrived for the on-site audit of the Garza compound. Olivia was present, having come home after staying with her aunt and uncle for two nights. Alex promised Olivia he'd buy her the recent new iPhone upgrade that she's wanted since its release three months earlier. In return, she had to return home and take part in the ADJC audit with no snide remarks or outbursts of anger.

Olivia made all the right noises about understanding the importance of helping a young person in need but she made no promises about being friendly. Her body language made her genuine feelings loud and clear.

Alex escorted the ADJC audit crew to the front door and shut it behind them as they poured into their government-issued SUV. He felt everyone gave satisfactory answers to their questions, even Olivia, but there was no way to know if it was enough. The audit team still had to do a background check and surely they'd find out about Edgar. Would that help or hurt their chances of becoming RIHARP JR hosts?

They would reveal the results of the audit in a week, but the anticipation of the pending outcome was always front of mind for Alex and Allison. They needed a distraction so that the next seven days didn't feel like a month. Alex passed the time by devoting even more hours to work, while Allison scheduled their annual preparation of Christmas treats. Tia Daniella came to their house to help guide the tamale making session with Olivia, Gaby, and Daniel. Daniella did less teaching and more observing as the three Garza kids were mastering tamale production, especially her namesake nephew, who seemed to have a knack for cooking. Next, Allison got to work on Christmas cookies, cakes, and pudding to continue their tradition of a multicultural Christmas celebration.

Alex arrived home the following week and found an envelope on the counter with the ADJC return address. Alex rushed into the bedroom to find Allison painting her nails at her makeup desk in the closet.

"Did you see this?" Alex asked.

"Yes, I did. I wanted to wait until you were home to see the news. Go ahead and open it."

Alex tore open the envelope and carefully pulled out the letter. A minute later, he looked up and smiled. "They approved us! ADCJ will drop him off in one week."

"It looks like the Garza family will grow to six people next week," Allison replied.

The entire family moved to the front porch when two black GMC Yukon SUVs pulled into the driveway.

Two ADJC corrections officers emerged from one vehicle. Linda Flowers and John Nickerson, the inventor of Sure Cuffs, exited the second SUV. Linda greeted the Garza family and introduced John while the two corrections officers stood by the rear passenger door. John extended his hand to Alex and Allison.

"Hello, Mr. and Mrs. Garza. I'm with Sectronix, the company that invented Sure Cuffs. Since this is a new program in the state of Arizona, Mrs. Flowers asked me to assist with the transition of your detained youth."

Linda took a few steps toward the parked SUV and turned around. "Are you ready to meet your RIHARP JR youth?"

Neither Alex nor Allison responded, but Daniel yelled out, "Yes!"

Linda nodded to the officers, and the passenger door opened. Alex held his breath.

Shoulder-length stringy blond hair was the first feature Alex noticed. A young man emerged and then stood fully erect next to the black SUV. His pale white skin looked like it hadn't seen the Arizona sun in months. Alex guessed the kid was at least six-foot-two and two hundred and ten pounds—three or four inches taller and twenty pounds heavier than Alex. He looked more like the lead singer of a heavy metal band than a teenage boy. Nothing like Olivia's scrawny friends that Alex was hoping for.

The boy did a slow 360-degree turn, looking up and down at his surroundings as his feet pivoted on the driveway. He nodded and scanned all the faces staring at him. He then locked his gaze on Alex and took two steps forward until he was even with Linda.

"Jared Gellar, meet the Garza family. Your new temporary guardians," Linda said.

"Hey," Jared said as he offered a quick half-wave to the family.

Everyone in the Garza family returned a weak wave. The scene was like introducing a new kid to a kindergarten class, with overflowing anxiety on both sides.

Linda gently linked arms with Jared. "Why don't we all head inside to continue the transfer."

Alex followed everyone inside. He noticed that Daniel and Gaby were close to Jared with smiles on their faces, but Olivia drifted back. She did not seem impressed with their new house guest.

The officers took Jared around their property's boundaries to test the GPS settings for Sure Cuffs. Linda and John followed the Garza party of five and everyone took seats around the dining room table.

"You have a beautiful home," John stated as he scanned the stacked stone fireplace in the large family room flowing into the gourmet kitchen next to the dining room.

"Thank you," Allison replied.

"Jared should be very comfortable here, and it's my job to make sure you also feel comfortable. Per RIHARP JR protocol, we've installed Sure Cuffs in Mr. Gellar. This will allow you to subdue and secure him in the unlikely event you need to detain him."

John slid a glossy folder full of flyers and pamphlets.

"First, a quick overview of Sure Cuffs. We insert ten rice-sized transmitter chips under the skin of each RIHARP inmate. They're located on each side in their inner knee, thigh, upper hip area, elbow and in the palm of their hand near their thumbs."

John pointed to his left thumb with his right index finger.

"This placement is important because these ten chips, when activated, secure the individual's knees together while bringing their arms and hands in tight next to their body, almost like a soldier standing at attention. In this position, Jared will be immobilized. If you activate Sure Cuffs, Jared will remain in this position until you deactivate Sure Cuffs on your smartphone app or by an ADJC staff member. The app notifies our Sectronix office in Austin, Texas, seconds after Sure Cuffs is activated, and we'll dispatch local authorities and ADJC officials to investigate."

John took a quick drink of water.

"RIHARP hosts have successfully used Sure Cuffs in hundreds of homes throughout Texas, so you can rest easy knowing that you have a way to subdue your detained youth if needed. We need to verify Sure Cuffs is functional, so we will test it on Jared when he returns."

Alex and Allison exchanged a look. He hoped this wouldn't be too scary for the kids to witness.

"First, I want to review all the ways to activate Sure Cuffs," John continued. "One is via GPS boundaries. The officers outside are calibrating and validating your property boundaries right now. It is my understanding that Jared will attend regular high school, so the school administration can choose if they want to activate an additional set of GPS coordinates for the campus or have Sure Cuffs off during school hours, based on their comfort level."

John held up three fingers. "You have two additional options to activate Sure Cuffs. They are your smartphone app and an emergency word. Of course, we need to establish that emergency activation word. Think of a single word that is not something you'd say in a normal course of your day, but you'll remember under stress or in an emergency."

Gaby picked the emergency activation word and Daniel chooses the temporary deactivation verbal command. Alex wanted his kids to be involved with their new RIHARP JR guest and selecting the words seemed to make Daniel and Gaby happy. Meanwhile Olivia continued to sulk in the corner.

John typed the words they selected into his app and stood up. "I'm going to check on the rest of the transfer protocol. Mrs. Flowers will help you with everything else."

John slid a binder across the table to Linda Flowers. She opened it and removed several brochures. "Bringing a minor child under your guardianship in your home is a big transition, and you will run into situations that nobody else will understand. I am the case manager for your RIHARP JR guest, so I'll be your first point of contact if you have questions, concerns, problems, or anything unusual that comes up with Jared."

Allison and Alex exchanged a quick glance at each other and nodded.

"Great," Linda responded. "Remember, the goal for RIHARP JR is to help your guest prepare for life as an independent young adult. Under the current rules of RIHARP JR, all participants age out on their eighteenth birthday, so you all have almost a full year before Jared turns eighteen on November fourth next year.

"What happens if he's not ready or makes a mistake after he's out?" Allison asked.

Linda closed her binder and rested her folded hands on top of it. "There are no more second chances after this for Jared. He has to be ready. If Jared breaks any more laws after he turns eighteen, he'll go to the state penitentiary as an adult. I have complete confidence that both of you can get him on the right path long term."

I wish I shared that confidence, Alex thought.

After the room was quiet for several seconds, John arrived back in the dining room. "Are you all done in here?"

Linda nodded, stood up from the oak table, and slung her bag over her shoulder. "You have all of my information, including my personal cell phone for emergencies. Contact me if you need anything."

Alex walked John and Linda to the front door and then out to their car.

John put his hand on Alex's shoulder. "I know this is overwhelming now, but you have everything in place now for the safety of you and your family. Now you can focus on helping this young man get his life on the right track."

Alex waved as they departed his driveway. He watched their SUV disappear down the hill and stood for another minute.

What did he get his family into?

Chapter 15

The house was so quiet when Alex returned that he could hear the hum of his pool filter in the backyard. When he returned to the dining room, Alex saw Allison, Jared, Gaby, and Daniel staring back at him, desperate for direction.

"Why don't we show Jared to his new room?"

Daniel smiled and stood. "Follow me."

The remaining foursome followed Daniel down the long hallway past Gaby's, Daniel's, and Olivia's bedrooms and finally to a room at the end of the corridor. Daniel paused outside the door and pointed into the bright room decorated in blue tones as if a new baby boy was coming home from the hospital.

"This is it. Go ahead, check it out," Allison encouraged Jared.

Jared walked around one side of the bed and then to the window. He pushed up one of the blind slats and peered out the window at the scene behind the home. Next, Jared shuffled around the bed and dragged his fingers across the dresser, still radiating a lemony scent from the furniture polish until he reached the nightstand. He stared at the devices on the nightstand.

"The remote works on the TV above your dresser. It has Netflix, Hulu, and Amazon Prime, so you can find something you like," Allison shared. "We also got you your own iPhone and iPad."

Jared slowly picked up the iPad. He turned it around and flipped it over. Gaby realized the problem and jumped in to help.

"You turn it on right here," she said while pushing a sleek button on the side. "Once it turns on, you use this button on the bottom to bring up all the apps you want to use."

The look on Jared's face screamed confusion, but he graciously replied, "thanks."

"You're welcome."

Alex sensed Daniel and Gaby's desire to help Jared might overwhelm him, so he intervened to give him space.

"Gaby and Daniel, thank you for helping Jared with his room. Let's give him some time to get settled now."

After they left, Jared moved his bag from the bed to the closet.

"Your bathroom is a couple of doors down the hall," Allison explained. "You can find clean towels and washcloths in the cabinet next to the shower. We have plenty of soap, toothpaste, and deodorant in the medicine cabinet for you. Let me know if you need anything."

"Thank you, Mrs. Garza."

"Is this going to work out for you, Jared?" Alex asked.

Jared smiled. "Yeah, this is way better than anything I've ever slept in."

"Did you have your own cell, or did you have to share one with someone else?"

Jared's forehead wrinkled, and his eyes narrowed. "I wasn't in a cell. I was in a room with a roommate. They told us it was like a college dorm room."

"I'm sorry, Jared. I thought you were coming from that juvenile detention facility up north of town."

Jared shook his head. "No, I was in Adobe Mountain School. It's kind of like a regular school, except it's run by ADJC, so they locked us in and we couldn't leave."

Jared pulled some clothes from his bag and put them in the top drawer of the dresser. He sat down on the bed.

"What did you do to end up in the Abode school?" Alex inquired.

"Alex, let's not pry into his past on his first day here," Allison retorted.

Jared put up his hand. "It's okay. They told me you'd want to know, so I'd rather tell you now and get it over with."

"You don't have to if you don't want to," Allison reminded Jared.

"I know. I want to tell you now."

Allison and Alex moved to one side of the bed and sat down. They all turned inward to face each other.

Jared cleared his throat. "I got in trouble a lot as a kid for shoplifting. You know, just to eat. They kept releasing me to my parents because nothing was big enough to get me out of there. Right after I turned sixteen, I tried something big. The Sheriff arrested me for drug possession of pain killers, possession of stolen property, and possession of a firearm by a minor. It was my dad's gun. During the court hearing, I was adjudicated delinquent for all charges. My old man also received a fine since it was his firearm, which sent him through the roof. They sentenced me to Juvenile Intensive Probation with home confinement with an electronic monitoring device for one year and suspended my driver's license for two years. So even that wasn't enough to get me out of there."

Alex couldn't believe his ears. This seventeen-year-old boy was deliberately getting in trouble to escape his family, then rattling off arrest charges and court sentences like he'd been doing this for a decade. Alex felt both sad and concerned.

"After a miserable couple weeks at home all the time, I realized what I had to do. I stuck a bag of pain killers under my seat and went speeding around town, driving on a suspended license. They caught me, of course, like I hoped, and found out I was on probation, so the deputy referred me to the Juvenile Intake Department in Phoenix. The Intake Probation Officer down there recommended detaining me until my court appearance after my parents refused to come down and take custody of me. I was so relieved. You have no idea."

Jared dropped his head and let his long hair hide his face. Alex thought he heard Jared sniff. Jared's head snapped back up, and he continued to tell his story.

"A week later, they put me in Adobe Mountain School and I started drug rehab for the pain killers. I got fresh sheets every week, regular meals; someone even got me into reading. After three months in rehab, I got clean. But some of the guys fought a lot, and that would freak me out. During an evaluation, my handler thought I needed a better environment. She told me about this RIHARP JR program and recommended that I join as part of my Continuous Case Plan to transition back to the community. I jumped at the chance to avoid going home, and now I am here."

Allison turned to Alex with her eyes wide open and she shook her head. "It sounds like you had a problem with pain killers. Did your parents ever try to get you some help?"

Jared chuckled and snorted. "Where do you think I got them?"

The room was quiet for half a minute until Jared spoke again.

"Look, both of my parents are junkies. My mom likes to keep to herself and pass out on the couch watching TV every night. Clint likes to mix his pills with whiskey and terrorize everyone around him. Their house would have garbage piled to the ceiling if it wasn't for me. That caseworker was right. I don't have a bright future if I live at home with them."

Alex stood up and motioned for Allison to follow him. Once they were near the door, Alex turned back to Jared.

"We are glad you are here and hope you'll find this to be a better environment for you. We'll let you get settled in your room now," Alex said and turned to leave.

"Can I ask you two a question?"

Allison and Alex moved back into the doorway.

"Sure. What's your question?" Allison asked.

"Why did you agree to take a troublemaker like me into your home? You have the biggest house I've ever seen, and your kids seem kinda like the goodie-goodie kids at my old school. Why take a chance on someone like me?"

Allison turned to Alex. He moved closer to Jared and leaned on the dresser.

"Jared, my older brother went to prison when I was growing up. We were very close until he changed, and I hated to see him in prison. Ten years ago, I started an organization that provides custom educational opportunities to prison inmates to succeed on the outside after serving their sentences. I vowed I'd try to help other people avoid the same pain I endured when Edgar went to prison."

"Is he still in prison today?" Jared asked.

"No."

"Oh, is he out? Did your education program help him?"

"No."

Jared's nose wrinkled. "Where is he then?"

"He's dead."

Chapter 16

J ared arrived with only a few days of classes before Winter Break, so Allison had a series of meetings at the school. All of Jared's teachers, resource officers, and the vice-principal were given the Sure Cuffs app and were briefed by Linda Flowers from ADJC on how to use it when he started after the holidays.

The Garza kids completed their last school day of the year and the Christmas season began in earnest. The house was decorated with lights, ornaments, stockings, and a Christmas tree. A handmade nativity scene filled a round table draped in a red cloth next to the well-lit spruce tree in the corner. Allison had a new stocking made with Jared's name, and they all watched him hang it on a sixth nail on the mantle above the gas fireplace. She noticed the quick but sure smile on Jared's face after seeing his name on a red and white stocking.

Jared's acclimation to his new environment continued. Gaby showed Jared how to turn on the TV with surround sound in the family room from his new iPad as well as how to turn on the hot tub from the wireless remote inside the kitchen. The entire time Gaby was sharing her tech knowledge of the Garza compound, Daniel followed close behind, offering his tidbits of advice.

"Daniel, give the new kid a couple of feet. You're going to suffocate him," Olivia quipped.

"What do you mean?" Daniel asked.

"You're like his shadow. Let the kid get used to our house before you follow him around everywhere."

Like most unhelpful suggestions Olivia offered Daniel, he ignored it and continued to show interest in everything the new teen male living under the same roof said or did.

Jared offered to help with chores so Allison had him do some simple tasks like sweeping the sidewalk and taking out the trash. Allison was shocked when she found Jared scrubbing the bathroom after she told Olivia to do it.

"I don't mind," Jared replied sheepishly. It was like he was expecting to be yelled at or even worse.

"I know you don't mind, but Olivia needs to do the chores I ask her to do."

Allison sent Alex and Jared to work outside. Jared was tall enough to reach the top of the archway to their front patio from Alex's inadequate six-foot ladder. It was a task she asked Alex to do every Christmas for the past four years but didn't have anyone tall enough to reach the top of the arch with the lights until now.

After they finished, Alex and Jared joined Allison adjusting ornaments on the tree in the family room.

"Thanks for your help, Jared. I've been wanting that done for a few years now."

"No problem."

"What types of Christmas traditions does your family have, Jared?" Allison inquired.

Jared chuckled. "Usually, it starts with my sister and me cleaning up the mess my parents left from the night before and then waiting until my dad wakes up around noon. Once he finishes his pot of coffee and sobers up, my mom goes into their bedroom and brings out a wrapped present for my sister and me. Last year, Chloe got a refurbished vacuum cleaner. I guess my parents were hinting that she needed to up her game. I got a used gun cleaning kit for a gun I don't even have. I think someone gave it to my old man or something."

"You don't have a Christmas tree or any presents under your tree at your house?" Allison asked.

"Nah, not since me and Chloe were little. The last tree almost caught on fire because nobody ever gave it any water," Jared replied as he shook his head.

"I'm sorry to hear that. I hope we can make this a memorable Christmas for you."

"Oh my gosh!" Olivia groaned.

Allison's attention snapped to Olivia. "What's wrong?"

Olivia rolled her eyes. "Can't you see he is just playing you? He's trying to make you feel sorry for him. Nobody has it that bad."

"Would you like to join me at my house for Christmas?" Jared responded coolly.

Olivia slammed down her frosting spreader and cookie onto the counter and bolted from the kitchen.

"I'm sorry, Jared. She's in a mood right now. She doesn't mean it."

Jared nodded.

"I didn't realize you had a sister. Would you like to send her something for Christmas?"

"Maybe if I knew where she was. She turned eighteen earlier this year, and she ran away a few days after her birthday. I haven't heard from her since summer. We've had no visits from the Sheriff telling us she's dead or in jail, so I guess she's doing okay."

Allison looked at the shell-shocked looks on the faces of Daniel and Gaby, who had never heard anyone talk like this before.

"Anyone want to test my new Christmas cookies?" Allison quickly asked.

For the next week, everyone counted down the days until Christmas morning. Alex attended his last holiday networking events of the year and his last day in the office was on December twenty-third.

On Christmas eve, Alex wrote out a check for his church and another for a special offering to help local families with food and other necessities. He checked his bank account and saw they deposited the first RIHARP JR stipend in his account.

He reached back into his top desk drawer and pulled his checkbook out again. It felt good to write a check to ESBB with the money from RIHARP JR. That was three thousand fewer dollars he'd have to raise and over time, the amount contributed to ESBB because of RIHARP JR could be significant. It was the first meaningful step toward the balanced life Alex sought.

That evening, they planned to attend Christmas Eve service at Mountain Shadows Christian Church in the matching outfits that Allison purchased for everyone. Jared shared that he did not want to go to church. He told Alex and Allison that he hadn't been to church since his grandma died and was too nervous to go to a Christmas service. Alex volunteered to stay back with Jared so the rest of the family could attend. After they left for church, he introduced Jared to *It's a Wonderful Life* and *A Christmas Carol* and the two watched the classic Christmas tales until everyone returned home.

On Christmas day, Gaby came into Alex and Allison's bedroom at six-thirty in the morning and asked if they could go into the family room to see what Santa brought them. They told her to wait until seven, and then the entire family would get up and open gifts together. By eight o'clock, they had strewn the family room with wrapping paper and piles of new clothes, games, and electronic gadgets. Allison made sure Jared also got to open multiple gifts.

Still, Jared sat apart from the family as if he felt he didn't belong there. Eventually, Daniel carried a new Lego set over to him and asked if he could help him assemble it later that day. After the family room was cleaned, everyone enjoyed their tamales and went their separate ways to enjoy their gifts. Olivia went to her bedroom, Gaby went to the game room to play her new video game, and Daniel went outside to try his new baseball glove. Allison went into her bedroom closet to find space for her new shoes while Jared remained in the kitchen with Alex while they downloaded several new movies onto Jared's iPad.

Alex's phone buzzed inside his pocket. He didn't recognize the number but answered anyway.

"Hello?"

"Get me Jared Gellar," a man demanded in a gruff voice.

"Who is this?"

"This is his old man."

Alex wasn't familiar with the term 'old man' for a father until Jared used it the day he arrived. Excited that one of his parents might try to do something nice for Jared by reaching out to him on Christmas, Alex brought the phone over to Jared.

"It's your dad. He wants to talk to you."

Alex was expecting to see a smile or a hint of happiness, but he saw instant tension in Jared's face. He took the phone from Alex's outstretched arm and put it to his ear.

"Hey, Clint."

Jared listened for a half minute and then closed his eyes.

"I don't have anything," Jared responded in a whisper.

Alex wondered what Jared's father could want from his son. He knew he was in temporary custody with another family. Jared told Alex that his father had a drug problem. Was he calling Jared to help him get drugs?

Jared's next reply was more roar than a whisper. "I said I don't have it." Jared pulled the phone away from his ear and shook his head. Alex could hear his father yelling into the phone.

"No, I don't. I'm not lying. Leave me alone."

Jared pushed the red end call button and tossed the phone on the counter. He rushed out of the kitchen and seconds later, slammed his bedroom door.

What was that all about?

Alex retrieved his phone, and the screen illuminated again. It was from the same number as last time, so Alex knew Jared's father was calling back.

"Hello," Alex answered.

"Get Jared back on the phone."

"He's not available right now. Can I help you with something?"

"That boy hung up on me. Nobody hangs up on me. I need to talk to him right now," Jared's father screamed into the phone. Alex could picture spittle flying everywhere as this man had a level ten meltdown over someone hanging up on him.

"He's still not available. Are you sure I can't help you with something?" Alex asked in a calm voice.

"You don't want to mess with me, buddy. Get my son on the phone!"

Alex couldn't find the words to respond.

"I know my son is getting money for this RIHARP program. His mother and I need a little cash this month to cover our bills, so I need him to send that money to us. He knows how much we need, so since you are his new babysitter, I need you to help him get it to me. I need it ASAP."

"He doesn't get any money from RIHARP."

"Are you saying my friend at ADJC lied to me?"

"No. I'm saying I get all the money from RIHARP."

"You're getting the money? I'm still his legal guardian. I should get that money. Not his new babysitter."

"I'm sorry, sir, but that's how the RIHARP JR program is set up. The stipend is to cover the expenses of Jared's care." No way was he going to tell this hostile stranger that he sent every penny on to ESBB to help other prisoners.

Clint snorted. "I know you don't need the money."

How could he possibly know?

"Take it up with the State of Arizona if you don't like how it's being administered."

"Don't get cute with me. I'm not someone to be trifled with."

"Not getting cute, sir. I'm just trying to explain to you that Jared doesn't have—"

The phone went silent. Mr. Nobodyhangsuponme had just hung up on Alex.

Alex stared at the phone for a full minute, waiting to see if Jared's father called back again. After the screen remained dark, Alex put the phone back in his pocket and found Jared and Daniel outside playing catch with Daniel's new glove.

It was obvious to Alex that Jared had spent little to no time playing catch with his father, but he appeared to be having fun with Daniel. Alex hoped that having fun with Daniel would take Jared's mind of the phone call so he could enjoy Christmas. Unfortunately, Alex couldn't get the call out of his thoughts.

It was clear that Jared's father is going to be a problem.

Chapter 17

Two days after Christmas, Olivia woke up Alex and Allison. She was standing next to their bed shortly after sunrise, so Alex knew it must be something serious.

"Mom, Dad, I have something I need to tell you. It's about Jared."

Alex sat up in bed, and Allison shot up and stood next to Olivia.

"Honey, we know you don't like that he is living with us, but we told you why we're doing this. We're not going to change our minds."

"I caught him sneaking around the house at night."

This got Alex up. He moved to the end of the bed and sat back down. "What happened?"

"Two nights ago, I thought I heard something, so I got up and saw Jared walking down the hall and into the family room. I checked my clock, and it was a little after two. I didn't follow him, so I don't know where he went. Then last night, I heard him again at almost the same time. He walked around the house for a bit and then went back into his room."

"Are you sure this wasn't just a dream?" Allison asked.

"I know the difference between a dream and someone creeping around my house, Mom," Olivia hissed.

"Did he try to go into Gaby's or Daniel's room?"

"No. I just told you that he went *all the way down the hall* and into the family room. Would it kill you to pay attention when I'm talking?"

"Okay, okay," Alex said as he stood and pushed both hands down as if trying to quiet down a raucous room. "Let's not start attacking each other right now. I'll look into this further myself."

Alex turned to Olivia and put his hands on her shoulders. He looked into her brown eyes and saw the genuine concern. "Thanks for telling us, Liv. Go back to bed or whatever you want to do now. I'm going to discuss some solutions with your mom."

Once Olivia left the room, Alex shared his plan.

"I'm going to install a security camera in their hallway so I can see if he is sneaking out at night."

"Will you put them all around the house so you can see what he's doing?" Allison inquired. "He's been through a lot in his life, and we're not sure yet what he's capable of."

"I agree his reasons for doing things make little sense to me. But I've seen him mostly being eager to please. I don't want this to turn into a prison for him or us. I just need to verify if he is leaving his room around two in the morning and what he does. Maybe he's just a sleepwalker. Or he gets thirsty at night and wanted ice water. Olivia didn't see enough to know if he's doing anything bad."

Later that day, when Jared and the rest of the family were in the backyard, Alex installed his new camera at the end of the hallway. His new camera had infrared capabilities, so he could identify a person in a dark hall. Once Alex installed it, he tested the motion sensor, and his phone vibrated as soon as Alex walked past Olivia's door. It was ready, and Alex just had to wait until later that evening to see if Jared was sneaking around at night.

A few minutes past eleven, Alex put down his book and turned off the nightstand lamp. He secured his phone, opened the camera app, and observed a black-and-white image of the dark hallway on the opposite side of the house. It was empty.

Minutes later, Alex fell asleep. The sound of his phone chime and vibrations on the nightstand surface woke him suddenly hours later. Alex opened the security camera app and saw an empty hallway on the screen. He continued to watch the live feed. Three minutes after the first chime, a person appeared in the hall and the chime went off again. Alex could only see the person's back based on where he positioned the camera, but he could confirm the person went into Jared's room, holding something in his hand.

"Olivia was right," Alex whispered.

Should I get up and confront him now? I'd have to knock on his door, and that would give Jared time to hide whatever he took. I'm too late tonight.

Alex decided it was best to catch him in the act, so he tried to go back to sleep. He couldn't fall asleep for another hour as Alex pondered why Jared may feel the need to sneak around and take something in the middle of the night. Sadness and concern battled each other in his gut. Concern was winning the fight.

Chapter 18

T he migration to a new email server over the holiday break at Emerson Churchill did not go as planned and Alex arrived at the office at six his first day back. During the migration, all of his appointments in his calendar for January vanished, so Alex spent the first four hours of his day transferring his handwritten appointments from his notebook back into his calendar software.

A little after ten, Alex received a call from Allison.

"Did you see anything last night on your camera?"

Alex inhaled and then exhaled loudly. "Yeah, I saw Jared get up in the middle of the night just like Olivia said. It was about ten minutes after two."

"Did you talk to him?"

"No, I didn't see him on the camera until he was almost back in his room, so I assumed he'd hide whatever he took once I knocked on his door."

"What? Did he take something? What did he take?" Allison asked in rapid-fire succession.

"I couldn't tell, but I could see something in his hand when he came back. If he does it again tonight, I'm going to confront him before he goes back to his room."

"Wake me up before you confront him," Allison demanded.

"I don't want to make this into a big deal. I'll get up and talk to him to find out what's going on."

"What if he gets upset and attacks you?"

Alex hadn't even considered that possibility. He assumed it was an innocent misunderstanding, but after Allison planted the seed, Jared's defensive reaction seemed like a potential outcome.

"What will you do if he does?" Alex asked.

"I'll do whatever I have to do to activate Sure Cuffs so he can't hurt you."

"Okay, fine, I'll wake you if I see him and get up to confront him."

The kids were playing a video game with a fictitious guitar in the family room when Alex arrived home that evening. Gaby and Daniel racked up the points as they strummed their plastic guitar chords to the notes on the TV and Jared gave his best effort for his first time playing the game. Everyone laughed at Jared's awkward fingers and poor performance, including Jared, but Olivia was not amused. She sat in the chair furthest from the big flat-screen TV and eyed Jared.

Alex stopped to watch his two youngest children and Jared having innocent fun. He couldn't have wished for a better dynamic among the threesome but then his eyes moved to Olivia watching carefully from a corner in the room. Something didn't add up. Jared's behavior in front of Alex did not send any signals of concern, yet the video evidence of Jared moving around the house at night didn't lie. Alex had to get to the bottom of why Jared was sneaking around at night.

Once all the kids were in their rooms for the night, Alex followed his usual routine of writing in his journal before bed. Like the night before, he turned out the light and checked the camera to confirm it was working. Sleep didn't come easy. He wondered why a young boy offered so much from a caring family would feel the need to steal. Alex had begun to trust Jared, but he felt that trust drifting away like a receding tide.

Alex stared into the dark room and prayed. He prayed Jared wouldn't get up tonight so he wouldn't have to confront him. He prayed that if he had to confront Jared, it would be a peaceful and productive conversation that led to an understanding. Thirty minutes later, Alex finally fell asleep.

The chime and vibrating phone woke Alex. He jumped out of bed and pulled on a shirt. He saw that it was two-sixteen in the morning, and Jared was on the move again.

Alex put his hand on Allison's shoulder and shook her gently. "Jared is up again, so I'm going to go see what he's doing."

Allison shot up and grabbed her phone. "I'll active Sure Cuffs if I hear a struggle or any yelling."

"Okay, I'm going now so I can catch him in the act."

Alex left his room and rushed into the family room. He could hear shuffling in the kitchen. Alex stalked his prey through the family room, and just as he entered the kitchen, Jared turned back toward his bedroom. Alex knew he had to catch Jared before he made it back to his room.

"Jared, what are you doing?"

Jared jumped at the sound of the voice and bolted for his room.

Alex chased him down the hall. He couldn't catch him before he made it to his room and slammed the door shut. Alex arrived a second later and pushed the door open without hesitation. He flipped on the light and put his hands up to defend his face in case Jared attacked. He didn't attack, but as Alex's eyes adjusted to the bright light, he saw Jared bend over his bottom dresser drawer and slam it shut.

"What are you doing?" Alex demanded.

"Nothing."

"I know you've been sneaking out when we're asleep. Why are you walking around the house in the middle of the night?"

"I'm not doing anything," Jared responded. His voice cracked, and his eyes welled up with tears.

Alex marched toward Jared and pulled open the bottom dresser drawer. His eyes widened, and he looked up at Jared, who was watching with regret in his eyes.

"What's going on?" Allison asked as she arrived in Jared's room. She had her phone in her hand while breathing heavily after running all the way from her room after hearing a door slam.

Alex stood up and looked at Allison.

"What is it?" Allison asked again.

Alex looked over to Jared as he leaned against the wall, slid down to the floor, and cried.

"He was taking cookies."

"What?"

"He was taking Christmas cookies and hiding them in his dresser."

Allison and Alex moved closer to Jared on the floor. His ribs shook with each labored breath. Tears streamed down his face when he looked up. "I'm sorry."

Jared ducked his head under both arms to shield himself like a boxer expecting a quick right hook.

Allison dropped onto both knees and lifted his chin with her thumb and index finger. "Why did you feel you had to get up in the middle of the night to get these cookies? You scared us by sneaking around. I would have been happy to make another batch if you just asked."

Jared wiggled his chin out of Allison's grip and let his head drop again. "I've never had so many amazing cookies."

Allison smiled. "I'm happy to hear that, but why not just ask for more?"

Jared looked away. "I don't know. At my house, we rarely had anything like this, and if we did, my old man would have smacked me just for asking. He would have told me how ungrateful I am. I just wanted some extra cookies and didn't want to make a big deal about it."

Alex extended his hand to Jared. "Let's get you up."

Jared grabbed his hand, and Alex helped him to his feet.

"I'm glad this is just a big misunderstanding. We will not yell at you for asking for something you want. We may say no if we don't think it's good for you or don't agree with your request, but we won't yell at you and we'll never hit you. Do you understand?" Alex asked.

Jared nodded.

It was quiet for a minute while all of them stood in Jared's room, assessing what just happened.

"This was a lot of excitement at two in the morning, so let's all try to get some sleep and start fresh in the morning," Allison said.

Allison and Alex turned out the light and closed the door.

Alex's heart sank when he thought of the life Jared endured at home with his parents. He knew in the upcoming year it would be a challenge to help Jared transform into a productive citizen, but like all other challenges, Alex generally expected to succeed.

But as he made his way back to bed, he questioned whether this challenge might be too big for him.

Chapter 19

After a week of hiking local trails and backyard barbecues, alarm clocks woke the Garza kids before the sun made an appearance. It was the first day of the new school year, and Olivia would start the second half of her sophomore year; Gaby seventh grade, and Daniel fifth grade.

It was also Jared's first day attending a regular school in over a year. ADJC received an exemption from the Arizona Department of Education, so Jared could attend Scottsdale North High School, where Olivia attended.

Once Olivia, Gaby and Daniel left the house for school, Allison saw Jared waiting with his new hunter green backpack at the kitchen island like a racehorse waiting for the gate to open. He fidgeted with the strap and then the zipper.

"You can wait in my car while I grab my purse and keys," Allison said.

A minute later, she arrived in her SUV with the nervous teen and began the short drive to Scottsdale North High School. Jared looked out the window and didn't speak.

Allison pulled to the curb for student drop off, "You'll have to take the bus next week too. All my kids take the bus until they have a driver's license to drive themselves to school. I'm taking you this week because it's a new school for you, and I don't want to add another wrinkle for you to have to worry about."

Jared nodded and clutched his backpack tighter as he prepared to exit the vehicle. Allison waved to Jared as he shut the door and returned to her empty nest at home.

During lunch, Jared forced a smile at two other students sitting together. He wished he could find some fellow teens open to meeting a new friend on his first day. When the boy with the shaggy black hair and black t-shirt moved his backpack to the empty seat, Jared knew this school year was going to be similar to Buckeye Union High School before his time at Adobe Mountain. It was the same in each class with the teachers. His first-hour biology teacher gave Jared a long stare after she called his name during roll call. The pattern repeated itself until lunch. It was clear all the teachers were aware of his history, and Jared knew that stare from adults and people in positions of authority well. In two silent seconds, they told Jared that they knew he had a past full of mistakes, and he'd better be on his best behavior in their classroom or he'd face swift consequences.

Jared's last hour was his social studies class. The teacher was also the assistant defensive coordinator for the football team. He didn't even attempt to hide his dislike for Jared like all the other teachers did.

"Jared Gellar?" The assistant coach bellowed to the room full of students.

"Here," Jared responded just above a whisper.

The coach shot his gaze over to Jared in the back corner of the room. Once he identified the source of the reply, he asked, "you're the *transfer* student?"

Jared nodded.

"I see. I'd like to see you after class."

A few of the other students shifted in their seats and turned to catch Jared's red cheeks before roll call resumed.

The bell sounded, and the rest of the students vanished from the classroom. Jared shuffled up to the teacher's desk and stood over him while he jotted down a few notes. The teacher saw Jared standing there, stood up, and walked around the desk. He looked Jared up and down.

"You're a good size for your age. What are you, six-three?"

"No, I'm six-two," Jared replied.

"Well, I can tell you think you are a big shot, so let's get one thing straight right now. I'm in charge of this class, and I won't tolerate any insubordination. If you follow the rules and do as you are told, we'll get along just fine. If you cross the line with me, I'll come down on you like a hammer on a nail. Is that clear?"

This routine was so old to Jared that it took all his power not to yawn. Countless teachers, counselors, corrections officers, and other people in authority always tried to establish that they were in charge of him.

"Yeah, it's clear."

"I hope so."

Jared sighed. "Can I go now? I'm going to miss my bus."

"Get out of here," the coach barked.

Jared jogged to the bus and caught it just before the door shut. He found a seat next to a boy leaning against the window with his hoodie pulled tight around his head. The unaware seatmate was perfect for Jared.

The bus pulled from the school lot, and Jared let out a quick chuckle.

"That went well."

With the kids back in school, Alex resumed his long hours at the office during the day and networking events in the evening. Allison's gigs as a freelance makeup artist slowed down after the holidays, and she had more time to help the kids with homework. At first, she was spending time equally with each of the four students in her home, but gradually she spent more time with Jared. Five weeks into the new year, Allison had to spend eighty percent of her time with Jared. It grew clear to Allison that he was a year or two behind the instruction he received at his new high school. Plus, Allison sensed Jared did not possess the same drive to succeed academically as her three kids. It was a struggle to get Jared to do his homework and when he did, it was with minimal effort.

As a staunch advocate for education, Allison worried about Jared's attitude about his studies. Her educational beliefs were a key reason she was such an energetic supporter for Education Stars Behind Bars when Alex first approached her with the idea. Allison recognized that Jared was coming from a much different place. She understood his lack of interest was the cumulative effect of years of neglect by his parents, and it would be impossible to undo that in one semester. She knew Jared could control one thing, however: his effort.

Allison clicked off the light on her nightstand and tried to fall asleep but couldn't get Jared out of her mind. She gazed into the darkness hoping for a solution, but not appeared.

"Alex, are you awake?"

"Yeah. Can't sleep either?"

"No. I keep thinking about how far behind Jared is compared to other Juniors. I'm at a loss on what to do to help him."

Alex was quiet for a few seconds and then responded, "I hear about that all the time at ESBB."

"What do you do?"

"Mateo and I can't help them. We leave it up to the professional educators and advisors to customize a plan for each student to address their specific deficiency or problem."

"Makes sense."

"Let's set up a meeting with Jared's guidance counselor so we can get everyone involved in a plan to get Jared on track. This shouldn't all be on your shoulders. We all need to chip in and help Jared, including me."

Allison liked the idea of a team effort to help Jared. She fell asleep minutes later.

Alex checked the clock on his office desk every two minutes. It was a quarter past four and in forty-five minutes, he had to leave for the Fourth Avenue County Jail in Phoenix. He arranged to show Mr. Park and another Emerson Churchill board member the ESBB classrooms that Mateo and Alex helped established last year. Hundreds of inmates had benefitted from all the resources provided by ESBB and Alex wanted to showcase one of their top training facilities.

The excitement to show Mr. Park and the board member turned to dread with each passing minute. Alex wanted to show off their remarkable facility and program, but his brain was already overflowing with anxiety. Although the Fourth Avenue jail had less security than Florence State Prison, he couldn't fathom passing through the steel and concrete corridor with Mr. Park today.

At four-thirty, Alex called Mateo and faked a personal emergency when he asked Mateo to escort Mr. Park and the board member. He didn't have time to make up a believable excuse and Mateo didn't have time to argue. Mateo raced from work in Chandler and arrived in Phoenix only minutes before Mr. Park.

The next day, Mr. Park called Alex into his office. He complemented the facility and the tour Mateo provided them.

"We would like to support ESBB."

Alex straightened up in his chair. The financial benefits that a corporate sponsor would provide ESBB could get Alex one step closer to the balance he desperately needed.

"Please send us the paperwork for the Adopt-A-Star program. We would like to get started next month."

Adopt-A-Star? Really? The monthly contribution was only ten percent of a full corporate sponsorship.

Alex couldn't contain his disappointment.

"Adopt-A-Star is a great program, but what about a corporate sponsorship? I think that is a better fit for Emerson Churchill."

Mr. Park's lips straightened and he stared at Alex for several seconds.

"We discussed the sponsorship options after the tour last night, but you weren't there. We're not ready for a full corporate sponsorship. Adopt-A-Star is the most we can do right now."

Mr. Park continued to share his thoughts on the facility and the tour, but Alex's mind was elsewhere. He knew that his work-life balance just flew up into a tree and perched on a high branch. Alex is going to have to do even more to convince Mr. Park to commit to a full corporate sponsorship in order to secure the balance he desperately needed.

Chapter 20

H omework sessions with Jared continued to be a challenge, but Allison didn't push him like she did Olivia, Gaby, and Daniel. Everything changed after the mid-quarter report cards were posted on the online portal for each school. Allison had never seen so many Ds and Fs. In fact, she had never seen one on a report card for any of her kids. US Geography was the only class in which he didn't have a D or F, and that was a B by a half percentage point. Although Jared wasn't her child and she'd only known him for six weeks, Allison felt her chest tighten every time she saw his report card in her mind.

The shock of observing his grades online prompted Allison to request the meeting with Jared's guidance counselor that she discussed with Alex. The guidance counselor agreed and suggested Linda Flowers from ADJC attend with the Garzas to discuss Jared's academic status at Scottsdale North High School.

During the meeting two days later, waves of emotion fluttered throughout Allison's body. She caught herself straightening her shirt and pants every time the guidance counselor looked up from the stack of papers in front of him. By the time he finished, Allison nearly rubbed the back of her neck raw.

Allison looked over to Alex in the chair to her right and Linda to the right of Alex and sensed they were not as anxious as she was. She inhaled deeply and closed her eyes as she let it out slowly.

"Mr. and Mrs. Garza and Mrs. Flowers, do you have any idea why Jared is struggling in all the areas I just outlined?" the guidance counselor asked.

Allison shook her head, "He's only been with us since before Christmas so there is a lot I still don't know about him, but I spend hours with him every night trying to help him. Jared will try for a few minutes, and then he gives up when he has any difficulty with his homework. I'm not sure what else I can do."

"He is getting a B in US Geography. Do you know why he does much better in that class?"

"I don't know, but I'll ask him," Allison replied.

The counselor nodded, "Please do. That may uncover some hidden motivation that you can try to bring out in other courses."

Allison was about to ask for a plan from each of Jared's teachers when Linda spoke up, "I may have something that will motivate him." Everyone in the room turned their attention to her.

"Jared will be eighteen in nine months, and legally he'll be an adult. Once he's eighteen, they'll evaluate Jared to determine if he should remain under the jurisdiction of ADJC and the RIHARP JR program. If Jared can't generate passing grades in high school by his eighteenth birthday, the committee may determine the juvenile system can't reform him and remand him to adult court. If that happens, he'll lose his eligibility to be part of RIHARP JR and will become the responsibility of the Arizona Department of Corrections."

"That doesn't sound like motivation. It sounds like more stress than any seventeen-year-old should have to bear!" Allison cried out.

"I'm sorry, Mrs. Garza, but that's the world Jared lives in. At ADJC, we are responsible for more youth than our resources can handle today, so if a youth doesn't respond to our limited reform programs, we have to give others a chance. Jared has until his eighteenth birthday to show he is on the road to reformation, or he'll be out of RIHARP JR."

The last words Linda said in the meeting hung with Allison like a thick fog during the drive home. Jared only had a few months to overcome a lifetime of neglect and become a model student. She knew that would be a significant challenge, but one she wanted to meet to help Jared.

Allison closed her eyes and prayed for the strength, wisdom, and patience to help Jared find a path to succeed in high school.

The next day, Allison sat next to Jared and waited for him to finish his algebra problems. He was getting a solid F in his math class, and Allison wanted to be sure he completed all his homework.

"Hey Jared, we had a talk with your guidance counselor at school yesterday."

Jared kept his eyes on his workbook. "The teachers all hated me the minute I walked in the door."

Allison almost replied, "they don't hate you," so he wouldn't feel bad, but caught herself. She assumed some teachers may not care to have a boy from a juvenile detention school in their classroom, but she didn't want to dismiss Jared's feelings. He was finally opening up to her, and she didn't want to say anything that could cause him to retreat. Instead, Allison nodded and shared her plan.

"We think we should get you a full-time tutor. You need someone who can answer all your questions and help you understand everything. I can't do that, but a tutor can."

Jared scribbled some letters and numbers that resembled an algebra formula on a sheet of paper.

"Are you okay if a tutor comes a few days a week to help you?" Allison asked.

"I appreciate it, but I don't think it'll help. I'm not as smart as the rest of those kids, plus I'm so far behind. I don't think you should waste your money on me."

Allison's heart sank to hear those words come from Jared. She tilted her head and leaned closer to Jared. "We are not wasting any money. We are investing in you because we believe in you, Jared.

You deserve extra help to catch up. You've been through a lot that most of those other students or teachers wouldn't understand."

"Thanks," Jared replied with a quick smile and then returned his attention to his math problem with intense focus.

Allison leaned back in her chair and waited for Jared to finish. She noticed he already completed his US Geography homework. Allison put her hand over his completed paper and raised her eyebrows. Jared looked up and nodded.

Allison reviewed all of his answers, and she estimated that ninety percent of them were correct. She smiled and looked up at Jared, "These all look good."

"Thanks."

"You're doing so well in US Geography. Do you have an interest in geography?"

"Yeah, I guess so."

"You seem to know a lot about geography. What made you interested in it?"

Jared looked down at his worksheet with figures that were supposed to be solutions to math problems.

He pushed the math homework to the side, "When I was little, I found a map of Arizona under the seat of Clint's truck and hid it in my room. For months, I studied the names of the cities and the roads that led to all of them. I also studied the national forests, parks, and rivers. I circled all the places I wanted to visit when I got older. A few years later, when I was thirteen, I took some money from my mom's purse and bought a full United States Almanac. That summer, I studied the other forty-nine states and even the ten provinces in Canada. I wanted to be anywhere but my house, so I also circled all the places in the USA and Canada that I wanted to visit. Clint found my map a year or two ago and burned it because he said it was filthy, but I still remember most cities and states. I guess that's why I do better in US Geography."

"That's great, Jared. So you can see that if you're interested in something, it's easier to learn that information," Allison replied.

Jared nodded and returned a half-smile.

"So, how many of the places have you visited that you circled?"

"None."

"I thought you said you circled a bunch of places in Arizona. Which places have you visited in Arizona?"

Jared didn't respond. He looked down at the desk.

"Have you ever been out of the Phoenix area?"

"Only once or twice."

Allison felt the tears welling up and pressing against her eyelids like a dam ready to burst. "I'm so sorry, Jared, I had no idea."

"I have to go to the bathroom," Jared said as he got up and left the room.

Allison stared at the blank wall in front of her. She knew the clock was ticking for Jared and he needed a lot of help.

Alex finished a rare dinner at home with his family and retreated to his home office to complete a fundraising flyer for ESBB. He increased the font size on his key bullet points and changed the background color when his cell phone buzzed.

It was Jared's father again.

"Hello," Alex answered.

"Get me Jared," Clint Gellar demanded at the sound of Alex's voice.

Alex sighed loudly into the phone. "He's doing his homework. A tutor is helping him so I can't get him right now."

Alex leaned forward in his chair to brace himself for the verbal assault he expected to receive from Clint.

"Oh, okay. When he's done can you tell him we need to know what he did with our tax stuff from last year?"

Clint's voice was smooth and cool.

"Did you say you want me to ask Jared about your tax documents?"

"Yeah, the kid is better than his mom or me at that stuff. He helped make sure we had all the numbers right. I can't find the returns, but I need them to prove we qualify for services I'm looking to get. They require a copy of our taxes for the state health insurance, the energy assistance program, and even the free legal aid."

Alex had so many questions circling his mind like swallows before dusk but couldn't find the voice to ask any of them.

"Okay, I'll let him know," Alex replied and the call ended.

Chapter 21

T he hum of the lights in the conference room added more weight to Alex's already tired eyes. He watched the finance director scroll through slides showing the February and year-to-date results for Emerson Churchill. Expense controls were always the first topic and the least interesting to Alex. He was all about growth, so he secretly checked his email on his phone until the more exciting revenue slides appeared on the screen. The consulting firm was eleven percent ahead of the same period last year, which caused lips to curl up and heads to nod around the room.

Alex straightened up in his chair, and his eyes widened when the finance director clicked to the sources of revenue slide. The pie chart showed new accounts generated nine points of the eleven percent increase. Alex was personally responsible for over eighty percent of their new revenue. After the fiasco at the Fourth Avenue Jail, maybe he'd at last redeemed himself. He turned to Mr. Park and saw what looked like a smile form and then vanish on his face.

Nailed it.

After the meeting ended, Alex checked his messages and noticed a text from Mateo. Alex closed his door and called his brother.

"Hey Alex, how are things going?"

Alex filled him in about Jared's arrival and all the challenges, but that he saw some great potential for growth. Jared was capable of doing well in a subject he liked, and had apparently even done his family's taxes last year, so he had to have some math skills.

"A teenager doing taxes? How'd you find that out?"

"I got the weirdest call out of the blue from Jared's dad. He wanted to speak with Jared and when I said he was busy, he shared that Jared helped do their taxes and that he needed his son's help to find the returns. His dad seemed much more friendly and cooperative compared to his previous call so maybe I just caught him on a bad day last time."

"Maybe you're starting to win him over." Mateo chuckled.

"I doubt that."

"That's wild. I can't believe Jared does taxes. How's work?"

"Funny that you should ask. I just got out of a meeting that highlighted how my networking efforts are paying off. We are growing three times faster than last year. I think I even saw Mr. Park smile."

"That's great news, Alex. I'm not surprised because you are working your tail off to bring new clients to your firm. I thought of something we briefly discussed several months ago but it was bad timing back then."

"Oh yeah, what's that?"

"What do you think about the ESBB All-Stars event for Emerson Churchill? You can invite your boss and other leaders so they'll get to see all the all-star certificate recipients that will thrive after their release because of their ESBB education and training. I still think it's the perfect event to showcase ESBB to a potential corporate sponsor. It's in five weeks, so I want to remind you now so you can invite your boss."

Alex was silent for a few seconds as he pondered the opportunity. He agreed it would be an ideal event to showcase to Mr. Park the benefits that ESBB provides to the community. His concern was that the event would be inside the Florence State Prison. Alex didn't want to have another panic attack, especially not in front of the Emerson Churchill leadership team, but knew after the Fourth Avenue Jail incident he had to try to overcome his anxiety. Emerson Churchill's support of ESBB was crucial for his plan to bring balance into his life. If he was going to be a partner at Emerson Churchill, he had to find that balance.

"Great idea, Mateo. I'll ask Mr. Park right away since he may be a lot more receptive to my invite after seeing the February results. I'll let you know if he accepts."

Alex hung up the phone and scheduled a meeting with Mr. Park for the following week. That gave him time to fine-tune his pitch for such an important invitation.

Sunday morning, Alex fixed his coffee, then strolled into the family room where Jared was relaxing in a recliner with his iPad.

"I didn't know anybody else was up."

Jared looked up from his screen. "Yeah, I couldn't sleep anymore. I thought I'd come out here and read."

"What about? If you don't mind my asking."

"I'm reading reviews on a couple parks up in northern Arizona that I'd like to visit someday. When they had me locked up at Adobe Mountain, I liked to imagine I was there."

"Oh, wow. Did it help?"

"Kind of. More often when I was feeling penned in, I would remember this place we went fishing, back when I was really little and Clint was still working as a cop. I'd remember how the water sounded and the sun felt and the air smelled and suddenly the walls that were crushing me just kind of melted away."

Alex realized he just gained a helpful insight from Jared about how to overcome his prison phobia to stay calm at the upcoming event.

"We like to camp once or twice a year, so we'll go to one of your spots as soon as school is out," Alex said with a reassuring smile.

Jared returned the smile and leaned back into the recliner. He pulled the iPad back in front of his face. Alex took the cue that the conversation was over, so he sipped his coffee and scrolled through his phone.

Thirty minutes later, Alex stood up. "Time to get everyone up."

He took three steps and stopped.

"Jared, we're all going to the ten-thirty service at church today. Would you like to join us?"

Jared sat up again with a pained look on his face. "Do I have to?"

"I'd love for you to come with us whenever you are ready, but I will not force you."

Jared exhaled. "It's been so long. Maybe someday, but I'm not ready today."

"Fair enough. I think Allison said we would go out for lunch afterward and then play a family game tonight."

Jared nodded, and Alex left to wake up the rest of his family to get ready for church.

After dinner, it was Daniel's turn to clean off the table and Olivia's turn to load the dishwasher. Once the table was cleared, Allison notified everyone to come back to the kitchen. Game night was about to begin.

"What are we going to play tonight?" Gaby asked.

"Monopoly!" Daniel yelled out.

"Oh no, I'm not playing Monopoly with you guys again. You add too many houses, and I go broke," Alex replied while he pulled the empty pockets out of his shorts.

"Plus, everyone gets a little too cutthroat with Monopoly, and I don't think we should play that during Jared's first game night with us," Allison added.

"Let's play Uno Attack. It doesn't take as long," Olivia whispered.

Alex looked around the room and saw heads nodding.

"Jared, do you know how to play Uno?" Alex asked.

He shook his head.

"It's easy. Anyone can play it," Olivia chimed in.

"It may be for you, but if Jared's never played it before, we have to go over the instructions and play a few practice games so he knows how to play too," Alex reminded Olivia.

Olivia rolled her eyes. Alex read the instructions and a few practice games followed. After the third practice game, Jared won, so Alex declared he was battle-ready for Garza game night.

Just as Alex was ready to make Allison add four new cards to her dwindling deck, the chime sounded from the security cameras. Alex checked his phone and saw that a grey pickup truck had pulled into his driveway.

Alex marched to the front door and looked at the vehicle idling outside. The truck looked to be at least a decade old and was equal parts rust and peeling paint. He watched as the man inside scanned their home and took pictures with his phone.

"I'm not sure who that is," Alex said as he peered out the window.

The comment roused everyone at the table, and soon six sets of eyes were looking out the narrow window next to the door.

Jared exhaled loudly. "That's Clint."

"What's he doing here?" Alex asked.

"I don't know, but I'm sure it's nothing good," Jared replied.

Alex motioned for everyone to move aside so he could open the front door. Before he could open it, Allison grabbed his arm. "What are you doing?"

"He drove all the way from Buckeye for a reason, so I'm going to see what he wants. Stay inside with the kids."

Alex opened the door and closed it behind him. He took several steps away from his front door and stopped. The man inside the truck was looking down at his phone. Alex waved, but the man did not look up.

Alex took two more steps toward the truck and called out. "Can I help you?"

Clint Gellar's head snapped up, and he locked eyes with Alex. A half-smile formed on his face, and he opened the truck door. It took him several seconds to pour himself out of the truck and shut the door. He kept his eyes on Alex as he walked in front of his truck while maintaining his hand on the hood to steady himself.

"Where's Jared?"

"He's inside. What can I do for you?"

"You can start by getting my son out here. I need to talk to him."

"Not until I know why you're here."

The expression on Clint's face changed in an instant. Alex imagined that Jared had seen this a million times before. Bulging eyes and pursed lips replaced the half-smile. He widened his stance and raised his chin.

"If you tell me why you're here, I may be able to help you," Alex offered.

Clint let go of his hood and took two steps toward Alex. Now only ten feet separated the men. Alex realized why he was hanging on to his hood. The slurred words and smell of alcohol confirmed Alex's initial suspicion that he'd been drinking. Alex had never been drunk before, but he could tell Clint shouldn't be driving in his condition.

"I drove all the way here today because you wouldn't let me talk to him on the phone."

"That's correct. You got nasty with Jared on the phone, and I'm not going to allow that to happen to anyone living under my roof. How did you find my house?"

The half-smile appeared again on Clint's face. He took two steps back and leaned against the right fender of his truck.

"You think you're the only one that's smart around here? I have friends, and I have access to the Internet. It's pretty easy to find somebody through public records if you know what you're doing, and I know what I'm doing. I said that you don't want to mess with me."

Alex pulled out his phone and prepared to dial 911. "I have no interest in 'messing with you.' You need to leave my property, or I'll have law enforcement make you do so."

"You mean Captain Morris? We go way back. I was in the academy with him and half his top lieutenants and I'm sure they'll take my word over someone like you. That state money belongs to me and I'm not leaving here until I get it."

Alex heard the door open behind him. He turned around and saw Jared coming through the door. His face was red with his chest puffed out. Alex thought he might charge his father and start a fight. Alex tried to remember the word to activate Sure Cuffs, but he couldn't remember under the stress of the situation. He pulled out his phone, opened the Sure Cuffs app, and placed his thumb above the activate button.

"Clint, I told you to never bother me again!"

The tension was thick as Alex stood halfway between Jared and his father. It was quiet for five seconds, which seemed ten times longer until Clint's grunt interrupted the silence.

"Why you little—"

Clint charged Jared. Despite his inebriated state, he was faster than Alex expected. A second later, he was passing in front of Alex and gaining momentum towards Jared. Alex didn't have time to think but reacted to protect Jared. He leaped towards Clint and tackled him just as he got his hand on Jared's shirt. Jared jerked away and backed up as his father ripped his shirt open. Alex had Clint entirely in his grasp and took him down to the concrete pavers in front of the narrow side window next to the front door with the rest of his family watching. Clint tried to fight back with his face planted in the pavers but quickly gave up. He turned his efforts to a verbal assault on Alex and everyone else within earshot. He aimed his profanity-ridden attacks at Alex and everyone in the house, but mostly at his "ungrateful" son.

Alex looked up from his position on top of Clint and saw five bodies standing over him on the front stoop. They all had wide eyes and open mouths, including Jared.

"Get back in the house!" Alex barked.

"Allison, call 911and tell them to send the police."

"You don't wanna do that," Clint yelled with his cheek pressed into the driveway. "Because then I'm gonna press charges against you for assaulting me."

"You have no right to be on my property. And I have five witnesses that saw you attempt assault first."

"If they catch you sitting on me like this, it will not look good, amigo. I know all the cops in these parts, and if they come to your house, I'm not the one that's going to jail."

Alex slowly lifted himself off Clint and backed away.

"You have ten seconds to get out of here. You can charge me for assault all you want, and I'll take my chances in court," Alex said through gritted teeth.

Clint sat up and dusted off his hands. He looked at the Garza family standing next to Jared on the front patio. He shook his head and then used a decorative boulder to help him stand up.

He glared at Jared and shuffled back to his truck. A minute later, he pulled out of their driveway and onto the dark road, heading back to the freeway.

"Allison, call the police and tell them a suspected drunk driver is heading West towards Scottsdale Road. I don't want that guy hurting anyone else tonight."

Allison punched some numbers on her phone and went inside the house. Alex looked over to Jared and noticed that the rage in his face earlier transformed into redness around his eyes.

"Come on, everyone, let's get back in the house. The excitement is over."

Alex was never more wrong.

Chapter 22

Allison, Gaby, and Daniel sat with Jared at the kitchen table when Alex came back into the house. Olivia was in her room.

"What's going on with your dad? Why is he coming here looking for money?" Alex asked.

Jared threw his hands up in the air. "I don't know. He's a piece of work, like I said before."

Alex leaned over the table and locked eyes with Jared. "I know you don't like to talk about him, but I need to know who I'm dealing with here. He's shown up unannounced once, and I don't want to be surprised by him again. I need to know more about him."

The creases in Jared's forehead and nose smoothed out. He looked at Gaby and Daniel, then back to Alex and Allison.

"Gaby and Daniel, please give us a few minutes to talk to Jared alone," Allison said.

After the room was clear of all Garza children, Jared straightened in his chair and cleared his throat.

"My mom said that Clint and her got married right after high school. She was pregnant with my older sister Chloe for the last few months of her senior year, and her parents wanted them to get married before Chloe was born. They got married a month after they both graduated from high school."

Jared took a deep breath and continued.

"Clint bounced around a few jobs until they had Chloe. He wanted to give her a better life so he joined the Army. After his two-year stint in the Army ended, he went to the police academy back here and worked for the Sheriff's department for a while. One day he had a driver pulled over alongside the highway when another driver hit the parked vehicle he pulled over. He said he was lucky to be alive but was in the hospital for weeks with broken bones and a back injury. He had multiple surgeries, and that's when he got hooked on painkillers. He couldn't sit in a car or desk for more than a few minutes and eventually, they let him go. Clint sued them and won a settlement for his injury and then turned to repairing appliances and engines as his new job. I was only about eight or nine when all this happened, but I felt a change in the house. Ever since he was injured, Clint has been bitter because he feels the world owes him more for his service in the military and law enforcement. He gets angry every time he thinks about it and then he drinks and that causes different problems."

Jared took a long drink of water.

"Clint soon pulled my mom down with him and by the time I was twelve, I was taking care of my parents with Chloe. It's been a real blast helping two grown adults get up in the morning and feeding them breakfast when my friends were out riding bikes, but that's the hand I was dealt."

Jared turned and stared straight ahead at the bone-white wall in the kitchen. Alex and Allison shared a quick glance.

"Can I go to my room now?"

"Sure," Alex replied as Jared hopped up from his chair and started toward his room. "I know it probably wasn't easy for you to share everything you told us about your parents. I'm glad you did so we know more about Clint and what he may do next."

Jared stopped and turned back to Alex and Allison. "Just be careful with Clint. I wouldn't put anything past him."

Jared left Alex and Allison alone in the kitchen.

"What are you going to do?" Allison asked.

Alex saw the concern in her eyes. He could feel the familiar terror Edgar's erratic behavior stirred up in him, but knew he had to play it cool and reassure Allison.

"I'll notify ADJC about this incident, so it's on the record that Clint came to our house and threatened Jared. I know he knows people in law enforcement, but the people at ADJC should be able to do something. Somebody has to stand up to this guy."

It was still dark outside when Alex woke up the next morning. He had too much on his mind to sleep, so he got dressed and went to the gym. As he jogged on the treadmill, Alex's thoughts turned to his teenage years and how it affected him today as a parent. The vision burned in his mind of his mama crying at the kitchen table when they learned Edgar's sentence included eight years in prison, a pain she bore alone while Papa left for another week-long business trip.

Forever and always, work came first. How differently would things have gone if Papa weren't so focused on success? Would Edgar have chosen a different path? Would Mama have divorced him and left the country? They were questions with no available answers.

After Alex showered, he emailed Mateo and asked him to meet for tacos halfway between their homes in Tempe.

Over lunch, Alex shared a recap of his encounter with Jared's father three nights ago. Mateo stopped eating and sat with his mouth open as Alex shared more details about Clint's checkered past.

"I can't help seeing parallels between Jared and Edgar," Alex concluded.

"What do you mean by that?" Mateo asked.

Alex put down the taco he was about to devour. "Jared got into trouble trying to escape his family, and it seems like Edgar did the same. Rather than try to meet Papa's expectations, he ran the other direction. And Papa refused to take any responsibility for pushing him away."

"Papa did the best he could with a bad situation. He worked really hard so we would have everything we needed."

"I know he worked hard, but we didn't need a bigger house. We needed Papa to help Edgar and keep our family together. I would have never done what he did."

Mateo stared at Alex but didn't respond. He picked up his fried fish taco and took a bite. Neither spoke again until they both finished their meals.

"Mateo, I'm sorry to dump all this on you. I'm just frustrated right now with poor fathers."

Mateo flashed a half-smile. "Parenting isn't easy. We all try hard to do what's best for our families and solve every problem, but sometimes we learn later that we were the source of the problem."

Chapter 23

At nine o'clock sharp, Alex tapped on the door frame of Mr. Park's office. Mr. Park waved for him to enter, so Alex got comfortable in the leather chair across from Mr. Park's enormous desk.

Alex started the meeting with the latest new business development results. Emerson Churchill billings from new clients were up eighteen percent year to date versus the same period last year. That exceeded Alex's target of fifteen percent growth, and he knew that would please Mr. Park.

"Very impressive, Mr. Garza. To what do you attribute this growth? The networking events?" Mr. Park asked.

Alex knew that this was his opportunity. "The networking events help some, but I attribute most of the success to the events I'm doing with businesses from the Education Stars Behind Bars."

This revelation surprised Mr. Park so Alex shared how the ESBB events are more relaxed for the business attendees. This makes them more accessible and comfortable discussing business, unlike some of the hyper-salesy networking meetings that scared away many prospects. Alex wanted him to see firsthand how a business partnership with a nonprofit like ESBB could provide tangible benefits to Emerson Churchill. He straightened up in his seat and invited Mr. Park to their biggest event of the year—the ESBB annual certification event at the Arizona State Prison Complex in Florence.

Alex finished his pitch and watched his boss closely.

Mr. Park leaned back into his chair and put his hands in a praying position. He rocked back and forth for a couple of seconds and then leaned forward again toward Alex.

"Yes, I would like to see how this nonprofit and business collaboration may work. I don't think my wife will want to come inside a prison, so it will be just me."

"Thank you, sir. I'll leave the rest of the details with Lisa, and I look forward to seeing you there."

Every day during the three weeks leading up to the event, Alex prayed longer each morning and practiced the breathing exercises Pastor Scott taught him. This was the first time he would attempt it inside a prison—the one environment where the gray walls turned into an angry elephant sitting on Alex's chest.

On the day of the event, Alex woke up before the sun. He crept into his backyard and caught the twilight dimming the stars in the inky black sky above the mountains to his east. He felt small but free. The nearest structure felt like a million miles away, and it was easier to breathe.

Alex got comfortable in a chaise lounge chair and lost track of time until the sun's crown showered the new day's rays onto Alex's cold skin. He closed his eyes tight and said one last prayer. Alex asked God to keep everyone safe at the ESBB event and to give him the strength to make it through without a panic attack. Convinced that God heard his plea, Alex went back inside and got ready for his big day.

Alex pulled into the visitor parking lot at the Arizona State Prison Complex in Florence a few minutes after five. He left work an hour early to beat the worst of the traffic heading home during their Thursday evening commute.

Alex hopped out of his SUV, and the familiar smell of the prison complex punched him in the nose. He was not aware of the source of the familiar scent, but it was unmistakable. Alex could tell he was near a prison with his eyes closed.

His pace slowed as his confidence waned at the sight of the first security point for visitors. For a moment, Alex considered returning to his vehicle. He could say he had to work late and just meet everyone at the banquet after the event, but he knew it would be best if he was present inside the prison walls when Mr. Park arrived. Alex looked over the complex and took a deep breath. His resolve for more balance overcame his concern, and he continued through the security checkpoint.

Ten minutes and three checkpoints later, Alex made it into the portion of the inmate cafeteria set up for the All-Stars certification ceremony. A handful of Florence prison residents lingered on the other side after completing their evening meal. A half dozen corrections officers stood between the inmates and the setup crew. Eventually, the officers encouraged the inmates to leave the cafeteria. Inmates who persevered in the most challenging environments, along with family, friends and business sponsors, would soon fill the entire area for the annual ESBB All-Star event.

Alex found Mateo and other ESBB team members hard at work to pull off the biggest event of the year. After exchanging handshakes and hugs with his team, Alex jumped in to help. Setting up chairs and tables helped him keep his mind off his location. Thirty minutes later, the cafeteria transformed into a room fit for any graduation ceremony. Friends and family members of the inmates receiving their certificates arrived and were escorted to their seats. Alex kept his eye on the door for Mr. Park.

Minutes before the certification campaign started, Alex saw his boss's familiar silhouette emerge in the doorway. Mr. Park was in the room, and now Alex just had to keep it together for two more hours until they could drive a mile across town and start the business sponsor banquet at the rustic Lake House at Windmill Winery. His chest was already feeling tight, and each breath labored. Alex closed his eyes and started his breathing exercises. So much was riding on this event, and Alex had already begun to crumble.

Alex escorted Mr. Park to the seat strategically near the aisle.

"Thank you for coming today," Alex said.

"I'm looking forward to it. Are the rest of the people here all family, or are some of them the business sponsors?" Mr. Park asked as he scanned the room.

"Most are family or friends, but some business sponsors are here. You'll have time to meet all of them at the banquet after the certification ceremony."

"Excellent. I'm looking forward to it."

The overhead lights dimmed, and the certification ceremony began. A meteorologist from a local TV news station was the emcee of the event. He announced that they were all attending the Fourth Annual Education Stars Behind Bars All-Star Certificate Celebration and shared a brief history of several certificate holders and their successes outside of prison. Next, the emcee introduced Mateo. He summarized ESBB and thanked everyone that helped make it happen, especially the business sponsors.

"Now, let's get to the real reason you are all here. Time to celebrate with some certificates," Mateo said into the microphone to jubilant applause.

Ten minutes into the ceremony, Alex felt heat inch up his back. He kept his eyes locked on Mateo as he called out the name of each inmate receiving a certificate. Alex clapped when an inmate walked on stage and received their framed certificate. The smiles on their faces reminded Alex of why he started ESBB a decade ago.

Ignoring the inferno growing inside of him did not work. Alex looked at his watch but it only made things worse. He still had over ninety minutes, and a full-blown panic attack stalked him like a lioness locked in on its prey.

Breathe in, hold, slowly exhale, one, two, three, repeat.

Alex started his breathing exercises to ward off the looming panic attack. After the fifth inmate received his framed certificate, Alex looked out of the corner of his eye to see if Mr. Park noticed him doing his breathing exercises. He was focused on the inmates on stage, giving Alex a brief reprieve. Alex was happy he had an aisle seat so he could slip away if needed.

After an hour passed, nineteen of the forty-two inmates scheduled to receive a certificate had crossed the stage. Alex was losing his battle against the siege of anxiety and claustrophobia. The heat grew in his stomach, and shooting pains in his chest felt like a python tightening its grip around Alex. He loosened his tie and pulled at his collar, hoping it would provide him with a few minutes of relief. Alex knew it was a race against time. Could he hold off an attack for another hour until he could leave the cafeteria that seemed to get smaller every minute?

Eight inmates later, Alex bounced his knees up and down while seated in his chair. He knew his fidgeting would soon get the attention of Mr. Park and others around him. He would not make it through the remaining forty-five minutes of the ceremony. Alex leaned over and whispered to Mr. Park. "I'll be right back."

Mr. Park nodded.

Alex slid out of his chair and crouched down as he scampered to the back of the room. Once out of sight, he paced behind all the guests and business sponsors. He needed to get his breathing under control and slow the stabbing pain that was exploding in his chest.

Alex looked to the one door that could give him instant relief. Fresh air and the end to this nightmare were inches away on the other side of the door. He turned away from the door and leaned against the concrete wall behind all the chairs. It was several degrees cooler, which provided a few seconds of relief, but then quickly ended.

Alex turned to the door again. He felt drawn to it and felt his legs wanting to move closer to the exit. When Alex got ten steps away, the corrections officer near the door saw him and pointed to the door. His eyes asked Alex if he needed to leave. This was Alex's chance to stop the pain.

"No," Alex whispered and shook his head.

Alex did a quick about-face and returned to the back of the room. He closed his eyes and tried Pastor Scott's breathing exercises but found he couldn't hold his breath with his heart racing. Next, he thought about the family vacation to San Diego and the Pacific Ocean the previous summer. He hoped the memory of the infinite view across the indigo saltwater horizon would transport his mind from the prison cafeteria that felt more like a coffin with each passing minute. Not even a vision of an ocean was enough to free him from his attack.

The growing desire to bolt from the cafeteria smacked Alex, and he opened his eyes to watch another inmate receive a certificate on stage.

Come on. Try to last a few more minutes.

Alex closed his eyes tighter and gripped the back of a chair in the last row, then he remembered what Jared had said about mentally escaping when he felt the walls closing in.

The view of the sunrise earlier that morning flashed in his mind. The dark sky with stars shimmering from millions of miles away grew more vivid with each measured breath. The vision of the night sky pulling back the ebony cloak to reveal the sun like a magician soothed Alex. Each ray of sun was a sign of hope—hope for a new day that wouldn't be the same as the day before.

Alex was no longer in the cafeteria. He was sitting on the chaise in his backyard, watching hope rise above the mountain peaks. A cooling calm flowed down from his head, through his neck, and down to his chest. It was like a cool glass of water on a hot day. Alex felt it moving through his body. Hope was the antidote to the army of anxiety battling inside Alex's chest.

He kept his eyes shut for another ten minutes, and by then, Alex breathed normally. Once he opened his eyes, Alex saw that only three inmates remained in their seats waiting to receive their certificates.

I made it.

Alex practically floated back to the seat next to Mr. Park.

"Is everything okay?" Mr. Park asked after Alex sat down.

"Yes, everything is fine."

Mr. Park searched Alex's face and must have found him to be truthful. He nodded, and the duo watched the remaining inmates receive their certificates. The ceremony ended, and the lights in the cafeteria illuminated the room.

"I need to wrap up a few things here and then I am heading over to the banquet. Do you want to wait here or meet me over there?" Alex asked Mr. Park.

"I'll meet you over there."

Alex watched his boss pass through the door he considered exiting one hour earlier. No matter what happened at the banquet, this night was already a victory for Alex. He had overcome a monster that haunted him for a decade. He knew he had not defeated the beast for good and that it would rear its head again, but now Alex was less afraid. He'd found the sword of hope, and that was enough to hold off the monster.

Chapter 24

V iewing the small man-made lake reflecting the dim patio lights washed off the remaining tension from Alex as he pulled into the banquet center parking lot. Alex bounded up the stairs and found Mr. Park eating shrimp alone at a high-top table. Alex patted Mr. Park on the shoulder and escorted him around the room to meet several business sponsors who raved about their sponsorship benefits with Education Stars Behind Bars. Soon a tall man wearing cowboy boots and a bolo tie approached them and gave Alex a handshake and a hug.

"Alex, that was another outstanding event. Thanks again for all you do," he exclaimed.

"Thank you. I'd like to introduce you to Mr. Park. He's the president of the Arizona branch of Emerson Churchill consultants where I also work." Alex turned to Mr. Park. "This is Earle Cooper. He owns Sun Valley Heating, Cooling, and Plumbing, the largest family-owned HVAC business in the state and a founding business sponsor of ESBB. They have a fleet of 40 vans with 316 full-time employees. Earle's grandfather started Sun Valley over fifty years ago."

Earle extended his hand and gave Mr. Park a firm handshake.

"Honored that you came to this event. Alex and I share a common history of family members spending time behind bars, and I jumped at the chance to do something positive for those inmates. The certificate ceremony is my favorite event of the year," Earle said.

Mr. Park nodded, "It was great to see the benefits for all the inmates that received a certificate firsthand. Has the sponsorship of ESBB helped your business?"

"Oh yeah, we've seen benefits in several ways. We've hired twelve of the certificate holders after they completed their sentences. So far, all of them have turned their lives around and grew to be reliable, productive team members. After seeing my uncle and co-founder of this business die behind bars five years ago, that is the number one benefit for me. The other benefit is goodwill, and that leads directly to higher revenue. At Sun Valley, we serve everyone in our community, and when potential clients learn we support turning around the lives of inmates and giving them a second chance, they choose to work with us."

Mr. Park smiled. "That's an amazing testimonial. It would be great if we could support you as a business partner at Emerson Churchill as well."

Earle turned and locked eyes with Alex. Alex wasn't sure if the abrupt business pitch offended him.

"Funny that you should mention that. Alex has been hounding me for years to give your firm a chance to earn my business, and we have our first meeting to discuss it later this month."

The broad smile on Mr. Park's face was what Alex needed to see after the last two torturous hours.

Alex basked in his successful mission while Earle and Mr. Park continued to talk. Minutes later, Earle excused himself to catch up with an old friend, and Mr. Park turned to Alex.

"I can see now why you have been encouraging Emerson Churchill to become a business sponsor of your organization. It was a pleasure meeting all the other sponsors, and I can see how sponsorship can be beneficial to our business."

Mr. Park extended his hand, and Alex did the same. Mr. Park held onto his hand after shaking it and said, "please send Lisa the business sponsor agreement, and I'll see that we review it in our budget meetings."

"Thank you, Mr. Park!"

"I really must go now, so I'll see you in the office tomorrow."

Alex watched Mr. Park meander through the other guests and back through the doors leading to the parking lot. As soon as he was out of view, Alex turned to the tranquil water below him and gave two fist pumps. At last, he could step back from ESBB for a while and get back on track to become a partner.

As the evening was winding down, Alex finally caught up with his brother. He couldn't contain his excitement and gave Mateo a bear hug.

"Everything was amazing. You and your team did a magnificent job. I can't thank you enough. Mr. Park was so impressed, he wants to become a business sponsor. ESBB will have even more funds available to help inmates."

Mateo beamed. "That's fantastic!"

"Best of all, I can finally get some balance in my life. With ESBB in better financial shape, I can focus on becoming a partner at Emerson Churchill."

Mateo nodded and put his hand on Alex's shoulder. "As long as that's what you really want, I'm with you."

Seventy minutes later, Alex pulled into his garage. He couldn't wait to tell Allison the excellent news. He closed the garage door behind him and sat in his SUV to recount the events of the evening, including overcoming a panic attack. The movie in his head of that evening's events ended with Mateo in the parking lot. The smile on Alex's face vanished when he thought of Mateo's last words.

This is what I really want. Right?

Chapter 25

The thrill of Mr. Park's agreement to sponsor ESBB lasted less than a week. During a meeting at work, Alex felt his phone vibrate in his pocket. He glanced at the screen and noticed that it was from Linda Flowers. For a moment, Alex considered leaving the room to answer the call but didn't want to interrupt the meeting's flow.

Once the meeting ended, Alex went into his office and quickly called Linda back.

"Hello, Mr. Garza, thanks for calling me back. Unfortunately, I have some bad news to share."

Alex took a deep breath. "Okay, I'm alone in my office now."

"I'm sure you'll receive your notification later today, but we just received a Notice of Claim of a lawsuit challenging the authority of RIHARP JR. Next, we will receive the suit and a notice to appear in state court."

"That's terrible news. Why am I also receiving a notice?"

"Jared's father, Clint Gellar, filed the lawsuit."

A million thoughts flooded Alex's mind.

"I guess that means we're also named in the lawsuit?"

"I'm afraid so."

"Wow, I don't have time for this right now."

"That's the other reason I called you as soon as I was able. I spoke to Legal here at ADJC, and they said they're going to file a joinder of parties with the judge so ADJC and the Garza family will be co-defendants. The ADJC legal team will represent all the parties in this suit. I wanted you to know all of this before you received the notice later today."

Alex exhaled into the phone. "Thank you for being proactive. I really appreciate it. What is the charge in the lawsuit?"

"I don't know all the details yet, so I recommend we jump on a call once our legal team has had time to review the lawsuit. After a quick scan, it looks like Mr. Gellar says he is the legal guardian of Jared and RIHARP JR unlawfully assigned him to another party for guardianship."

"Hmm. He didn't seem all that interested in taking care of Jared when he had the opportunity before RIHARP JR."

"I know, but sometimes parents will see the error of their ways or regret the mistakes of their past and want to make things right again."

"I don't think that's the case with Clint Gellar. He just wants access to the host stipend."

"That's a strange way to make money, but it explains the lawsuit," Linda replied.

Alex remembered the anger in Clint's eyes when he left their driveway a couple weeks ago. He said that we were messing with the wrong person, and this must be the way he planned to get even.

Alex turned back to his desk to the photo of his family in front of their house. He remembered the look in Jared's eyes when his father staggered toward him in their driveway. The look of horror, disgust, and shame on Jared's face would be forever burned in Alex's memory. Now, Jared needed someone to protect him from his self-serving father. Alex pulled a picture of Edgar out of his wallet. He touched Edgar's face and then committed to protecting Jared from Clint and Becky Gellar.

"Jared needs an ally right now. I'll do as much as I can for him and help ADJC beat this lawsuit."

Saturdays always buzzed with activity at the Garza house. Baseball games, piano recitals, swimming in the pool, and visits with Tio Mateo and his family were standard each weekend. After a long day, Alex and Allison went to bed after Daniel and Gaby just past eleven. Jared struggled to sleep now that he knew his parents were fighting to pull him away from the Garzas, plus his tutor worked him so hard, he saw algebraic equations float across his mind every time he closed his eyes. So he stayed up to finish watching his movie on his tablet, hoping it would help him wind down. Hungry when the film ended a little before twelve, he left his bedroom to get a late-night snack before he turned in for bed.

Olivia arrived home just before her midnight curfew. She passed Jared in the hallway as she scurried to her bedroom. After he was a few feet past her, an unexpected, but familiar scent stopped Jared in his tracks and he turned to face her. She pushed open her door and saw Jared staring at her.

"What's wrong with you?" Olivia snapped.

"I could ask you the same thing," Jared replied.

"What are you talking about?"

"I can smell what you've been smoking from here. I don't think your parents would be too happy if they knew you were smoking weed."

Olivia's eyes widened, but she quickly tamped down her surprise. "It's not weed. One of my friends smokes cigarettes, and she was smoking in the car. It must have gotten all over me." Olivia responded in a pleasant tone.

Jared smiled and shook his head. "That may work on some people, but I've smelled people smoking marijuana hundreds of times. I could spot that smell a mile away."

Olivia pursed her lips but did not respond.

"I don't think you should start doing that. A lot of the guys I met at the Adobe High School started with weed and kept trying stronger stuff until they got hooked on oxy or heroin or meth. It can happen to anyone. Don't do it, even if it means you have to find new friends."

Olivia took two steps toward Jared. "I don't take orders from kids from juvie. Mind your own business and stay out of mine." She turned and went into her room.

"Please don't do it again," Jared whispered.

Olivia popped back out of her room and into the dark hallway. "Or what? What are you going to do if I do it again? Narc on me to my parents?"

"Only if you force me to," Jared responded so fast that it caused Olivia to take a step back.

"Oh my gosh, you're a narc? You're worse than I thought. Stay away from me!"

This time, Olivia shut the door behind her.

Jared waited in the hallway for a minute to see if she would come back out, but when she didn't open the door, he continued to the kitchen to get his snack.

The tension between Jared and Olivia thickened. It was not as noticeable at home, but at school, she told her friends that Jared was a narc, so they made fun of him whenever they saw him.

On a Tuesday evening, Alex was at a networking event, and Allison was at baseball practice with Daniel. Gaby was playing Go Fish with Jared when Olivia came home. She darted past both of them sitting at the kitchen island. Gaby stayed focused on her cards, but Jared noticed the smell again. Olivia turned around to face Jared just before turning down the hall, and they locked eyes. They communicated a full conversation without a single spoken word. This was her last warning.

Later that Friday, Alex came home from work and started up the barbeque grill in the backyard. Just as the sun set, everyone but Olivia enjoyed a feast of carne and pollo asada. After dinner, they all moved to the kitchen island to enjoy a spread of warm brie cheese topped with strawberries and blueberries for dessert.

Just like Tuesday, Olivia arrived home and darted past the rest of the family.

"Hey, hon, we have some of the brie cheese that you like. Why don't you have some?" Allison asked before Olivia could reach the hallway.

"No thanks, Mom. I'm not hungry right now."

"Where did you and your friends go?"

"We went out for some tacos. It was good, but I'm exhausted now."

Olivia pivoted and continued to her bedroom.

Jared inhaled deeply. He smelled the distinctive odor of marijuana again and could tell that she had smoked again tonight. She was choosing the wrong path in life, and Jared respected Mr. and Mrs. Garza too much to not tell them about the critical information he possessed. Olivia left him with no choice.

Alex pushed his chair away from the table and opened up his phone to check his email while Allison did the same. Gaby and Daniel finished putting the dishes away and they passed Jared entering the kitchen. He hovered near Alex for a few seconds until he looked up.

"Can I talk to both of you about something?"

Alex and Allison turned to each other and put their phones away.

"Sure, you can talk to us about anything," Allison replied.

Jared turned to the hallway where he last saw Olivia and then blurted, "Olivia is smoking weed."

Chapter 26

Jared's four-word statement felt like a baseball bat across the chest. Alex knew the impact of the accusation and the long list of undesirable outcomes attached to it. The weight of the lawsuit and Jared's claim pushed the remaining oxygen out of his chest. This was the last thing he wanted to hear, but even more so today.

Alex put both hands on the counter and bent over while Allison put her hand over her mouth.

"Why would you think that?" Allison asked.

"I smell it on her."

"Are you sure it's marijuana? I know a couple of her friends smoke, but Olivia says she would never even do that. She thinks it's gross," Allison responded.

"I'm sure."

Allison paced while Alex straightened up and moved next to Jared. "I think we need to ask Olivia. She has always been honest with us, so let's see if she is smoking something or if this is just a big misunderstanding."

A few minutes later, both Allison and Olivia were standing across from Jared and Alex at the kitchen island. Olivia had just gotten out of the shower and changed into her pajamas. She wrapped her long hair in a towel.

Well played, Jared thought.

Allison spoke first. "Olivia, we have something important to ask you, and we need you to be honest with us."

Olivia nodded.

"Jared says he smelled marijuana on you tonight. Have you been smoking anything?"

Olivia snapped her gaze toward Jared. "Oh my gosh, I can't believe you'd stoop that low." She turned to Alex and Allison.

"Jared is just mad because I won't let him hang out with my friends and me at school. I gave him a chance to meet them, but they think he's weird and they don't like him. I told Jared to find his own friends, and he got furious at me. He said he'd get even with me, but I didn't think he'd go so low to falsely accuse me of doing drugs."

"Olivia, you never answered the question. Did you smoke anything today?" Alex asked.

Olivia's displeasure swung to Alex. "No, I haven't smoked anything. Is that a clear enough answer for you?"

Allison turned to Alex. "I smelled nothing on her when I went to her room. I think she's telling the truth."

Jared dropped his head and stared at the floor. He only wanted to help but knew that he made things worse by speaking up.

"Jared, is it possible you made a mistake on what you thought you smelled?" Allison asked.

Jared looked at Olivia. The daggers lurking behind her brown eyes spoke volumes, and he didn't want to go to war with her.

"I guess."

"Can I go back to my room now and finish getting ready for bed? My hair is still soaking wet."

Alex responded. "Both of you go to your rooms now."

Jared shuffled back to his room several steps behind Olivia. She reached her room first and entered. As Jared walked past, Olivia whispered, "Don't mess with me again. I can make up wonderful stories about you too."

She shut the door and Jared continued to his room. He fell back into his bed and stared at the ceiling. Jared got off to a positive start with his RIHARP JR hosts, but now he once again had an arch-nemesis living under the same roof. His future living with the Garzas was uncertain after feeling safe and secure in a home for the first time in his life. Jared knew they'd believe Olivia over him, a troubled teen, and he didn't blame them. It had been that way most of his life. He just hoped that they would understand that he was only trying to help and let him stay.

But Jared knew that even if they allowed him to stay in their home, they would treat him differently. Life was about to get rough again.

The following week, Alex drove to the four-story ADJC building in downtown Phoenix that looked more like an old high school than a state government office. Alex gave his name at the security desk, and minutes later, Linda escorted him up to her office on the third floor.

A lanky man in his early to mid-thirties arrived in a navy-blue suit. His shaggy brown hair bounced with each step. The man reached out his hand and gave Alex a firm handshake.

"I'm Evan from ADJC Legal."

Linda turned from her computer monitor and faced the two men across her desk. "Evan, please fill us on the Gellar lawsuit."

"Sure. The plaintiff is seeking custody of the minor child, Jared Gellar, during his enrollment in the RIHARP JR program. Clint and Becky Gellar are the claimants and the legal guardians of Jared. They object to the temporary guardianship granted to the Garza family through the RIHARP JR program and are seeking immediate custody of their son."

"Wouldn't Jared still be in ADJC custody at the Adobe School if he wasn't part of RIHARP JR right now? Wouldn't sending him back to his parents to live with them be like an early release or something?" Alex asked.

"Yes and no," Evan quickly responded. "Yes, Jared's current sentence runs through his eighteenth birthday, which is in seven months, but since he is not serving his sentence at the Adobe School as originally cited in the last judgment, he's in a gray area now. We try to think of everything when we write these new programs like RIHARP JR, but they found a small crack in the program's wording, and they're trying to exploit it."

Alex nodded. "Makes sense, I guess. When do we have to go to court?"

"Since this is a civil case, the plaintiffs' attorneys will conduct sworn depositions in front of a judge in a couple of months. It will be a bench trial, so no jury or courtroom for this case."

Alex was both relieved and disappointed. He'd never been in a real courtroom before, not even for a speeding ticket, so part of him wanted to get a front-row seat to a scene like the legal drama shows he loved. The thought of entering a courtroom with a jury, bailiffs, and judge in a black robe was daunting for Alex. Plus, he'd seen cases on the true-crime TV shows where they sequestered juries for days trying to convince the twelfth juror to break the deadlock. He didn't have the nerves or the time for such a dramatic event in his life right now.

The conversation in Linda's office continued until Evan answered all their questions.

"Mr. Garza, we'll be in touch soon with a location and time for your deposition. In case you are not aware, a deposition is your testimony given under oath in front of a judge, attorneys and court reporter. This creates a legal document for the court, so we'll want to get together a day or two before your deposition date to give you some pointers and do a dry run or two."

Alex pulled out of the ADJC parking garage and began his journey home. The full gravity of the lawsuit didn't hit him until now.

"I can't believe I'm getting sued with all the other stuff going on right now."

He pushed a button on his steering wheel, and after the chime, Alex told the voice coming from his Bluetooth to call Mateo.

Mateo answered and Alex immediately launched into his dilemma. "You'd never believe where I'm driving from right now—the ADJC office in Phoenix after meeting with the legal team. We are getting sued by Jared's parents. Suddenly, they want custody of their son now that they know a paycheck comes with him every month from RIHARP JR."

"Wow, when do you have to go to court?"

Alex explained the deposition process to Mateo that he'd just learned himself minutes earlier.

"So I get to look forward to being grilled by Clint Gellar's attorney in a conference room somewhere in a month or two. This couldn't have come as a worse time with everything else going on. I feel like a shaken-up soda that's about ready to explode."

"Why don't you get away for a while?" Mateo asked in a calm, measured voice.

"Get away?"

"I've seen the stress in your face that last few months, and I know you love to escape into the woods to blow off steam. Why don't you take everyone camping for a long weekend or something? I think Allison and all the kids could probably use some time away from their phones, friends, and distractions. It's also an excellent opportunity for everyone to bond together as you enter some brewing storms, especially for Jared."

Alex's eyes widened, but he didn't respond.

"It's just an idea. You can do something else," Mateo responded to fill the silence.

"No, it's a great idea. I can't believe I never thought about it."

Mateo laughed, "That's what smarter older brothers are for. I have all the answers."

The call ended, and Alex straightened in his seat and readjusted his grip on his steering wheel. He was going to take his family camping.

Chapter 27

A lex stood in front of the bay window in their bedroom as the sun climbed higher above the craggy mountain peak and turned to Allison scurrying from the bathroom to the closet.

"I want to take everyone camping."

Allison inserted one earring and stopped, "Right now? With everything else going on?"

"Yes, that's exactly why I think we should go. We could all use a change of scenery right now."

Allison moved back to the mirror in her closet and inserted the other earring. "The cooler temps would be nice and I think time away could be especially beneficial for Jared and Olivia."

"Why's that?" Alex asked as he leaned against the archway to the closet.

"Olivia has been acting strange this school year, and I know Jared has struggled to find friends and fit in at school. The tension is so thick between those two that maybe the pressure got the best of both of them. I suspect that may be why Jared made that wild accusation about Olivia."

Alex nodded. "Yeah, could be."

Allison kissed Alex and darted for the door. "I've gotta go, but let's go camping over the long Memorial Day weekend and see if we can all start fresh when we get home."

After the kids arrived home from the pre-holiday half day at school, Alex tightened the gear bulging on the roof rack while Allison filled up the cooler. Once they finished, everyone packed into the SUV and they headed north to the national forest.

Three hours later, they arrived at their destination seven thousand feet above sea level and twenty-five degrees cooler than their home in the Valley of the Sun. Ponderosa pine trees rose thirty stories above the forest floor and huddled together as far as the eye could see. They chose a campground near Willow Lake and set up both tents on adjoining campsites.

After stories and smores, Jared sat with Allison and Alex around the crackling fire. Everyone else was asleep or listening to music in their tent.

Alex closed his eyes while Allison and Jared continued to watch the orange and yellow flames dance around the logs.

"Alex, go to bed if you are tired. You're falling asleep in your chair," Allison said.

Alex opened his eyes and let out a quick laugh. "I wasn't sleeping. I was praying."

Allison put her hand over her mouth and then removed it. "I'm sorry. Keep praying. I won't bother you this time."

"That's okay. I'm done."

Everyone around the fire pit grew silent again until Jared asked a question. "Why do you pray?"

Alex turned to Allison and then to Jared. He leaned forward in his folding chair. "Tonight, I was giving thanks. I was thanking God for this beautiful forest and the company of my family. I also thanked him for you."

"But why?"

"God is my Heavenly Father, and I want to talk to him. I talk to him when I am thankful, sad, angry, worried, and when I do something that I'm not proud of so I can ask for forgiveness."

"You ask for forgiveness? Is that because of all the rules?"

"Not necessarily. It's because I want to have a strong relationship with God, and he wants to have one with all his children as I do with

Olivia, Gaby, and Daniel. I don't want to do something that offends him, like talk behind somebody's back, feel pride or greed, or whatever disappoints Him. I want to have a good relationship with Him, just like my family here."

Jared stared at Alex but did not reply. He turned back to the fire.

"Does any of this make sense, or is it confusing?"

"It's confusing. I thought God wanted us to follow all His rules or He would punish us. I've never heard of anyone talking about God like an actual father. I sure hope he's not like my father."

Alex stood up and moved his chair closer to Jared's. He leaned over his armrest and whispered. "God is not like your father or my father. He is the most loving father in the universe. He even loves Clint, even though he's not a very good person."

Jared shook his head. "How can anyone love him?"

"That's the thing. God loves everyone, even when we don't deserve it. It's called grace. Unlike all of us, God is free of sin, and to live with him in Heaven, you have to be perfect or sinless."

Jared nodded. "So that's what all the rules are for. But, how does anyone—"

He stopped himself and leaned back in his chair. Alex could see the confusion on his face highlighted by the crackling fire.

"How does anyone what?"

Jared leaned forward. "How does anyone get to Heaven? The rules seem impossible not to break at least once in a while. I mean, come on. Everybody lies, cheats, or gets mad at someone, so how does anyone ever get into Heaven?"

Alex turned to Allison and they both smiled. He turned back to Jared. "That's why we call Jesus our Savior. God loves us so much, and He knows all of us on earth are sinners. He knows life on earth is full of pain, suffering, and temptation, so God sent his son Jesus to save us. When Jesus died on the cross, he took the penalty of sin upon Himself, so we can get to Heaven if we have Jesus on our side."

"If he took all the sins, why do we still have to follow all the rules?"

"Great question." Alex laughed. "It comes back to that relationship I talked about earlier. When you know that someone loves you as much as God loves us, you don't want to hurt or disappoint Him. He loves us more than we can comprehend and sin disappoints Him, so I don't want to sin."

Jared leaned back in his chair but asked no further questions.

Alex bounced his attention back and forth from the fire and Jared. He could see Jared was in deep thought. The wheels inside his head were turning, and that's all Alex could ask for.

"Does any of this make sense?" Alex asked.

"A little. I still have more questions, but you've given me enough to think about for now."

"Come to Allison or me anytime with questions."

"Okay. Good night."

Alex remained by the fire until it burnt out, long after everyone else went to bed. He was at peace, and he wanted to soak in the moment for as long as possible.

Chapter 28

A week after the camping trip, Alex drove back to downtown Phoenix to meet with Evan, the lawyer for ADJC, as well as the outside counsel for Jared's custody case. Evan ushered Alex and Linda into the corner conference room with floor-to-ceiling windows that showcased one-hundred-and-eighty-degree views of the Phoenix metropolitan area. Alex marveled at the excellent vantage point of Camelback Mountain compared to the one he had in his Scottsdale office and then turned his attention to the man and woman sitting at the conference room table. Evan introduced him to the outside counsel who would help with the case, Kristen, an attorney in her upper forties with long blond hair that flowed over the left side of her dark jacket, and Ted, a junior attorney with a neatly trimmed goatee who looked to be barely thirty years old.

Kristen kicked off the meeting by explaining the deposition process step by step. Ninety minutes later, she called for a break. "Now that everyone is familiar with the process and what to expect, let's reconvene here in ten minutes to do a dry run with Alex."

After everyone left the room, Alex strode over to the windows. He looked across the low-rise buildings, red stucco-roofed homes and trees dotting the landscape. "I could get used to this view," Alex whispered to himself. "Maybe I'll have an office like this someday when I become a partner."

The meeting resumed. Ted had seated himself directly across from Alex so he could play the role of Clint Gellar's attorney and ask Alex questions they expected from the plaintiff during the deposition.

"I have one last reminder before we start the role-playing portion," Kristen interjected. "Alex, during a deposition, the key is to take your time and think about your answer before you respond. Always be one-hundred percent honest with your answers, but don't worry about filling any silence in the room. Remember that a deposition is an official transcript for the court, and nobody knows how long it took you to answer, so take your time and respond when you are ready. Does that make sense?"

Alex nodded. "Yes, it makes sense."

"Okay, great. Go ahead, Ted."

Ted smiled and stood across the room from Alex. For the next ten minutes, Ted asked him a half dozen simple warm-up questions.

Ted put both hands on the table and leaned toward Alex. "The opposing counsel will probably be friendly to you in the beginning. They are trying to gain your trust, so you'll let your guard down. They are not your friend or ally, so keep that in mind when they switch to the harder questions that I'm about to ask you."

Maybe they don't know what I do for a living. I can handle questions from an attorney.

Alex snickered. "Okay, I'll be ready."

Everything about Ted changed. He stood over Alex and his voice deepened. Ted asked Alex about his childhood, current position at Emerson Churchill, and his marriage with Allison.

Although they were only mock questions, Alex grew more defensive with each one. He wondered why they had to ask about his family or his past when they were there to discuss the custody of a seventeen-year-old boy he'd only known for six months. Alex's body stiffened and he abruptly answered the last two questions nanoseconds after Ted asked them.

Kristen put her hand up to stop Ted before his next question. "Alex, you're not taking your time to think about your response to each question. Are you getting frustrated?"

"Yeah, I guess I am. I don't understand why those questions apply to this case."

Kristen smiled. "They may or may not apply, but expect that they will ask questions on topics you feel are off-limits or irrelevant. The key is to relax and not get defensive."

"How do you relax with questions like those?"

"Sit with your hands on your knees and then turn your palms up," Kristen demonstrated through the glass table.

Alex mirrored the position of Kristen's hands, and he looked up with a furrowed brow.

"Don't worry, the table for the deposition won't be glass, so nobody will see what you are doing with your hands."

"Does it work?"

"It does. I read it years ago in the book *Love Does* by Bob Goff. He was an attorney and recommended it to his clients. I tried it and it worked, so I've been recommending it ever since then. It hasn't failed me yet."

The team concluded the dry run forty minutes later.

Kristen stood up first. "Alex, you did great. You're as ready as you'll ever be. Go home and get a good night of sleep, and we'll see you tomorrow."

The next day Alex arrived thirty minutes early. He dressed in his finest business suit and sported a freshly shaven face.

He sat with his legal team across from Clint and his attorney in the horseshoe set up of the tables while the judge and court reporter sat at the middle table. The elderly judge leaned into the microphone and said, "The plaintiff will start, followed by cross-examination from the defense."

They placed a microphone in front of Clint and the questioning by his attorney started the proceeding. Clint smiled and spoke slowly with his responses to all the basic questions about his history in the military and the Sheriff's department. Once Clint's attorney finished, the ADCJ legal team started their line of questions designed to expose some of the less stellar periods of Clint's recent past. He was unflappable during the questions about his post-injury addiction and even claims from Jared that he and Chloe took care of their parents. It was evident that Clint had experience with intense questioning and his attorney prepared him well for this trial. By the time the ADJC attorney sat down to end his questions, Clint had portrayed himself as an innocent victim trying to clear up a silly misunderstanding so he could get his son back.

The plaintiff rested and after a short recess, they moved the microphone in front of Alex. After Alex was sworn in, Clint's attorney started out with basic questions. He asked Alex where he lived, worked, and how he found out about RIHARP JR. After seeing the ease with which Clint breezed through his questions, Alex felt more comfortable with Clint's attorney and he relaxed with each additional question. He'd been in high-stakes business negotiations in the past, and this was not as stressful as those meetings.

"Mr. Garza, who is Edgar Garza?"

The abrupt change in the content and tone of the question caught Alex off guard.

"Excuse me?" Alex whispered.

"Please explain your relationship to Edgar Garza."

Alex clenched his knees under the table at the audacity of the question. He couldn't believe his late brother was being brought up during this deposition.

"I don't understand what this has to do with this case."

The sleepy judge appeared to wake up. He leaned toward the microphone on the table and said, "Please answer the question."

Alex sighed. "Edgar Garza is my brother."

"Where is he today?"

"He passed away ten years ago."

"Was he incarcerated at the time of his death?"

Heat shot up Alex's back. He clenched the fabric of one of his pants legs in his fist and twisted it under the table. He didn't expect Edgar would be on trial during a deposition for Jared's custody.

"Yes, he was," Alex responded coolly.

"What was he in prison for?"

Evan leaned into his microphone. "I object. Relevance?"

Clint's attorney responded before the judge could snap back to attention, "Your honor, I'm making a case to the court that a family with a questionable history and criminal behavior has custody of the plaintiffs' minor child. We need these questions to establish—"

The judge raised his hand to stop Clint's attorney. "I'll allow it but get to the point on this line of questioning quickly and move on."

"Thank you, your honor."

Clint's attorney faced Alex again. He smiled and leaned forward into the microphone in front of him. Alex felt his face flush red with anger at the smug look on the attorney's face. He knew he was losing his cool but couldn't stop himself. Somebody had to stand up to these bullies.

"What was the last charge against Edgar Garza, and how long was his sentence?"

"Since my brother was murdered, I've spent the last decade helping inmates turn their lives around. Nobody in my family today has any kind of problem with—"

Evan interrupted. "Alex, remember what we talked about."

Alex furrowed his brow and then it hit him. He wasn't using any of the techniques that they taught him. Alex remembered Kristen's tips and his commitment to helping Jared get away from the horrible environment he left at home. The best way to do that was to keep his cool and beat Clint Gellar and his baseless lawsuit.

Alex took in a deep breath, let it out, and nodded. He opened his palms and relaxed them on his knees. He felt the tension dissipate like a slow leak in a balloon.

"Mr. Garza, what did you and your attorney discuss?"

Alex smiled and paused. "He told me to answer succinctly and honestly."

"Move on, counsel," the judge barked with irritation evident in his voice.

"Yes, your honor."

For the next two hours, Alex kept his palms open under the conference room table and answered every question without a hint of anger or irritation.

The judge adjourned the deposition. Alex looked across the conference room at the hollow gaze of Clint Gellar that he felt during each question. Alex knew their questions almost rattled him as they hoped, but he caught himself and finished strong.

Brimming with confidence, Alex stared back at Clint, a classic stare-down contest that would make any fifth grader proud, but with higher stakes. Alex promised himself he wouldn't look away until Clint did. A minute later, Clint's attorney tapped Clint on the shoulder, "Let's go."

Clint seemed to lock in even harder. Alex wasn't sure he even blinked until the attorney waved his hand in front of Clint's face. "Come on, let's get out of here."

Clint pointed at Alex and whispered, "Watch yourself."

Alex returned a smug smile. He knew it wasn't a good idea to antagonize an unstable bully, but he was so tired of his tactics that the victory felt sweet.

Alex won the battle today, but the war was just getting started.

Chapter 29

Alex pushed the button to call the elevator as he recalled his answers from the deposition. His confidence waned as he thought of better answers to the questions from Clint's attorney. It was too late to rephrase his responses now. He hoped they were good enough to save Jared.

Ding.

The elevator arrived and escorted Alex to the third floor of the parking garage. When the doors opened, Alex observed his SUV at the far end of the concrete structure and hurried toward his vehicle. Each footfall echoed off the concrete ceilings and walls as he passed empty stalls of workday commuters in the comfort of their homes by now.

Despite the nearly empty parking garage, Alex sensed he wasn't alone. He stopped and scanned the monochromatic gray structure but didn't detect any company. Alex slowed his breathing to listen for the faintest sound of movement, but there was none. Clint Gellar and the daggers he shot at Alex during the deposition flashed fresh again in Alex's mind. The look of contempt on Clint's face caused Alex to stammer more than once during the deposition and was now causing the hair on his arms to stand up in the empty parking garage.

Alex jogged the final twenty feet and arrived at his vehicle seconds later. He immediately locked his doors and exhaled once he was inside.

"Come on. Don't let him get to you. That's exactly what he's trying to do," Alex said to himself.

Alex pushed the button to start the engine, and a sweet melody from the radio filled the cabin. His favorite country music tickled his ears, and Alex's mind drifted back to ease. He drove down the three levels and paid his fee to exit the parking garage. He looked in the rearview mirror as he left and saw a familiar faded gray pickup truck pulling out of the garage behind him. It was Clint Geller.

Alex told himself it was a coincidence, but he straightened up in his leather seat and readjusted his grip on the steering wheel. Alex checked his mirrors every few seconds to see if Clint was still behind him. Once Alex reached the freeway entrance, he knew he would understand Clint's intentions. Alex had to turn right on the eastbound lanes to head back to his Scottsdale home from downtown Phoenix, but Clint lived in the opposite direction, so he should turn left and head west on the freeway. Alex descended the freeway access ramp and watched in the rearview mirror for Clint to turn the other direction. Instead, the unmistakable cross-eyed headlights—one headlight pointing a few degrees too much to the sky and the other pointed down too much—turned onto the same eastbound ramp.

Alex swallowed hard and slammed his foot on the gas pedal. He knew that Clint's bucket of bolts was no match for the three hundred horses under the hood of his luxury SUV. Alex accepted the potential risk of a speeding ticket to distance himself further from Jared's unpredictable father.

For the next twenty minutes, Alex raced up the freeway toward his house while he kept checking the mirrors for signs of Clint. The headlights with one side looking like a droopy eye were nowhere to be seen.

Alex exited the freeway and waited at the red light to take the local road to his house in the foothills. It felt like the light was red forever. As he sat through three radio commercials, Alex kept looking in his rearview mirror and waited to see the unmistakable headlights of Clint Geller each passing second he sat at the light.

The light turned green, and Alex was ready to dart off the freeway ramp, but the car ahead of him did not move. Alex threw his hands up in the air, muttered, "What's going on?"

He saw the silhouette of the driver ahead of him, looking down at his phone. Alex laid on his horn for a full three seconds. The driver got the message and drove through the intersection just as the light turned yellow. Alex knew he should stop but couldn't bear to sit for another rotation of the longest-lasting traffic light of his life. The light turned red when he was halfway through the intersection, and Alex was up to the speed limit a few seconds later. Just before the first curve, he looked in his rearview mirror, and his heart sank. The cross-eyed headlights on a pickup truck veered off the freeway a quarter-mile behind Alex.

Clint had traveled over thirty miles in the wrong direction, and it was apparent to Alex that Clint was coming after him. Clint knew where Alex lived, so he couldn't guide him away from the house and his family. Alex knew he had to prepare for an altercation with Clint.

Alex took a deep breath and pushed the button on the steering wheel to call Allison.

"Hey, hon, how'd it go?" Allison asked when she picked up the phone.

"Gather all the kids and get them to the backyard. Clint Geller has followed me all the way from Phoenix, and I don't know what he's up to, but I'm sure it's nothing good. I don't want anyone near the driveway or the front of the house when I pull in."

"Where are you now?" Allison shouted.

"I'm only a few minutes away. He was fuming during the entire deposition, so I'm not sure if he's coming after Jared or me. I just want to make sure you all are as far away from him as possible. Get them out right now."

Alex hung up the phone as his headlights illuminated his home. He slowed down and pulled into his driveway. He stopped at soon as his SUV was off the street and jumped out with his vehicle still running.

Alex walked to the street to investigate and saw Clint's pickup truck lurching up the hill. Twenty yards before Alex's driveway, the truck came to a halt. Alex could hear the worn belts under the hood and smell the exhaust burning too much oil. The truck sat with the engine idling for several seconds, so Alex moved onto the street to get a better look.

"What's he doing?" Alex whispered to himself.

The truck sputtered and died.

Clint exited from his vehicle and slammed his door so hard, Alex was sure the entire truck would collapse. He opened the hood, popped his head under it and then slammed it back down harder than the door.

Alex took several steps toward the stalled vehicle when Clint noticed Alex.

"Go away," Clint shouted. His voice was raspy and lacked all the confidence Alex heard hours earlier.

Alex walked within ten feet of Clint and noticed he was wiping his eyes.

Is Clint crying?

Clint put his head down on his hood and Alex was sure he heard crying. He turned to his running SUV at the end of his driveway and then back to Clint. He wanted nothing more than to pull his SUV into his garage and pretend like Clint Gellar's truck didn't break down in front of his house, but he couldn't.

"What's wrong?" Alex asked.

Clint raised his head and slammed his hand on the hood. "It broke down again."

"Why did you follow me here? You used to be a deputy, so you know that attempting to intimidate a witness can hurt your chances with your lawsuit."

"I'm not trying to intimidate you. I just need that RIHARP money so I can finally fix this junky truck and a few other things."

"And what about your son? Do you need him, too?"

"I haven't had a clean bathroom in ages. And Becky hates watching fishing shows with me."

Alex imagined the condition of their home since Jared left and shuddered. He felt a strange emotion well up in him. Pity.

"Do you need some help with the truck?"

"I know how to fix it, but I don't have my tools with me."

"Good, because I know nothing about trucks, but I do have a lot of tools. What do you need?"

Clint stood up straight and cleared his throat. "A socket set and a pair of pliers."

Minutes later, Alex returned with pliers, bottled water, a flashlight and a socket set that had never been used. He placed it on the hood and stepped back.

"You need anything else?"

Clint opened the set and examined it, "No, this will do."

Alex walked back to his driveway but turned around, "Keep the tools. I never use them."

Chapter 30

T he trial was stressful and the outcome unclear, so Alex decided to take the boys away for the weekend to visit the place on Jared's list, Bear Canyon Lake. The girls had their own weekend plans for fun. Allison and her friend Rebecca would treat Olivia and Gaby to a day of shopping for their summer wardrobes, followed by a day at the spa to relax and unwind.

After the familiar trek north, Alex guided his two companions to set up their primitive campsite in a clearing they found around a half-mile from Bear Canyon Lake. They completed the setup of the sleeping tent, shower tent, and kitchen canopy. The last task was to complete the fire pit, which would serve as their family room for the weekend.

Daniel placed the final large rock to complete the fire ring circle while Jared and Alex unfolded the chairs.

"What are we going to do first?" Daniel asked.

Alex looked up at the sun high above the trees in the west and said, "we have a couple of hours before we need to get back here and start dinner. What do you two want to do?"

"Shoot BB guns!" Daniel shouted.

"Do you want to shoot BB guns, Jared?" Alex asked.

"Sure."

"Great, let's each grab some empty cans we packed and head out. The best shot gets a break from dinner duty tonight."

The boys raced each other to select their weapons. Once properly armed, they hiked for fifteen minutes until they found the perfect hill to assault. They strategically placed their cans in the same place they envisioned the enemy and began the shooting competition. After two hours of a constant assault on the hill and never-ending trash talking about who was best, Daniel emerged as the sharpshooter among the threesome.

Back at camp, Alex and Jared prepared their dinner of hot dogs and beans over an open fire and followed by s'mores for dessert. Once darkness engulfed camp, Alex told the same ghost stories that his father and brothers told him growing up. Exhausted, they all climbed into their sleeping bags and fell asleep before ten o'clock.

Alex woke up as the sun penetrated the blue nylon on the east side of their tent. He heard birds cheering on a new day and encouraging the rest of the forest to wake up. Alex raised his head and saw Daniel and Jared still in a deep slumber, so he grabbed a jacket and quietly left the tent.

The cool air hit his face, and he retreated under his hoodie like a turtle in a shell. It was a welcome relief from the scorching heat six thousand feet lower in elevation in Scottsdale. Alex positioned a chair near the fire pit with one slit of sunlight beaming through the pine trees that stood like soldiers soaring fifty feet above. Alex closed his eyes and let the sunlight warm his stiff body.

Next, his thoughts turned to his brief talk with Mateo on the day of the All-Stars event. Alex smiled and drifted into deep prayer. For the first time in months, his mind felt clear enough to pray and listen for God to whisper into his soul.

Alex was in deep thought for the next thirty minutes until he heard the tent zipper. He opened his eyes and watched Jared emerge from the tent into the cool morning air.

Once Jared found a seat near the fire pit, Alex assembled several logs and started a fire. Minutes later, the fire danced up the logs and shared its warmth with the twosome. Jared pulled his chair closer to the stone ring and put his hands out to warm them. They stared at the fire without talking until Alex broke the silence. "Want some coffee?"

Jared pulled his hood down tighter and nodded, so Alex placed a pot of water on the metal rack above the flames. Ten minutes later, they each had a cup of coffee to warm their hands and body.

Once Alex's cup was half empty, he leaned forward. "Jared, what is it about Bear Canyon Lake that put it at the top of your must-see list?"

Jared straightened in his folding chair and smiled. "That's easy. It looks like Heaven on earth based on the pictures I've seen. I can't wait to see it."

"I've been there before. You're going to love it."

Alex topped off his coffee and asked another question weighing heavy on his mind. "How are you feeling about the lawsuit?"

Jared's shoulders slumped, and he fell back into the chair. "I want to feel like Clint filed the lawsuit because he wants me back, but I know that's not true. He just misses the maid that did everything for my mom and him. I sure hope he doesn't win and force me to move back in. Nothing I do will ever be good enough for that man."

Alex nodded and let his attention drift to the surrounding forest. Jared's response felt eerily similar to one he often heard Edgar complain about Papa, but Alex couldn't fully understand. If Alex managed to win a game or do something well, sometimes Papa showered him with praise. It was a key motivator for Alex to keep pushing harder and harder to do well and receive the praise he craved. It came less frequently over time and then dried up as Edgar's problems took center stage in their family as Alex grew up, but that did not stop Alex from trying just as hard to hear "great job" from Papa.

"A part of me can relate," Alex stated over the quiet crackling fire.

Jared tilted his head, "How can you relate? You have a great life and seem to have everything together."

"I am very grateful and blessed for the life I have, but don't let the shiny exterior fool you. I have issues with my dad and that's why I focus on my father in Heaven. God is constantly working on me to grow as a father, brother, son, and husband and that will never stop. Even this conversation with you shows me how much more I need God in my life."

The pair sat silently around the fire until Daniel emerged from the tent and their day in the woods started.

After lunch, Jared scrambled behind Daniel up the rocky hill while Alex followed. They'd already hiked a third of a mile over rough terrain, and Jared knew the lake he'd dreamt about for years was on the other side of the hill. Daniel stopped to wipe the sweat off his forehead and take another drink of water.

"Drink up, fellas. Although it's thirty degrees cooler up here, you still have to drink a lot of water or you'll get dehydrated," Alex said as they all tipped their water bottles to their lips.

Once everyone hydrated, they continued to climb the boulders to the peak of the hill. Twenty yards from the top, Jared could feel the expanse of water beyond the ponderosa pines in his bones. Daniel reached the summit first and stopped. Jared pushed his sore legs to join Daniel, and the view was everything he'd imagined.

Two stories below, the sixty-acre serpentine lake shimmered under the afternoon sun. Just like the pictures Jared etched into the pages of his mind, the steel-blue water kissed the granite shoreline while pine trees stood guard like sentinels.

The water pulled Jared toward the shore like a giant magnet, but he didn't want to forget this feeling. He scanned the area ahead of him and the climb he just completed behind him. He grinned wide and jumped down to a pile of loose rocks that caused him to slide toward the icy water. Jared grabbed onto a tree to prevent a tumble all the way to the lake.

"Be careful!" Alex shouted.

A couple minutes later, all three stood on a rocky outcropping several feet over the lake. It was so quiet that they could hear the wind tickle the pine needles with each gust and the crows calling their mates deep in the forest. Jared's eyes remained fixed on the beauty in front of him until movement caught his attention. A bald eagle appeared on cue and took a swipe at the surface for a mid-day fish snack. The eagle was unsuccessful and he vanished just as quickly over the forest, but Jared's show was a success.

Jared stood next to Alex and Daniel as they took in the scene like a museum painting.

"Just like you said, Jared. It's like Heaven on earth," Alex whispered.

"If this is Heaven, I just got a lot more interested in going there."

Alex turned to Jared. "For real?"

The words came out so fast and natural that Jared never gave it much thought, but it was true. If Heaven was anything like this, he wanted to learn more about it.

Jared pulled his gaze away from the lake and looked Alex in the eye. "For real."

Chapter 31

A fourth backpack dropped onto the pile just inside the door from the garage as Olivia arrived home on the last day of school. Gaby, Daniel, and Jared had already stripped their bodies of any evidence of school and were playing their guitar video game.

Allison ordered each of them their favorite item to be delivered from a local restaurant for dinner to celebrate the end of the school year. They celebrated the honor roll for Gaby and Daniel, Jared pulling his grades up to C's and one B and Olivia squeaking by with low B's after getting straight A's her freshman year. For Olivia, the B's weren't a reason to celebrate. They were celebrating the end of the school year. Her grades were on track to fall to C's had the school year continued another month. Her focus was no longer on achieving good grades so she could go to a respected university; she spent all of her time with friends and wanted little to do with anything else. For the first time in her life, Olivia was content with B's.

After dinner, the celebrating continued outside with ice cream sandwiches and several hours in the pool. Once the excitement dwindled, everyone left the backyard to retire for the evening.

Alex found Allison brushing her hair in front of the bathroom mirror before bed and gave her a hug.

"What's that for?"

"We survived another school year," Alex replied.

Allison stopped brushing and turned toward Alex. "Yes, we did. I'm not sure we'd be in a good mood if Olivia's grades had slipped to C's. She was on that path the last few months."

"I know. We've got to get her back on track this summer."

"How do we do that?"

"I'm not sure, but I think time away from her current group of friends would help. We should keep the plans to visit your family back in Boston like we do every summer. I think that will be helpful for everyone, especially Olivia this year."

Allison put her hairbrush down. "How can we visit Boston when Jared can't leave the state?"

"I'll stay home with him so you all can go."

"That's not fair. None of us have to go this year."

"It's okay. I want you, Daniel, and the girls to go. Plus, I think it will be good for Jared. I can spend some quality one-on-one time mentoring him while you're gone. I believe that intensive mentoring could have helped Edgar and we may not get another chance like this with Jared before he turns eighteen."

Allison pondered his idea. "This is important to you, isn't it?"

"Yes, it is."

Allison kissed Alex and then started brushing her hair again. "As long as you're okay staying back with Jared, I'll take the kids to Boston. I think you're right about getting Olivia away. I'm hoping my folks have some wisdom, too. I know I wasn't the easiest teenager."

"And look how well you turned out." Alex said and squeezed her shoulders.

Alex arrived home after dropping off Allison and the kids at the airport and found Jared reading a magazine at the kitchen island.

"It's just you and me, kid."

Jared looked up from his magazine and smiled.

"Any ideas of what you'd like to do? We can do whatever you want."

Jared looked down at the granite counter and back up. "I don't know."

Alex tossed his keys on the counter. "Give it some thought. I'd like to make this summer an unforgettable experience for you. Until you give me a list, we can start with visiting some local attractions. That sound okay?"

"I don't know what there is to do, so I'm cool with whatever you want."

The summer slump in networking meetings started as locals departed the desert in droves to escape the intense summer heat. Mr. Park planned to be in the Bay Area for the next two months, so Alex worked from home.

The first week, Alex finished work early each day, and he took Jared to the aquarium and the famous Heard Museum for Native American Art. Jared seemed to enjoy the museum so later that week Alex took him to the Arizona Science Center in downtown Phoenix. They moved together through all the exhibits slowly as Jared shared everything that he learned in his biology class the last school year.

Jared lingered around the brain exhibit longer than any of the others. He grew quiet and his smile disappeared while he read every single sentence displayed near the vivid artist renderings of the brain.

"You interested in the brain?" Alex asked.

"Sort of. I like to know what makes people tick."

Alex nodded and scanned the cross-section of the brain on the wall near him.

Jared continued, "I'd like to do something with substance abuse counseling when I'm done with school."

Alex raised his eyebrows and put his hand on Jared's shoulder, "You'd be a great counselor and I'm sure it would be a very rewarding career to help people get their lives back on track. If you're interested in substance abuse counseling, you should definitely pursue it."

"It probably would have made a big difference in my life," Jared responded and turned away from the exhibit. "I'm ready to go now."

Every night after dinner, Alex talked to Allison and the kids on video calls. Olivia wasn't interested in a video call with her dad, so Alex texted her jokes and funny videos to let her know he was thinking of her. He remembered how Papa would go weeks without saying a word to Edgar, and now that he was spending so much time with Jared, he realized how the little moments can add up to a lot in terms of kids feeling a parent really cares.

That weekend, Alex surprised Jared with a visit to more destinations circled on his map when they arrived at Walnut Canyon National Monument outside of Flagstaff. They hiked the ancient cliff dwellings just before sunset and then drove to their next destination in the dark. Jared awoke the next morning on the South Rim of the Grand Canyon. Alex could barely keep up with Jared as he rushed to the edge of the canyon to drink in the awe-inspiring beauty of one of the natural wonders of the world. They hiked, enjoyed dinner on a patio overlooking the canyon and rushed to a prime location to watch the sun set in the canyon.

As the sun descended and the shadows changed the colors of the canyon walls like a chameleon every few minutes, Jared and Alex watched in silence. Neither could say anything to improve the display on the nineteen hundred square mile canvas.

Once the sky was dark and the stars took over illuminating the canyon, they returned to Alex's SUV in the parking lot. Minutes into their three-hour journey back to Scottsdale, Jared turned to Alex.

"That was amazing. Thank you."

Alex beamed at the unexpected comment, "You're welcome. I hope you're having a good time visiting these places."

"I am. It's like I've seen Heaven three times this year and you took me to all of them. Do you think that's what Heaven really looks like?"

Alex rubbed his chin and replied, "I'm not sure what it will look like. I just know I want to be there someday."

"Why?"

"Because I get to live with Jesus and all the other people I love who passed before me. I get to live with God, the perfect Father."

"You're a good father," Jared replied.

"I appreciate that Jared, but I'm nothing like God."

"Can you tell me more about Him?"

"You bet."

For the next three hours, Alex shared Scripture about the Holy Trinity and personal stories about why he chooses to believe in God and give his life to Jesus. They even talked a few minutes after they arrived back home and parked in the garage after midnight.

"Jared, it's getting late. You better get inside and get ready for bed while I unpack."

Jared exited the SUV and turned to Alex, "I want a father like God. Will you tell me more about Him later?"

"Absolutely."

Alex remained in his SUV as he processed the past week with Jared. He could see the confidence emerging in Jared's face and body language after years of being told he couldn't do anything right. Over the next month, Alex wanted to stoke the emerging fire of faith and self-confidence growing more evident in Jared.

Alex sat in the silence of his vehicle in the dark garage and pondered his future for several minutes. For the first time since Alex could remember, a glimpse of what was ahead didn't involve being a partner at Emerson Churchill. He felt the tug to use the pain of his past to help others like Edgar and Jared.

Was this the whisper from God he asked for?

Chapter 32

F or the next four weeks, the duo continued to visit other places on weekends that Jared circled on his map and talked about faith during their long drives. Alex understood that he could permanently change the trajectory of Jared's life and wanted to maintain his momentum.

The day before the rest of the family returned, the house was a wreck. The sink was full of dishes, the trash was overflowing, and the countertop was barely visible under the collection of items brought back from each weekend trip. Alex and Jared spent all day cleaning the house so Allison could relax after a long time away from home.

The next morning, Alex ate a late breakfast and departed for the airport. He waited outside the arrival doors and jumped out of his SUV when he saw his family emerge onto the sidewalk.

Gaby reached him first and slung her arms around him in a firm embrace. Daniel ran out next and joined the group hug.

"Hi, Dad," Olivia said as she jumped into the front seat.

Allison reached his SUV last. She let go of her suitcase, dropped her bag, and fell into Alex's arms. He put both hands on her face and gave her a kiss. "I missed you."

"I missed you too. We had a great time, but I'm so happy to be back."

They left the airport, and Alex heard about their time in Boston for the next thirty minutes.

When everyone arrived home, Jared helped Alex bring in the luggage. Daniel and Gaby chatted happily with Jared, but Olivia walked past him as if he didn't exist.

"Did you two have a good time?" Allison asked Alex as she watched Jared interact with Daniel and Gaby.

"Yes, it was great."

"Jared seems… different."

Alex squinted. "How so?"

"He seems happier and more confident. I can see it in the way he walks and talks."

"I think we made a breakthrough while you were in Boston, but let's see how he reacts when everything gets back to normal," Alex replied. "How was it with Olivia? Any breakthroughs?"

"She was quiet at first and then she warmed when all the cousins arrived for the first Sunday dinner. It was great to see the old Olivia having fun with her grandparents and cousins again. I just hope it sticks."

For the next seven days, everyone was busy with preparation for the new school year. Clothes shopping, school supplies, dentist appointments, and haircuts filled their days. Mr. Park returned from vacation, and Alex resumed long days at the office. At night, they ventured outside after the scorching sun set to swim. All the kids stayed in the water until they had wrinkled skin. Alex arrived home after his networking events and joined them in the pool on most nights.

On the first day of school, all the kids got ready and posed together for pictures in front of the house so Allison could get her annual first day of school picture. After two quick shots, Olivia left the group and loaded up her car for school. Although she was going to the same campus as Jared, she never offered him a ride.

Instead, he left a few minutes later to walk to the bus stop. He thought about how the start of previous school years was often the start of fresh trouble in his life. Jared hoped this school year would be different. He bowed his head and closed his eyes to pray like he'd seen Alex do many times. His first prayer was short and sweet, but Jared felt it helped.

Jared paid for lunch and balanced his beverage on his tray through the cafeteria and into the courtyard. A sea of fresh-cut grass surrounded a square concrete island dotted with metal picnic tables bolted to the pavement. One large metal ramada provided shade against the unrelenting Arizona sun. The single-story, horseshoe-shaped high school complex surrounded the courtyard, with only the south end open to the student parking. The asphalt lot of cars belonging to juniors and seniors separated the grassy yard with a wrought-iron fence painted in the school colors, crimson and gold. Sun-bleached concrete trails led students from the central island to the different classroom buildings.

Jared meandered through the tables and stood next to a boy scrolling through his phone. The boy moved his tray a few inches like a guard opening a gate to an ancient walled city, signaling it was okay to sit down.

"Hey," Jared said after he sat down.

"Hey."

"I'm Jared."

"Dustin."

It wasn't much, but it was nice to have another person at the same table for lunch. Jared mirrored Dustin and scrolled through the images in his social media feed on his phone as he alternated between bites of his club sandwich and potato chips.

Ten minutes later, Dustin got up. "See ya, Jared."

"You, too, Dustin."

Jared crunched his last chip and glanced toward the opposite side of the lunch area. Olivia and her friends were sitting at the same table they claimed every day. Five girls and two boys leaned in and spoke softly to keep their special world hidden from outsiders. Jared didn't dare engage Olivia or her friends at school after the failed intervention with her parents. They all loathed Jared, and he knew they would never welcome him into that tight circle.

Today was different. Olivia wasn't engaged with her friends like usual. Her attention broke away from her group as she looked around at the other students at the nearby tables every few minutes. Olivia maintained a stoic look while her friends broke out in laughter. Her body language screamed that something was wrong.

Jared kept his eyes locked on Olivia as he finished his lunch and packed his books for his next class. He watched a new member of the group at Olivia's table open her backpack and share it with each of the other boys and girls at the table. The boys exchanged high-fives after viewing the contents, and Jared could tell one girl said, "wow," but Olivia's reaction was different.

Instead of acting surprised or excited, she straightened up and moved to the end of the metal picnic table. A frown formed, and she shook her head. This reaction did not appear to please the other six members in her circle. Olivia took her longest scan of the other students at the nearby tables. At one point, she spun all the way around and looked in Jared's direction, but he ducked behind the offensive tackle on the football team between them.

What's going on, Olivia? What are you planning now?

Jared dropped off his tray at the cafeteria and returned to his table. He had one more minute before the passing bell rang, and students would flood the courtyard heading to their sixth-period class. Jared inched closer to Olivia's table to watch her next move.

The chime sounded. Hundreds of students emerged from the buildings to reach their next destination of science, English, or math class, but not Olivia and her friends. They headed south toward the student parking lot.

"That's what she was so worried about. She's going to skip class again," Jared whispered to himself.

His stomach did a quick somersault at the turmoil she was about to cause his host parents. Unlike his parents, they were so supportive of her, but she insisted on hanging out with the wrong crowd. For a split second, he considered reaching out to Olivia to warn her of the path she was about to take, but he remembered the thin ice he was on with her.

Jared didn't want to be late for class, so he started toward his US History class. Just as he grabbed the door handle to enter the building, he heard a scream. It came from the same direction that he last saw Olivia headed, so Jared rushed back to the courtyard and saw one of Olivia's girlfriends tug on her arm.

"No, I don't want to!" Olivia cried out.

The new girl in the group rushed to the side of the friend who was harassing Olivia, and together they walked her toward the parking lot. The commotion drew the attention of other students passing nearby, and a small crowd formed around them.

Jared took several steps toward Olivia, and before he had time to think, he was in a full sprint toward the group. Seconds later, he arrived next to Olivia and the three girls surrounding her. They were ten feet from the gate to the parking lot.

The bell rang, signaling that everyone in the courtyard was late for class. This caused a few onlookers to disperse, but Jared knew he had to act fast. Olivia's friends moved in unison, with Olivia trapped in the middle until they were five feet from the gate.

"Leave her alone! She doesn't want to go with you today," Jared roared.

Two of the girls jumped at the unexpected intrusion, and when they saw it was Jared, they turned their attention back to Olivia.

"Everyone is nervous the first time. Come on, we're all doing this together," one of the girls tried to convince Olivia as they guided her closer to the gate.

Jared lunged forward and blocked their path. They were only two steps from the gate that would lock behind them as soon as they exited.

"Let her go!"

That's when a boy in the group got involved. He pushed Jared to the side and stood in front of him.

"Stay out of this, juvie boy. We don't need any narcs around here."

Jared looked down at the high school junior, six inches shorter and fifty pounds lighter than him.

A sinister smile formed on Jared's face like the villain in an action movie. "I said, let—"

Before Jared could finish, the other boy got a running start and lunged into Jared. It knocked him back several steps.

"Oh yeah? What are you going to do about it?" he asked after Jared regained his balance.

The scuffle among the boys and Jared stopped the girls from pushing Olivia, and she broke away. She darted several steps from the group and then turned to look at the growing tension between her friends and Jared.

It was only for a split second, but Jared locked eyes with Olivia. He saw fear radiating from her brown eyes, and that was all he needed to know.

Jared took a few steps to position himself between Olivia and her friends trying to force her to the parking lot moments earlier.

"Go ahead and go to the parking lot. She doesn't want to skip school with you."

"Is that true?" one girl asked Olivia.

Jared turned to see Olivia's reaction, and that's when the boy charged him again. The boy drove Jared back to the building's wall by the gate, but that allowed Jared to regain his leverage. He picked the teenage boy up by the back of his shirt and hurled him into a nearby metal trash container, which flew into the metal gate. The sound echoed throughout the courtyard and caught the attention of Jared's PE teacher as he rushed across the courtyard toward the gymnasium.

He saw the commotion and dashed over to the three intertwined students in the courtyard grass. Jared had both boys in a tight headlock. The teacher yelled for them to stop and break it up, but none of them listened. The teacher pulled out his phone, but Jared was too busy trying to keep the boys from slipping out of his grasp to see why.

Suddenly, Jared felt his arms release from the two boys and slam tight against his side. His ankles and knees did the same. He felt defenseless against the two boys as he laid stiff on the courtyard grass and prepared for Olivia's friends to kick or hit him. Instead, the PE teacher lifted both boys to their feet by their collars.

"All of you are going to see Mr. Patterson."

He turned to Jared, "Get up."

"I can't. You need to deactivate Sure Cuffs."

The teacher deactivated Sure Cuffs on his phone, and Jared stood up and wiped grass clippings from his jeans and t-shirt.

"Let's go," the PE teacher barked.

As the teacher escorted the three boys across the courtyard to the admin building that housed the vice-principal's office, his phone rang.

"Yes, I activated Sure Cuffs," Jared heard his PE teacher say into the phone. "I'm his PE teacher, and I caught him fighting. I'm taking him to the vice principal's office right now. Yes, sir, I will let them know to notify ADJC as well."

Jared's heart sank. He knew that fighting could get him kicked out of RIHARP JR.

The coach hung up the phone and completed the three boys' transfer to the assistant to the vice-principal. All three boys sat together, with one seat between each of them, as they waited for Mr. Patterson.

Chapter 33

Each boy got to tell his side of the story to the vice-principal. It seemed like the first two boys were in his office for hours when Jared finally shared his testimony with Mr. Patterson.

The punishment was probably pre-determined as soon as the coach marched in with three boys fighting in the courtyard. Mr. Patterson didn't seem to care that Jared was defending himself. All of them received five days of out-of-school suspension for fighting.

"You need to leave the campus now. Drive home if you have a car or call for a ride and wait for them in the parking lot. You're banned from campus for another week. Do you have any questions?" Mr. Patterson asked after he shared the punishment.

Jared shook his head and stood up to leave the office. Mr. Patterson stopped him after a few steps.

"Jared, you realize that I have to report this to ADJC?"

Jared nodded.

"You better hope this doesn't revoke your eligibility to the RIHARP JR program."

Olivia waited for Jared outside of the administrative office building. She approached him as he passed through the double doors.

"Need a ride home?" Olivia asked.

The question stopped Jared mid-stride. Olivia had only been rude and hostile to Jared the entire time he'd known her, so her offer to help him caught him off guard.

"Don't you have to go to class?"

"No, I told my sixth-hour teacher that I felt sick, so he excused me to go home. I really do feel a little sick about what happened, so I'm heading home now. Do you want to go or not?"

Jared nodded and followed Olivia to her SUV. He crawled into the passenger seat, buckled up, and put his backpack between his knees. Jared swallowed hard when he saw the school disappear in the side mirror.

An awkward silence filled the SUV for the first five minutes of their commute home until Olivia turned to Jared at a red light and asked, "Why did you do that?"

"That kid tried to attack me, so I was just defending myself against both of them."

"I know. I saw that. That's not what I'm talking about. Why did you get involved? Why did you help me?"

Jared knew that was her original question but didn't want to rush into this discussion. He took his eyes off the sun-bleached road ahead and turned toward Olivia. He'd never seen her look and act so vulnerable during the nine months they lived under the same roof. Jared noticed her jaw trembling and sensed tears were not too far off.

"I could tell you needed help. I don't know why they were pulling you or why you didn't want to go, but I just knew that you didn't want to go, and that's all I needed to know to get involved."

Olivia's eyes welled up, and her voice cracked when she spoke, "I've been so mean to you the entire time you've lived with us, so why would you do that for me?"

Jared looked out of the passenger window at the passing palm trees dotting the entrance to another Scottsdale shopping plaza. He ran his right hand through his thin blond hair and exhaled loudly.

"While you were in Boston, I went to the high school ministry after your dad and me talked about God and stuff. Well, during a life group event, they taught us about the Good Samaritan. They taught us about helping our neighbor and that everyone is our neighbor, so we should help everyone. It didn't mean too much to me until I saw those girls trying to drag you out of the courtyard. When I saw them doing that to you, I didn't care that you haven't been nice to me. I saw you needed help and didn't even think about it. I just did it. I know you may hate me even more now because I got your friends in trouble, but I believe I did the right thing back there and would do it again."

"I don't—" Olivia blurted but stopped herself.

As they neared their house, Olivia paused at the stop sign longer than usual as she stared at Jared. It was like she was trying to tell if he was real or not. Several seconds later, she turned on the road to their house.

Neither one said another word until they got home.

Allison looked at the clock on the stove when she heard the garage door open and shut. She wasn't expecting anyone home for another ninety minutes, so she left her laptop at the kitchen counter and investigated who was home so early.

Allison saw Olivia and Jared walk in together. The early entrance and the two rivals coming into the house together increased her concern.

"Why are you both home so early? Did I miss something about an early release on the first day?" Allison inquired as they entered the kitchen.

Olivia and Jared shared a quick glance, and Olivia turned her attention to the floor. Jared turned to Allison and responded, "I got an out-of-school suspension for five days for fighting. Olivia isn't feeling too good, so she offered to take me home instead of calling you to pick me up."

"What? Why were you fighting, Jared? You know you can't do things like that if you want to stay in the RIHARP JR program. It's the first day of school and this could jeopardize your ability to live here and go to a regular school."

Jared dropped his head. "I know. I was just defending myself against these two guys, but the vice-principal didn't care. My PE teacher caught the three of us scuffling together in the courtyard, so all three of us got suspended."

"That's not good, Jared. Why did those boys come after you?"

Jared's body stiffened and he pursed his lips. "I don't want to talk about it right now. I just want to go to my room."

Jared rushed past Allison toward his bedroom.

Allison turned to Olivia. "Do you know what happened?"

Olivia shrugged her shoulders and started on the same path to her bedroom.

Allison called out to Olivia, "We're not done talking about this. We're going to talk about this again when your father gets home."

Alex arrived home just before nine after another long networking event. He placed his keys on the counter and saw Allison sitting by herself in the family room. Alex joined her and fell back into his recliner.

"Ahh."

"Don't get too comfortable. We need to have a talk with Jared and Olivia about a fight and suspension at school today," Allison informed Alex.

"What? Jared got into a fight? On his first day? Why? With who?"

"I don't have many details, so I'm going to get Olivia and Jared out here to explain everything themselves."

Allison walked down the hallway past Gaby and Daniel's closed bedroom doors and found Jared lying across his bed. She knocked on the door frame, and when Jared looked up, Allison asked, "can you come to the family room now?"

Jared nodded, put down his iPad, and started toward the family room.

Next, Allison knocked on Olivia's closed door. When Olivia opened it, Allison told her to head to the family room. "Your father is home, and we're ready to talk to both of you about what happened today."

Alex leaned forward in his recliner when Allison, Jared, and Olivia walked into the family room. He stood up and pointed to the couch, commanding, "you two have a seat."

Alex paced a few times in front of the coffee table and then turned toward Jared. "Why were you fighting today?"

Jared and Olivia turned to each other at the same time and then quickly snapped their heads back towards Alex after their eyes met.

Jared cleared his throat. "Those two boys went after me first. I was just defending myself. Just because I was winning, the PE teacher assumed that I started the fight with them."

"Okay, I understand that, but why were these two boys coming after you? Who are they?" Alex asked.

Jared shifted his weight and scooted back on the couch a couple inches. He leaned on the armrest and shook his head. "I don't know."

Alex tilted his head and asked, "you don't even know who these boys are? I can't believe two random boys would just come after you for no reason."

Jared's face flushed red. "I said I don't know who they are."

Alex paced again, and this time he stopped a few steps closer to Jared. "That makes little sense. I think there is more to this story than you're telling us. Be honest, Jared. What's going on?"

The room was silent until Olivia stood up and yelled out, "They were my friends. They attacked Jared, and he was just defending himself."

Chapter 34

A lex and Allison turned to each other wide-eyed after Olivia's outburst. Alex marched around the coffee table and stood shoulder to shoulder with Allison in front of Olivia.

"Honey, why would your friends go after Jared?" Allison asked.

Olivia sat back down on the couch and gave Jared a long look. She stared at him for what seemed like a minute and then turned back to Alex and Allison with tears in her eyes.

"He was protecting me from them. They were trying to get me to skip class and do drugs with them, but I didn't want to go. Jared saw them trying to force me into the parking lot and helped me get away from them."

Alex put both hands on his head as if he was trying to extract an answer buried deep inside his skull.

"That sounds horrible," Allison said. "Why would they think you'd ever want to do drugs with them?" Allison asked in a whisper.

Olivia leaned back and exhaled. She twirled the hair behind her right ear. "I smoked with them before, okay? Jared was right when he told you that he could smell it on me. I never liked it—it always made me feel weird. But I didn't want them to think I was uncool or a baby, so I did it to be part of the group."

"Olivia Garza! You did what?" Alex roared.

"I know it was dumb, Dad, and I'm never doing it again, especially after what just happened. Today, Stephanie stole pills from her stepmom. It was some type of pain medicine that I've heard is really addictive, and I wasn't willing to do that. They wanted to leave the lunch courtyard and take the pills in the parking lot. I said no, and they tried to force me to go with them. That's when Jared helped me."

"I can't believe you'd do that after all you've heard about Tio Edgar!"

Allison put her hand on Alex's forearm, "Not so loud, Alex. I don't want Gaby and Daniel to hear this."

"I'm sorry. It'll never happen again!" Olivia sobbed.

Alex walked away and stood near the fireplace. He put one hand on the rock wall and ran the other through his hair.

Olivia wiped away the tears on her left and then her right cheek. "I have heard everything, but I thought this was different. I thought my friends were different, and I thought I was different, but I realize now that it was all the same. I'm so sorry about all this."

Alex walked back, but Allison held up her hand to stop him. She knelt in front of Olivia until they made eye contact.

"Olivia, I'm glad you told us today, but you've been lying to us for months and that's not okay. We always tell you to come to us with any problem and we'll help you. Although there may be consequences, we will always support you. Instead, you deceived us and let us question Jared and his motives when he was just trying to help you. You need to know all of that was wrong and that you owe Jared an apology. You are going to have serious consequences for what you've done."

Olivia wiped away more tears, sniffed, and said, "I understand." She turned to Jared and said, "I'm so, so sorry."

He nodded and Olivia turned back to her parents.

"Can I be grounded from my car and everything else but school for two months?" Olivia asked.

The same confused looks Alex and Allison had earlier returned to their faces.

"Okay, I was thinking one month with no car or no phone, but if you want two months, you've got it," Alex replied with anger still alive in his voice.

"I do. I don't want to see my old friends anymore. There are not who I thought they were, and this will make it easier for me to make sure I don't hang out with them again."

"That's a very mature decision," Allison added.

"Plus, this gives me some time to hang out with Jared. I realized today that he's kind of like the big brother I've never had."

At the unexpected revelation, everybody's head snapped towards Olivia, including Jared's.

Alex turned to Jared and saw the widest smile yet from his teenage guest.

Linda Flowers insisted on a site visit with the Garzas after she heard of Jared's suspension for fighting. She arrived two days later and sat at the dining room table with Alex and Allison as Jared recounted his version of the story. Alex and Allison verified he was defending Olivia from several students mixed up in drugs.

"That's admirable to help someone like that, Jared, but that still doesn't excuse your suspension for fighting. This puts ADJC, RIHARP JR, and you in a precarious position. Plus, this will be even more ammunition for the plaintiff in your guardianship hearing. I don't know what's going to happen because of this, but none of it will be good."

"I'm sorry, Mrs. Flowers. I won't get in any more trouble. I promise."

Linda jotted down a few final notes and shuffled several files strewn in front of her on the table. "I know you don't intend to, but that's one of the teaching aims of the RIHARP JR program. We need to help you understand how to react to situations more constructively and not put yourself at risk of criminal activity. It's something you must work on for the rest of your life."

After twenty minutes of discussion, Linda packed her files and rose from the table. "Thank you for meeting with me tonight, Mr. and Mrs. Garza."

"Anytime," Allison responded. "What's going to happen now?"

"I'm going to submit my report to the RIHARP JR review board, and they'll determine if Jared is still eligible to participate in the program."

"Could they really kick Jared out of RIHARP JR?" Allison asked.

"It's a new program, so anything is possible."

"It seems counterintuitive to pull a boy from a supportive environment and put him back into a toxic one that caused so many of his problems to begin with. I don't get it." Allison countered.

"I understand your perspective, but remember that ADJC is taking a risk allowing a teen in their custody to attend a regular high school. This is the second notification from Scottsdale North High School to ADJC regarding Jared. The first was on his grades and now for fighting. There will be concern among some leaders at ADJC about whether it is safe to allow Jared to continue at a public high school."

Linda put her bag back down on the dining room chair and looked across the table at Jared. "I'm going to do everything I can to keep Jared in the RIHARP JR program, but it will not be easy. His future in RIHARP JR is hanging by a thread right now."

Allison escorted Linda to the front door and returned to the kitchen.

"Let's all try to be positive," Alex stood and said to Jared and Allison. "We've got a lot going on, including the decision on Jared's custody next month, so let's stay positive on all this."

Alex wanted his pep talk to boost Allison and Jared's spirits, but he was the one that most needed to stay positive. The pressure from

Mr. Park to increase revenue month after month was taking a toll on Alex. Despite trying to step away from ESBB, he kept having new fundraising ideas and emailing them to Mateo. His drive to become a partner seemed only a few steps closer today than when he committed to driving hard after his promotion one year earlier. Alex realized his goal was going to be much harder and would take longer than his original plan.

How long can I keep doing this? Will I ever become a partner?

For the first time since his commitment to become a partner, he asked the tough question he hoped he'd never ask himself.

Is it worth it?

Alex shook his head to shake the negative thought out of his mind. Then his own words to his brother came back to him: *"we didn't need a bigger house. We needed Papa to help Edgar and keep our family together."*

Chapter 35

A lex finished his response to an email and noticed it was past five-thirty, so he packed up for the day. He had another networking event at six. After he zipped up his backpack, his phone buzzed, and he saw it was Linda Flowers.

"Hello, Alex. I have Evan in my office with me. Do you have a minute?"

Alex swallowed hard. "Yeah, I have as much time as you need. What is it?"

"Unfortunately, I have some good news and some bad news."

Lines formed across Alex's forehead as he fell back into his chair. "Okay."

"The good news is that the board felt that Jared's incident was an isolated mistake and that overall he's made significant progress under the RIHARP JR program, with much improved grades and no discipline problems other than this one. They are going to give Jared his last second chance in the program."

Alex exhaled loudly. "That's great news. What's the bad news?"

"I'm going to let Evan explain that to you," Linda replied.

"We heard from the judge on the Clint Gellar custody case a little bit ago," Evan said.

Alex had almost forgotten about the case. It had been four months since his deposition, and Clint hadn't harassed him since the night he helped with the truck breakdown.

"The judge ruled that RIHARP JR can't grant temporary guardianship of a minor without the consent of his or her current legal guardians. Since Clint and Becky are still legally Jared's guardians, he can remain in the RIHARP JR program, but he has to live with them if they choose."

"What? I thought RIHARP JR's goal was to help the kids learn how to become productive citizens and sending Jared to live with his parents back puts him back into the environment that got him into trouble. Can't we fight this?"

"We will file an appeal, which will buy us three to four weeks. During that time, we'll see if updating the RIHARP JR program's legal language will help. We'll do all we can to prevent Jared from having to live with Clint and Becky Gellar again."

Alex ran his hand through his hair. "Okay, I know you're working just as hard as we are for Jared. Thank you for the update and let me know if I can help."

"Will do."

The call ended, and Alex looked at the clock on the wall. He was going to be late for a meeting he didn't want to attend.

Alex grabbed his keys, phone, and laptop bag in one motion and then hurried out the door. He trotted down the aisle of the empty office and jumped when he encountered someone around the corner. It wasn't just any Emerson Churchill employee; it was Mr. Park.

"Hi, Alex, are you heading home now?"

"No, I'm on my way to the Financial Executive International Arizona chapter networking event."

"Of course," Mr. Park replied with a smile.

"Were you coming to see me?"

"Yes, but it can wait until another day."

Alex put his laptop bag down on an empty desk beside him. "I still have time to get to the event," Alex lied. He wanted to know the reason for the unusual visit from Mr. Park.

"I want to get your forecast for the fourth quarter."

Alex smiled. "I'm five percent ahead of plan and eighteen percent ahead of last year. I expect to maintain that pace through the end of the year."

Mr. Park shifted his weight and then looked down at the floor before looking back up at Alex. He sensed that Mr. Park had something to tell him or ask him that was uncomfortable.

"Can you do any better?"

Alex let out a brief chuckle. He didn't mean to, but he'd hustled every day since the beginning of the year to achieve the impressive results he shared. "Better, Mr. Park?"

"I know you've been working very hard, Alex, but one of our IT consulting clients had to redo their entire enterprise software package because of our mistake. We are going to miss our profit target for the fourth quarter if we don't find a way to make it up."

The office suddenly went quiet. Alex could hear the elevator bell chime on the floor below them. He hoped Mr. Park couldn't hear him swallow the sudden lump in his throat.

"I'll do what I can, but I'm already putting in twelve to fourteen-hour days almost every day of the week. Have you talked to the other business development people to see what they can do?"

"Yes, I already talked to them, and they said the same thing. I wanted to ask you last because I think you may have extra motivation to help fill the gap in the profit."

"Why would I have the extra motivation?"

"Your education charity."

"ESBB?"

"Yes, if Emerson Churchill is going to be a business sponsor of your charity organization next year, I need to ask corporate for more money in the budget. I can't ask for more money next year if we miss our profit target this year."

Heat raced up Alex's back and into his neck and face. He was sure that Mr. Park could see the frustration in his flushed red cheeks. Alex rubbed the back of his neck and looked at his watch. "In that case, I better get to my networking event so I can write some new business this year."

"Thank you, Alex," Mr. Park replied.

Alex snagged his laptop bag and dashed for the elevator. He couldn't be around Mr. Park another second, or it would be impossible to hide his anger.

During the drive to the networking event, Alex caught himself going twenty miles over the speed limit and slamming on the gas at every green light. He couldn't attend his networking event right now. He needed to stop somewhere to collect himself before he talked to a prospective customer about the benefits of working with Emerson Churchill.

He pulled into a grocery store parking lot, stopped in a distant spot, and dialed Mateo.

"Hey, little brother, how's it going?"

Alex took in a deep breath and exhaled. "Not great. Jared might have to go back to his parents, plus I just found out a few minutes ago that an Emerson Churchill sponsorship of ESBB depends on me getting my act together and generating a lot more revenue this year."

"Are you serious?" Mateo said.

"My boss will do anything to hit our quarterly results. Heck, he may even fire me if I don't deliver the results he wants."

"They'd be crazy if they let you go, and I don't think they're crazy. Mr. Park is just trying to motivate you, so he doesn't get any heat from his boss at corporate."

"That's probably true. Sometimes I wish..." Alex could feel an idea just beyond his grasp. A life where he wasn't constantly hustling —a life where he was helping.

"You still there, Alex?"

"Sorry. Guess I was daydreaming there for a minute."

"No shame in having dreams, little brother. And please let me know if there's anything we can do to help, okay?"

"Thanks, Mateo."

Alex leaned forward in his home office chair and scribbled down numbers and then reclined back to gaze into the air. He repeated that activity multiple times as he pondered how to balance his family budget from a potential pay cut of his current executive salary. Dipping into savings wasn't a viable long-term solution, so cutting back on expenses was the best option. Alex, Allison, and all the kids enjoyed luxuries and amenities from his position at Emerson Churchill, but most of them would disappear if Alex took a pay cut.

The RIHARP JR stipend for Jared was generous and a second one could make up a good portion of his existing income. Alex reasoned that Jared was such a pleasant experience that they could easily host a second teen.

Alex stood up and paced in his office as he considered this option. A minute later, he returned to his desk. He understood that RIHARP JR wouldn't be a reliable monthly income but a way to offset the expense of another person living under their roof. It wasn't the solution to his potential income problem.

"It's going to hurt, but we may all have to cut back a little," Alex whispered to himself.

October brought cooler weather, and Alex and Allison took advantage of the perfect evening temps to sit by their backyard fire pit. Ever since they had kids, they sat by the fire pit and talked after putting them to bed. Now they were often in bed before the kids, but they still liked to catch up with each other beside the golden glow of the natural gas flames.

It had been a long work week, so Alex and Allison talked for hours about the kids' progress, their work, their worries. Alex shared his concern about his future at Emerson Churchill.

"I've been very worried about you burning out, honey," Allison confessed. "And what if your boss gives partnership to someone else?"

"Mateo would be thrilled if I left Emerson Churchill tomorrow and joined him at ESBB, but that would come with a huge pay cut. It seems unfair to you and the kids."

"We could find a way to make it work. I don't want us to end up like your parents. The amount you've been gone this past year helps me understand your mother so much better. If I have to work more and cut our spending, it's a sacrifice I'm willing to make."

Alex couldn't speak; he was so surprised. Allison and his mother had rarely interacted. Was Allison concerned they'll end up divorced like Mama and Papa?

"Not to be a cliché," she continued, "but I need your presence more than presents."

New options for balance swirled in Alex's mind that he assumed were not possible minutes earlier. Alex nodded. "You've given me a lot to think about."

Allison looked at her phone. "Hey, babe, it's ten ten. Make a wish."

"What? It can't only be ten o'clock. We've been out here for hours."

"No, it's after midnight, so it's October tenth now. Make a wish."

Alex nodded and smiled. "That's easy. I wish for no more drama."

Allison snuggled closer to Alex on the outdoor sofa and put her head on his shoulder. "Amen to that. No more drama."

Chapter 36

Alex slept in and spent most of his Saturday morning lounging around in his PJs. He got dressed for lunch and puttered around the yard doing some light landscaping in the afternoon. Alex was about to ask Allison and the kids what they wanted to do for dinner when his phone rang. It was Linda Flowers from ADJC.

Why was she calling on a Saturday?

Alex answered, and Linda didn't waste any time with small talk.

"Alex, I have terrible news. They denied our appeal, and the judge ordered Jared back into the custody of his parents."

"What? Does the judge know about Clint's past?" Alex shouted into the phone.

"Yes, we shared all of that during the appeal, but this judge has a strong bias for keeping kids with their biological parents at any cost, so he ruled against us."

"Can we appeal to someone else? The state supreme court?"

"No, we need to deliver Jared to his parents today."

"Today?" Alex couldn't believe his ears. A few hours ago, he joked with Jared over some pancakes and sausage, and now he was being yanked from their home.

"Yes, I'm leaving soon to pick him up. I have to deliver him to his parents by six tonight, or we will be in contempt of this judgment. We don't like it either, but we have to comply with the decision of the court."

"Alright. I don't know how to break this to Jared. He will not want to go."

"Do you want to wait until I get there, and I'll tell him?" Linda asked.

"No, I want him to have some time to prepare. He's had so much sprung on him, and I don't want to do that to him. I just don't know what to say."

"Tell him he just has to tough it out for three and a half weeks."

"What do you mean?" Alex asked.

"He'll be eighteen on November fourth, so he'll automatically age out of RIHARP JR. This order is just for the rest of his RIHARP JR term, so Jared can leave after he turns eighteen."

A half-smile flashed on Alex's lips. "Well, that's a little good news among this avalanche of bad news. Jared's a strong young man, so he can probably handle living with Clint and Becky for a few weeks. I'll see you in an hour or two. I'm going to tell Jared now."

Alex hung up the phone and his heart sank. Jared had grown so much in the last eleven months, and Alex didn't want any setbacks to ruin his progress. Moving back with Clint was like sending a deer into a den of wolves. It was the worst possible scenario for Jared's growth, but Alex wanted to give him some hope to persevere until November fourth.

First, Alex called Allison back to their bedroom. He shared the bad news with her and how Linda was on the way to pick up Jared. After Allison got over the shock of the report, they agreed they'd tell Jared together and encourage him to go peacefully with Mrs. Flowers and to do his best for the next three and a half weeks.

Jared was scrolling through his phone as he lounged on the plush leather chair when Alex and Allison entered the family room.

Allison and Alex sat down together on the couch. They turned their attention to Jared, so he swung his feet to the floor and faced them with a questioning expression.

"Jared, we have some news to share with you," Allison said in almost a whisper.

Jared put his phone on the end table. "Okay."

"The judge ruled against us in your custody case, but we're still fighting it. We will do everything in our power to overturn this."

Jared leaped to his feet. "What? What does this mean?"

Allison opened her mouth, but the words seemed to stick in her throat, so Alex responded. "It means that you have to move back in with your parents."

"No!" Alex shouted and darted to his bedroom.

Alex and Allison gave him a minute and then proceeded to his room at the end of the hall. Alex knocked on the door and opened it. Jared was sitting on the floor, hugging his knees.

Allison leaned down with tears forming in her eyes. "I'm sorry, Jared. We can't believe it either. We were hoping you'd be here for as long as you wanted to stay."

That caused Jared to sniffle and look up at Allison. "When do I have to go back?"

Allison took in a deep breath and let it out. "They are on their way to pick you up right now."

"Clint?"

"No, Mrs. Flowers has to take you home by six o'clock today based on the court order."

Jared sobbed and banged the back of his head against the wall. Allison stood up and put her hand over her mouth. Tears streamed down her cheeks.

"Jared, stop it!" Alex roared.

The abrupt outburst from Alex caused everyone to freeze. Jared looked up through his tears, and Alex bent down on one knee next to him.

"Don't hurt yourself over this. You're so much stronger now than when you arrived here. I believe in you. I think you can handle living back home for a little bit, can't you?"

"You don't understand. I don't know what Clint will do to me when I get home. I'm sure he's going to smack me around more than ever. I don't know how much of that I can take."

"Can you avoid him for a little over three weeks?" Alex quickly replied.

Jared stopped crying and tilted his head, "what do you mean three weeks?"

"Jared, you'll be eighteen in twenty-five days, and then you get to decide where you live. That's all the time the judge said you had to live with them, and then you can move out right away. Can you try to dodge Clint for three weeks?" Alex asked with a reassuring smile.

Jared sniffed and wiped his nose. He let his bent legs flop straight on the carpeted floor and looked at both Allison and Alex. "Yeah, I guess I can try to avoid him for three weeks. It's going to feel like the longest three weeks of my life, but if I know I can leave and never come back, that will make it easier."

Alex ruffled his hair and handed Jared the iPad from his nightstand. "You've grown so much this year, so I know you can do it. Take this iPad with you too so you'll have this and your phone. Message me every day to let me know how you're doing and how they're treating you. If Clint touches you, let me know and I'll get ADJC involved so they can get you out of there."

Nobody spoke for a half minute, so Alex broke the silence.

"Jared, we'll give you some time to pack before Mrs. Flowers arrives."

He nodded, so Alex and Allison left his room.

Minutes later, Allison returned to Jared's room with Alex following close behind. He had a suitcase on his bed filled with shirts, shorts, and socks.

"I was planning to give this to you on your birthday, but it's getting chilly at night, so pack this," Allison said as she handed Jared a jacket.

"Is it an Arizona Cardinals jacket?" Jared asked with a smile as he pulled it over for closer inspection.

"No. It's cardinal red, but no fancy logos. It will keep you warm on these cool nights."

"Thank you."

Allison and Alex retreated to the family room to wait for Linda to come and take Jared away. Gaby, Daniel, and Olivia found out what was happening and spent time in his room with him, saying their farewells.

Ninety minutes later, their security camera chime notified them that a vehicle was in the driveway. When Alex opened the front door, he saw Linda Flowers and a police officer.

She must have caught the look on Alex's face because she answered his question before he asked. "This is Deputy Cole. ADJC requires a law enforcement officer during all transfers, so he's just here to assist me while I drive Jared to his home in Buckeye."

"Hello, deputy," Alex replied with a wave. "He's still packing, so wait out here and I'll get him."

Minutes later, Jared walked out of the front door with Alex and Allison behind him. He stopped at the end of the front patio as soon as he saw the SUV with the Sheriff's logo emblazoned on the passenger door.

Jared turned back to Alex and Allison. His face was as red as the new jacket he was wearing. "What's this? I thought you said Mrs. Flowers was going to take me."

"That's what we thought too, but I guess it's the procedure for an officer to come with her," Alex replied.

While Jared had his back turned to him, Deputy Cole walked up behind him and placed cuffs on one wrist. Jared yanked his other hand away before he could put the cuffs over his other wrist. Jared ran off the patio, past Linda and the deputy.

"Why are you doing this? Nobody said you were going to handcuff me!" Jared shouted with fear and anger in his voice.

"It's for our safety, son. I won't put them too tight," Deputy Cole replied.

Linda put her hand up to stop him, "Let me handle this."

She took several steps toward Jared, and he took the same number of steps away from her to maintain his distance. Linda sighed, "Jared, please. Nobody is happy about this, but let's not make this any harder than it already is."

"That's easy for you to say. You're not getting forced to live with a monster. I'm not going."

The smile on Linda's face vanished. "Come on, Jared. We need to go now."

Jared turned and marched off the driveway into the front yard toward the back of the house with the handcuffs dangling from one wrist. "I'm not going back there, and I'm not going with you. Nobody is going to—"

Jared stiffened and fell like a young redwood tree into the grass. He landed on his chest, and the thud echoed all the way to the front patio. Allison screamed, and Alex looked over at Linda. She had her phone out and her thumb on the Sure Cuffs activate button.

In this tragedy, the irony that the victim was lying on the ground in handcuffs while the perpetrator was comfortably perched at home waiting for his prey to arrive dumbfounded Alex. He jumped off the patio and started toward Jared.

Linda commanded Alex, "No, let him be. Deputy Cole is going to get him in the vehicle, so we can get going."

"Why did you do that?" Alex asked, but nobody responded.

After Linda deactivated Sure Cuffs, Deputy Cole grabbed Jared's dangling handcuffs and clicked them around both wrists. He helped Jared to his feet and guided him to the backseat of the SUV.

Linda turned to Alex and Allison. "I'm sorry I had to do that. We'll keep fighting for Jared administratively and through the courts, but I will not fight him in your front yard. I need to fulfill this judicial order today and we're running out of time."

She got into the front passenger seat, and the Sheriff's vehicle drove out of their driveway.

Alex could see the silhouette of a boy in a red jacket leaning against the window in the back seat as they drove away. He looked over at Allison to see tears racing down her cheeks. Alex also wiped away several tears.

Chapter 37

A lex checked his phone for a text from Jared every twenty minutes that first night. He paced in the bedroom until he heard the ping on his phone just after eleven. It was only a two-word text, but it spoke volumes.

I'm here.

Alex sensed the anger seething through Jared's fingers as he typed each character. Surely, he felt betrayed by Alex, Allison, and especially Linda Flowers. They were all people he'd learned to trust and didn't expect that they'd hurt him.

Now Jared was back in the toxic environment that introduced him to ADJC in the first place. Alex hoped Jared would do his best to avoid Clint, but hope wasn't enough. Alex put his phone down and walked into his closet, where it was quiet and prayed for Jared.

Over the next three days, Jared texted Alex more frequently, but they were short messages. Based on the texts, Alex gathered that Jared was getting along okay with Clint and that his mom Becky was happy for him to be in the house.

"Hang in there, Jared. Only twenty more days to go," Alex said to himself as he counted down the days until Jared could move out.

Alex was extremely busy at work. It was a welcome distraction from worrying about Jared, and the days passed quickly as Alex hustled to boost fourth-quarter revenue. That is until Alex received a text from Jared early in the morning with horrible news.

Clint is drinking again. It's bad.

Alex felt nauseated at what that meant for Jared. He knew Clint could be nasty when he was sober but turned meaner than a rattlesnake when he was drunk. Nineteen days was a breeze for Alex in his safe, climate-controlled house and office, but it would be agony living with an angry, abusive drunk like Clint.

Could Clint's drinking be grounds for ADJC to remove Jared? It wasn't safe for Jared to be there with his father in that condition.

Alex debated his options but just couldn't sit idle while Jared dealt with Clint. After his ten o'clock meeting was over, Alex called Linda at ADCJ. Maybe she could do something.

"Hi Linda, it's Alex Garza. I got a message from Jared that Clint drank heavily again last night. I wondered if ADJC could investigate Jared's living arrangements with Clint to be sure it is safe for him to live there. Is there anything you can do?"

"Sure, we can open an investigation, but it will take at least two weeks before we'll be able to get anyone out there for a site visit and then a hearing up to a month after that. Hopefully, Jared will be out of that house long before an investigation could remove him."

"So there's nothing else we can do right now?"

"I'm sorry, not in the short time we have. How many days does—"

"Nineteen," Alex replied before Linda could finish the question.

"Tell him to hang in there. He has less than three weeks."

The call ended, and Alex stared at the stack of customer leads on his desk. The urgency to increase revenue for Emerson Churchill felt trivial to Alex when he compared it to the concern for Jared's health and safety. He couldn't concentrate on work, so Alex left for lunch and didn't intend to return. Instead, he headed toward home to talk through his concerns with Allison while the kids were at school.

Alex arrived home after a quick stop for food and took his array of sandwiches, soup, and salads to the backyard. He pulled the bistro table out of the shade and into the sun to soak up the rays still warming the air. As he waited for Allison to join him, Alex poured both of them a glass of sparkling water with a lime. Two minutes later, Allison arrived with a smile.

"This is such a pleasant surprise," Allison said as she sat down and assembled her lunch. "Why did you leave work early?"

Alex put his sandwich down. "I want to talk to you, but let's enjoy lunch first. We don't get to do this very often."

Allison nodded, and Alex took a bite out of his Cuban sandwich.

When they finished eating, Allison put her napkin on her plate. "Okay, what did you want to talk about?"

Alex scanned the beautiful vistas from his backyard and exhaled. "I'm worried about Jared. He said Clint was drinking heavily again, and I know that's going to lead to some type of confrontation between him and Jared. I feel like I should do something, but I don't know what to do."

"Have you talked to Linda? What does she think?"

"Yeah, she thinks we need to encourage Jared to hang in there until he's eighteen, and then he can bolt like a racehorse, but I don't know."

Wrinkles formed between Allison's eyes as her eyebrows pinched. "What else could we do?"

Alex felt the heat of Allison's gaze on his face. He was rarely indecisive, and she could suspect that his dilemma meant that he was considering something that he shouldn't do.

"I don't know. He's still a kid, and he's all alone with Clint. I just don't know."

"Alex, you're not considering going down there, are you? That man is a loose cannon! Who knows what he is capable of if you go down there. We need to do what Linda recommends. We need to encourage Jared to stay strong for a couple more weeks and then help him get out of there as fast as possible. Okay?"

Alex nodded and looked away.

"Alejandro, you can't go down there!" Allison's face turned red, and her voice got louder. "It's too dangerous! Promise me you won't try to help Jared by going to visit him."

Alex put his hands up in surrender. "Okay. I'll keep texting Jared to keep tabs on him and help boost his spirits so he can last a few more weeks."

"Thank you," Allison replied as she stood up from the bistro table. "I have a call, so I have to get back inside. I'm glad you came home early so we could have this talk."

Allison gave Alex a kiss on the cheek and took the empty lunch containers back inside. Alex remained outside. He couldn't stop thinking about Jared and the stress he was under living with Clint. Alex was okay as long as he received regular texts from Jared and had confirmation that he was okay.

For the next week, Alex received one or two texts a day from Jared describing Clint's growing annoyance toward his mom and himself. Then Alex got the text he hoped he'd never see from Jared.

He got so drunk last night he hit me. Never again!

Alex wanted to jump in his SUV and drive down right away. He wanted to save Jared from this monster, but he didn't have a plan. Jared was ten days from freedom, and Alex hoped he could make it.

Jared didn't respond the next day or the day after. A pit grew in Alex's stomach every day that he didn't hear from Jared. He was only days away from freedom, but Alex wasn't even sure Jared was okay. He always thought Clint was a monster but was he capable of severely hurting his own son?

Alex thought about the possibilities, and none of them gave him a sense of hope. He hated to break his promise to Allison, but he had no other choice. He needed to help Jared.

Chapter 38

On the first day of November, Alex went to work, but instead of attending a networking event afterward, he headed West on the I-10 freeway towards Buckeye, Arizona. Alex found Clint Gellar's address online from the county assessor's website and put it in his GPS.

The sun settled behind the distant mountain range as Alex left Phoenix's urban density and drove deep into the furthest suburbs. It was completely dark when Alex turned off the freeway onto a blacktop road dissecting a small cluster of homes carved out of the chaparral shrubs in the desert. Even the houses appear to scream "stay away" to outsiders who dared to enter their turf.

The GPS indicated that Alex arrived at his destination. It was a large lot with a mobile home perched on a cinder block foundation twenty yards from the road. A single light illuminated the gravel driveway and a front-yard full of junk. Alex assumed these were all the projects Clint started and didn't finish. Clint's familiar gray pickup truck was steps from the front door, and it looked like it had a recent kiss from a guardrail on the passenger side.

Alex rolled by at normal speed so he didn't draw attention to himself. He was in enemy territory, and he knew he had to be extra cautious. He passed a neighbor's house across the street and came to an intersection with a dirt road. Alex turned left and drove slowly along Clint's corner lot until he could see the back of the trailer. Lights were on and the flicker of a TV showed someone was home. Alex continued down the dirt road until his headlights splashed light on a dip ahead. It was a dry wash, and it ran directly behind Clint's house.

The stars and the waxing crescent moon cast a dim light on the desert, so Alex killed his headlights and stopped at the wash. Once his eyes adjusted, he backed his SUV onto the soft gravel and parked under the canopy of a mature palo verde tree.

He shut off the engine, took in a deep breath, and slowly let it out. When he departed the office, his plan was to get here and check on Jared but wasn't exactly sure how he would do it without getting noticed.

Should he wait until someone left to see if Jared was there, or should he try to get closer to the trailer and look inside a window?

Alex closed his eyes and let the cool desert air envelop him through his open window as he considered all his options. He said a quick prayer and opened his eyes again. He strained his neck to get another look at the mobile home. Allison would be angry if she even knew that Alex drove to Jared's house but would be furious if she found out he tried to sneak up to the mobile home. She knew it was a risky exercise.

She's right. I don't know what I'd do if I saw Jared sitting on the couch or if it was only Clint and Becky. It's too dangerous.

Alex put his finger over the start engine button of his SUV and turned his eyes back to the mobile home. He stared at a broken screen on a dark window and wondered if that was Jared's room. The sounds of the desert seemed to rise in volume, and then Edgar's image appeared in his mind. The crickets' rhythmic song reminded Alex of all the times he would follow Edgar and Mateo into the desert at night. They'd descend hundreds of feet into the wild desert to sit quietly and listen to animals come alive as the moon rose higher in the sky. They could hear the scratching of mice, the laughter of the coyotes, the patter of javelina feet, and if they were lucky, the flapping wings of an owl on the hunt.

Alex remembered those nights like it was yesterday. He felt so brave sitting in the dark with his older brothers.

Before Alex could give his plan additional thought, he was out of his SUV and moving up the wash toward Clint's house. A few minutes later, he arrived near the back windows with light beaming onto the rocky ground. Alex crouched below the window and raised up slowly to peer inside. He was outside some type of eat-in kitchen and could see Clint and Becky in the next room over while they each sat in a chair and watched a TV. They were facing the opposite wall, so Alex felt confident they couldn't see him. He could hear the voice of a news anchor on TV through the paper-thin walls. Once the anchor covered the news of the day, a female voice talked about the weather. That's when Alex heard movement and saw Clint stand up and pace in the small area between their chairs and the TV.

"I need to find that kid."

Was he talking about Jared?

Clint continued to pace. "You see how I'm trying hard, don't you? Now he runs away after one little fight. First thing tomorrow, I best get looking for him or we can kiss our RIHARP checks goodbye."

Becky said something Alex couldn't make out over the TV. The sports segment of the news started, and Clint returned to his chair.

Alex wondered if he was hearing everything right through the walls and over the TV. Did Jared really run away?

The questions tugged at Alex like a giant hand. He needed to get closer to be certain Jared was missing and that Clint was preparing to go after him. Alex needed to move to the front of the mobile home so he could get a better view.

The hair on the back of his neck rose as Alex turned both corners and headed toward the covered patio he was sure Clint built himself. Moving closer would expose Alex to the beams of the front porch light, but it was his only option.

"I'll just look inside to verify Jared is not there and leave," Alex whispered to himself as he crouched against the trailer. He was about to move onto the concrete patio when he stepped on a piece of wood from one of Clint's failed projects hidden in the shadows. The wood splintered. It sounded like a cannon blast to Alex but he wasn't sure if they'd hear it inside the structure.

"What's that?" Clint barked.

Alex froze and moved closer to the mobile home to be less visible.

"What's what?" Becky asked. Alex heard her voice clearly this time.

"Are you deaf? Something's stirring outside."

"That's just that pack of coyotes looking for mice again around your junk pile," Becky stated with a slow slur of someone who'd had too much to drink.

Alex slowed his breathing and listened for movement inside the trailer. After several minutes, he heard the familiar intro music to a courthouse drama on the TV. Clint bought the coyote story.

Alex crawled past the front door and under the front window. This was the view he needed to know for sure if Jared was inside the mobile home or not. He moved to the corner of the window and strained to see the room with one eye, but he couldn't. Alex raised a couple more inches and saw Clint and Becky sitting in the chairs with the TV's light flickering on their faces. Nobody else was in the room.

Alex glared at Clint's blank expression. He couldn't believe a father could do what he'd done to his own son and daughter. Just as Alex took a step back to duck away and leave, Clint's head snapped in the window's direction. Alex jumped and hit his head on some rusty wind chimes.

"We have a trespasser! Get my shotgun!" Clint roared.

Alex turned and sprinted toward his parked SUV. He rounded the corner and tripped over an old bathtub in the yard while he heard the front door slam against the side of the mobile home. Alex found his footing and continued his retreat. He heard Clint yell as he descended several feet into the wash.

Boom!

The shotgun blast drove Alex to the ground. He had one ear in the sand while the other heard the lead shot ricochet off the rocks above him and fall to the ground. Alex was halfway to his SUV, so he bounced up, bent over, and plodded down the dark wash as if boarding a helicopter in a war zone.

"Garza? Is that you?" Clint yelled out as he neared the wash. Alex ducked down and continued inching toward his SUV.

"I can see shiny bits of that fancy sport-yute of yours! What are you doing here?"

Alex ducked behind a dying shrub and faced Clint. He tried to quiet his breathing but had too much adrenaline pumping through his veins. Alex spun to locate his SUV and estimated he had another forty to fifty yards to reach it.

Could I reach my SUV before Clint could get off another shot?

"Gosh-darnit, Garza. I know it's you. Did my boy tell you about our fight? I bet he did. Well, it's too late to pull him outta here if that's why you came. He's gone."

Alex got the confirmation he was seeking, but needed more information.

"Please don't shoot," Alex called back.

Clint sighed. "I get nervous when I catch people sneaking 'round my property. I'm gonna put down this gun, okay? Come on out. We need to talk."

Alex debated whether he could trust Clint. Was he serious or was this a trap? After a quick deliberation, he determined it may be the best opportunity to help Jared and stood up in the wash.

"I'm sorry for scaring you. I was just worried about him. If he's not here, I'll just be on my way."

"No!" Clint hollered.

Alex froze.

"I mean, er… um… *please* come on out and talk to me," Clint spluttered, like using common courtesy was a foreign language. "I'm worried, too."

"You're worried about Jared or about losing the stipend?" Alex shot back.

"Well, both, but… I don't want my boy hurt, or dead. I might be a screw up, and, well, not that good at looking out for him, but I'm not a monster. Or at least I don't want to be."

Alex took a moment to absorb this. His head was telling him to run, his heart was telling him something extraordinary was going on, and if he ran, he would miss it. "Why should I trust you?" he asked.

"I owe you. That night when I was sore about the trial, and you helped me get my truck going? You didn't have to do that. You could've called the cops and won the lawsuit. But you didn't. You gave me a second chance; you gave my boy and me a second chance. I've messed it up again, like usual. Garza, man, I could really use your help."

"My help?" Alex was incredulous.

"I know you care about my boy. If we worked together, maybe we can find him before something terrible happens."

Alex stared at Clint for what seemed like an hour and reached into his pocket. He pulled out his phone and dialed Linda Flowers. He was grateful she answered after only one ring.

"Is everything okay?" Linda answered.

"I'm sorry it's late, but I'm concerned about Jared."

Alex shared that he was texting regularly with Jared, but his communication stopped suddenly after his last text was about Clint striking him.

"Now, he's not responding to any of my texts. What can we do to help Jared?" Alex asked while he watched Clint shuffle back and forth in the sand.

"The first thing we'll do is send an officer to the Gellar property for a wellness check."

"What if he's not there?"

"We'll get a statement from Clint and Becky and then have the Sheriff issue an APB to start a formal search for him."

"But can't you just locate Jared with the Sure Cuffs GPS tracker?"

Linda did not respond. Alex wondered if he dropped the call.

"Are you still there?" Alex asked.

"Yes, I'm here. I'm just kicking myself for disabling Sure Cuffs before we dropped Jared off at the Gellar residence."

Alex stopped pacing. "What? Why did you do that?"

Linda cleared her throat. "Well, I didn't want to give Jared's father another weapon to use against Jared. When I saw Jared fall in your front yard and lay there helpless until we disabled Sure Cuffs, I thought of all the horrible things that could happen if the Sure Cuffs app were in the wrong hands. I figured it was just a few weeks and wouldn't be an issue."

"I never thought of that. What happens if he really has run off and they find him before his birthday?"

"That would be up to a judge, but if he ran away from his legal guardians under RIHARP JR, it's like fleeing any ADJC facility, so that wouldn't be good. Let's find him first and make sure he's alright, and then we can worry about all the rest."

"Okay, keep me posted."

Alex turned to Clint. "Bad news. If we don't find Jared before the police, he could end up in adult prison. I don't want that. Do you?"

"No. No way. So you'll help me?"

Alex sighed. "I'll help you."

Chapter 39

The two men walked into the light of the front porch and Clint leaned up against a picnic table that screeched under his weight.

"How we gonna find Jared?" Clint asked.

"Well, I think we should split up. You can go check with any extended family he may reach out to and I'll look for friend connections. We'll cover more ground faster that way."

Clint nodded, "He's got an aunt that I'll pay a visit."

"Great, call or text me as soon as you find out anything about Jared."

Clint looked to the ground and kicked at a pebble. "I ain't got a phone right now. My minutes dried up on the prepaid phone I have."

"You don't have a phone?"

Clint hopped up from the picnic table, "You know I don't have any money. That's why I keep harping on you about that stipend."

Alex put both hands up in surrender. "Okay, I was just asking."

The desert seemed to come alive when the chirps of crickets filled the silence between the two men.

"You know what?" Alex asked, "I think I may have something for you. I got a new phone with service when I extended my contract last month. I was holding it to give to my son for Christmas, but I can let you use it now."

"Oh, okay. That would help."

"We need to look for Jared right away. I'll go get it and drop it off later tonight."

Alex drove home trying to decide if the events he experienced on the Gellar property were real. He couldn't believe Jared bolted from home and that he was now working with Clint to find him.

Did I really agree to help the same guy who shot at me tonight?

All the kids were in their rooms playing games or reading when Alex arrived home. He rushed into the closet and pulled out his bottom dresser drawer. Below several summer t-shirts and shorts, he found the phone he'd hid from Daniel for a future Christmas gift. Alex powered it up and noticed the battery was at forty percent.

"I'll charge this up on my way."

Alex turned to head back to his SUV when Allison walked in.

"Where are you going?"

Alex took a deep breath, "I'm taking this phone to Clint Gellar."

"What?"

He shared the whole story with Allison. The sneaking up to the trailer, the gunshots, the truce with Clint, his story about the fight with Jared and finally, the need to give him a phone.

"I still can't believe it, but Clint and I are going to work together to find Jared."

"Does he really want to find Jared or do you think this is an act?"

"I—I think I believe him. He's still a wildcard and I'm going to be careful with him, but I genuinely believe that he wants to find Jared before anything bad happens to him."

"I hope so."

"I have a long drive back to Buckeye so I'm going to head out now."

"Okay. Be safe," Allison said as Alex left for the garage.

At work the next day, Alex called a number he found in Jared's file that he heard him mention multiple times. It was the home of a boy he shared a room with at Adobe School before RIHARP JR who he talked about most often. It was the closest thing to a friend Alex recalled from his conversations with Jared. He hoped he was hiding out with this boy, but the man who answered the phone wouldn't admit it. Alex told the man to have Jared call him if he showed up and assured him that he wouldn't get the police involved.

For the rest of the afternoon, Alex jumped at every ring and ping on his phone, hoping it was Jared. Alex felt Jared was still in the area but considered the possibility that he might have left town.

"Where are you, Jared?" Alex whispered to himself as he scanned the mountains from his office window.

Alex finished his October revenue report for Mr. Park and closed his laptop. He planned to leave early to drive around some areas where he suspected Jared might try to hide from Clint. Alex slid into his jacket and his phone rang. He fished the phone out of his pocket and saw Linda Flowers on his caller ID.

"Hi, Linda, did you find Jared?"

"No, when the deputy showed up at the Gellar residence for a wellness check, only Becky was there. She said he and Clint had gone on a fishing trip."

"What are you thinking now, Linda?"

"Your hunch alone isn't enough to go on, unfortunately. His lack of communication could be that he's just out of range of cell service. When his own mother won't report him as missing, we can't really send out search parties."

Alex silently cheered. Becky had bought them some time with her fine acting.

"Please keep me posted if you hear of anything or get an update from the sheriff."

Alex was out of his office seconds after ending his call. He had to find Jared before the deputies, so he drove from Scottsdale to Phoenix. His destination was the home of the man he spoke to on the phone earlier about Jared. En route, he texted with Clint and shared the good news that the police wouldn't be on Jared's trail until the fake fishing trip was over. Clint reported he had checked with several of Jared's aunts and uncles, but none of them had seen his son.

Alex pulled off the freeway and into a neighborhood jammed with single-level homes that looked like a cookie-cutter formed them. Alex dodged the large potholes in the street and noticed many houses had bars on the windows behind the shadows cast from every other broken streetlight. He slowed to confirm the address he wrote down and came to a stop in front of an eggshell white home with light peering out of multiple rooms. It had a chain-link fence surrounding the dirt front yard with a large Beware of Dog sign. Alex couldn't sneak up on this home, so he'd have to wait outside until someone left the house.

Alex searched the area and saw several open parking spots two spaces down among the cars parallel parked in front of the homes. He pulled his SUV into the closest space and parked at an angle to maintain an unobstructed view of the target house. Alex flashed a brief smile at the thought of a stakeout he'd seen many times in the movies.

Alex snickered. "Special agent Garza, you are going to be here a while."

He wasn't sure what he would do if he saw Jared. He hadn't called for over a week, so if he was hiding out there, maybe he didn't want to talk to Alex anymore. Alex didn't want Jared to get hauled in by deputies, so he decided that if he saw him, Alex would help him if he needed anything and keep his distance if he asked to be left alone.

Over the next hour, dozens of cars sped through the residential street until one slowed and parked behind Alex. He slumped down as the high school age boy slid out of his car and strolled toward the house Alex was staking out. He passed through the fence and walked through the front door.

"This may be it," Alex whispered as he straightened up to get the best view of the house.

Two minutes later, three people emerged from the front door. They were all wearing hoodies with the hoods pulled tightly over their heads, so Alex couldn't identify if one was Jared or not. He watched them walk around the house and vanish into the backyard. One of them appeared to be Jared's height and had his unique gait when he walked.

"The alley!" Alex shouted to himself.

He started his SUV and pulled around the cluster of homes until he reached the alley behind that row of houses. It was dark, but Alex could see the silhouettes of three people walking. He turned to enter but stopped.

I'm not even sure that's Jared. What if that isn't him or his friend? Should I wait until I can be sure it's him?

The silhouettes were getting smaller under the moonlight, so Alex knew he had to act fast or he'd miss them.

He continued into the alley, and his headlights lit up the three figures at the end of the dirt path. None of the trio turned around to see who was behind him until Alex was only ten yards away. Then they all turned around at the same time and started walking toward him. Alex could tell Jared was not in the group and that they weren't happy to see him.

Alex jumped out of his SUV. "I'm looking for Jared Gellar."

The three boys stopped and exchanged glances until the one nearest to Alex spoke. "He ain't here. Why are you looking for him?"

"Do you know him?" Alex asked.

"It depends. Why are you asking?" the boy said with a level of seriousness that caused Alex to take a step back.

"He was living with me, but now he's missing, and I think he's in trouble. I want to find him so I can help him."

The boy turned to his friends and the tallest one nodded.

"Yeah, I know him. I was his roommate at Adobe but haven't heard from him since he entered a program to live with some rich family. Are you the rich guy?"

Alex flashed a half-smile. "A judge forced him to move back in with his parents, and now he ran away. I want to find him before the police do, so will you tell him to call Alex if you hear from him?"

The boy shook his head, "Ah man, his old man is crazy. Even crazier than mine. I always told Jared he should pound on that nut job after all those years he hit him. Jared was bigger than his old man but still wouldn't defend himself. Yeah, I'll tell him to call ya. I hope you find him before the law does because he'll be going to the big house this time."

"Yeah, I hope so, too," Alex said.

The three boys turned and left the alley.

"Me too," Alex whispered to himself as he got back into his vehicle.

Alex barely slept as he thought about where Jared could be hiding. He didn't appear to be staying with old friends, and Jared hadn't attempted to contact Alex or anyone else in his family since he ran away.

Where could he be?

Alex asked himself that question over and over until exhaustion took over and he fell asleep.

Alex opened his eyes and shot up in bed. The sky was still black with no sign of a looming sunrise. He looked at his clock on the nightstand and saw that it was five forty-eight, so he stretched and plopped his feet onto the carpeted floor. His body cracked in protest after each step he took toward the closet. He planned to head north to search for Jared, and had to get dressed for the trip.

After rummaging through the hallway coat closet for his winter jacket and downing a cup of coffee, Alex walked to the sliding glass door in his family room. He saw hints of blue in the sky, which meant that the sun would be up once Alex reached the Arizona High Country.

Just before leaving, Alex went back into his room to kiss Allison goodbye. He placed a soft kiss on her forehead and darted for the door.

"Are you going to work early?" Allison asked in a gravelly voice as she sat up in bed.

Alex returned to the side of the bed and sat down at Allison's feet. "No, I'm going up north to look for Jared. I'll take one of my personal days that I've been hoarding all year."

"Why are you going up north? Don't you think he'd stick around an area he knows?"

"We've looked and looked and nothing. I'm going to check some of our camping sites, starting with Woods Canyon."

Allison leaned over on her elbow and propped up her head. She was fully awake now, and Alex could tell she was processing his plan.

"It's cold up there. Do you really think he'd try to hide out up there?"

"You saw the look on his face when we went camping this summer. Plus, it's isolated, so it's a perfect place to hide out," Alex replied.

"I guess, but why do you have to go? Can't the police send the local sheriff or something to look for him so you don't have to drive all the way up there?"

Alex leaned over on his elbow until he was eye to eye with Allison.

"I need to find Jared first. He turns eighteen tomorrow, so if he can make it one more day without getting caught by the authorities, he'll be free from the juvenile justice system and can live where he likes. If they find Jared before me, he might have to do some time in prison for running away from ADJC custody."

Allison remained expressionless in the dimly lit bedroom but then nodded.

"You better get going. Take that crazy fur hat and sheepskin mittens your dad brought you from Alaska—they're boxed up behind Gaby's skates. Keep me posted if you find him or any clues. I'll do the same around here."

This time Alex planted a kiss on Allison's lips, grabbed the hat and mittens from the back of the coat closet, and darted to his SUV.

When he got outside, he texted Clint a list of campgrounds to check for Jared, promising that he would check out several others.

Clint replied, "Thanks, Garza. I don't deserve your help, but I'm thankful for it."

Chapter 40

Two hours later, the RPM's in Alex's SUV increased as he climbed the steep hill to reach the Woods Canyon campground's turn off. When Alex exited his vehicle, the brisk air from seven thousand feet of elevation greeted him. He zipped up his coat and put on the fluffy hat from Papa that had seemed like an enormous joke when he got it.

For the next thirty minutes, he searched the area near their old campsite from their summer trip. Then he walked the perimeter of the fifty-five-acre Woods Canyon Lake until he reached the general store near the boat launch. Surely, if Jared was in the area, a store worker, camper, or boater must have seen him.

Alex approached a woman behind the counter with white hair and an accommodating smile.

"May I help you?"

Alex pulled out his phone and scrolled to a couple of recent pictures of Jared. "I'm wondering if you've seen this young man in here in the last day or two."

The woman pulled the glasses secured by a chain up to her face and inspected the images. She shook her head, "I'm sorry, I haven't seen him."

"Do you think any of your co-workers might have seen him?"

"This is our last weekend open, so I'm the only one working until we close up for the winter on Saturday."

"It is pretty chilly up here, so I guess not too many people want to camp this time of year," Alex said.

"Nope, just the diehards. I'm surprised we don't have snow yet, but I saw that it's in the forecast for next week."

That was a stark reminder that Alex had to find Jared soon if he was hiding up here.

"Thank you for your time," Alex said as he turned to leave in a rush.

He wasn't paying attention to the customer standing in line behind him, and Alex ran right into the chest of one of the diehard campers. The mountain of a man was wearing camouflage gear from head to toe, while a long, graying beard hid his face.

"I'm sorry, I didn't see you standing right behind me," Alex said, looking up at the man's cold eyes.

"Don't be in such a rush next time. I'm kind of hard to miss."

"I will. I'm just in a hurry to find someone."

Wrinkles appeared on what Alex could see above the man's nose. "Who you looking for?"

Alex wasn't sure he should tell the man. He seemed hostile toward strangers, and Alex wanted to get back to his search for Jared.

"I'm up here scouting sites for elk," the man continued. "I got a permit this year, so I've been scouring this forest for a few days now. If someone is up here, I may have seen him."

Desperation overcame concern, so Alex showed the man the same pictures of Jared that he shared with the woman behind the counter.

"Oh yeah, I saw him."

Alex straightened up and took a step closer to the man. "Where did you see him?"

The man stroked his beard a few times as he looked up at the ceiling. "I saw him at the supercenter in Payson. We were both in the camping section, which is dead this time of year. It caught my eye because he was buying camping gear."

"Do you know where he was heading?" Alex asked as soon as the man finished his last word.

"I didn't speak to him, so I have no idea where he was going."

"When did you see him at the supercenter?"

The man pursed his lips. "It had to be two nights ago because I had to buy some extra ammo. Yep, it was two days ago."

"Thank you, sir. I appreciate all your help."

Alex stuffed his phone into his front pocket and jogged to his SUV. He had to get to the supercenter in Payson to get on Jared's trail.

Sixty minutes later, Alex pulled into the parking lot of the supercenter store in Payson, Arizona. Alex quickly found the camping section of the store. He browsed several aisles until he came to a counter with a boy not much older than Jared, working behind a glass counter filled with knives and expensive rifle scopes.

As he'd done at the general store at Woods Canyon, Alex shared Jared's pictures with the young man behind the counter. He looked carefully and broke into a wide smile.

"Oh yeah, I saw him. He was one of the few people who purchased camping gear this week, so I did a double-take when he plopped a cold-weather sleeping bag on the counter."

"What else did he buy?" Alex asked.

"I remember he didn't have enough money to buy a tent, but I believe he had enough for a sleeping bag, a tarp, and a few boxes of granola bars."

"Did he mention where he was going?"

"Nah. He didn't say anything. He seemed to be in a hurry, so I just rang him up and bagged everything real quick."

"Where would you go around here if you wanted to hide from your dad for a few days?"

The young man laughed. "I don't have to guess on that question. I ran away a few times when I was in high school and I slept under the bridge over the East Verde River or the Flowing Springs Campground just up the river a bit. Both are a few miles outside of town."

Alex nodded, "Got it." He took several steps and then turned back to the counter.

"Can you look at the pictures one more time to be sure it was the same person I'm looking for? If he's outside in a sleeping bag, he may be in trouble with these nighttime temps."

The young man leaned over the counter to get a closer look at Alex's phone. "I'm pretty sure that's him."

"Did he pay with a credit card? Can you check receipts for a name?" Alex asked.

"I remember he paid in cash. He pulled five twenty-dollar bills out of his red jacket and laid it on the counter."

"Did you say red jacket?"

"Yes, it was bright red like an Arizona Cardinals football team jacket, but it was just plain. Never saw—"

Alex turned and was out of the camping department before the young man finished his sentence.

The confirmation that the store employee saw Jared put a fresh gust of wind in his sails. Alex reached his car a minute later and found the bridge over the East Verde River on his phone that the supercenter worker mentioned. It was only a twenty-minute drive when Alex crossed over the bridge and came to a stop along the shoulder behind another truck. Alex jumped out of his SUV and plodded down the worn dirt path while he zipped up his coat. He arrived on the bank of the East Verde River, which was more like a gentle creek after several months of dry weather. Alex looked around all the areas under the bridge where a person could find proper shelter from the chilly wind. The concrete and steel bridge absorbed more of the strong Arizona sunlight than any area in the forest, so it made sense that some could hide out here for a few days, but Alex didn't see any sign of Jared.

An older gentleman was fishing a hundred yards downriver, so Alex walked in his direction.

"Catching anything?" Alex asked, pretending to be interested in the answer.

"No keepers yet, but I'm not going home until I have dinner," the older man replied with a deep belly laugh.

"I'm sure you'll catch a full stringer for dinner."

"I sure hope so."

Alex took a few more steps and asked what was really on his mind. "Have you seen a tall kid wearing a red jacket around here? He's about six-two and around eighteen years old."

The man kept turning his reel as he looked hard at the water and then looked up at Alex. "I've been out here every day this week and haven't seen any kids. A bunch of old fogeys like me trying to catch Moby Dick, but that's it."

"Thank you and good luck," Alex said as he turned back toward the bridge.

The boy at the supercenter said something about a campground nearby.

Alex checked his map app on his phone and found the campground about a third of a mile upstream. He climbed up to the path along the river and headed toward the campground.

Alex's phone rang in his pocket. He hoped it would be some news from Allison, so he pulled it out and checked the caller ID. It was Clint.

"I hit the first two places up in North Phoenix, and I've got nothing," Clint reported. "How about you?"

"I have a lead! Meet me up at the bridge over the East Verde River outside of Payson."

"Aye, aye, cap'n. I'll be there in a little over an hour."

A minute later, his phone rang again. Did Clint need directions?

But Clint wasn't calling back. It was Linda Flowers.

"Hi, Linda, any news about Jared?"

"No, but he and his father didn't return the day his mother said, so I'm concerned you may be right. I'd like to get the sheriff's department out looking at this point. Did Jared mention any friends or places he wanted to visit while he was living with you?"

Alex looked over the tall grass along the bank at the river noisily bubbling. He hoped Linda didn't hear that because it would tip her off that he wasn't in the Phoenix area. He shuffled his feet and kicked a small rock with his shoe.

"I've been racking my brain to come up with something that he might have said, but I can't think of anything. The only guess I have is one of his friends at Adobe, but I just assumed you would have already suggested that."

It was quiet on Linda's end for several seconds. It was quiet for too long. Did she hear the swoosh of the water or the crow calling nearby?

"That's a good idea. We hadn't looked into his friends yet."

"Okay. Jared's birthday is tomorrow, so all this can end soon. I just hope he's okay when we find him."

Alex ended the call and picked up his pace down the path. He needed to find Jared as soon as possible. Ten minutes later, he arrived at a fire pit and Alex knew he was in or near the campground. It appeared to be deserted, so Alex searched the area until the shadows covered all the open campsites. The sun would be behind the trees in thirty minutes.

Alex started back to the bridge when his phone rang again. It was Papa. Alex debated whether he should answer. The light was fading and he didn't have time for small talk, but he answered after the fourth ring.

"Guess where I'm at?"

Alex rolled his eyes. "I don't know. Another fancy restaurant?"

"Nope."

"I don't know then. Where are you?"

"Hear those waves, son? That's the sound of the beach in Hawaii."

Alex pursed his lips and squeezed the phone until his knuckles turned white. He felt like an over inflated balloon that has to let some air out before it bursts.

"You know where I am? I'm in the middle of the freezing cold woods hunting for someone else's runaway son because I care about something besides impressing others with toys, lavish vacations, and the biggest house on the block. I'm tired of everything being about money and status with you! I can't do this right now, Papa."

Papa did not respond for a few seconds, which was unusual, but then he asked a question. "Are the local authorities not cooperating with you? I donated to the congressman's campaign for that district several times when I was still living in Arizona. Do you want me to make some calls and rattle some cages?"

Alex ground his teeth. "That's not necessary. The fur hat you got me from Alaska has been help enough. I really need to go."

Alex hung up the phone and rushed up the path only to realize he had gone the wrong direction. He spun around and stopped after a few steps. Alex took in several quick breaths until he could hold one and slowly exhaled.

It was hard to talk to Papa that way, but he had it bottled up for so long that the virtual container cracked under the stress and truth oozed out. Alex felt lighter for being honest about his feelings instead of always contorting himself to live up to Papa's expectations. He resumed his journey back to the bridge.

Half the sun slipped behind the mountains, and the path back to his SUV was getting darker, so Alex picked up his pace. The sun was down once he arrived, and Alex knew he had to find Jared soon.

Even with a cold-weather sleeping bag, the nights were dropping into the low thirties in town and the upper twenties in the higher elevation forests. Alex waited in his SUV until he saw the familiar headlights from Clint's truck pass over the bridge and park behind him.

Alex met Clint wearing a fur-lined camouflage trapper hat as he pulled gear out of the bed of his truck. He held up two old camping lanterns. "I thought we may need these."

"Great idea, Clint. So, a guy at the supercenter saw Jared buying camping equipment a couple days ago. He said a lot of kids will hide out around here." Alex motioned toward the banks of the river.

"Let's get looking."

The two dads search the area for another hour. Their breath was becoming more visible in the light of the lanterns with each passing minute. Alex was thankful for the warm hat, though thoughts of Papa made him grind his teeth again.

"Where could he be?" Clint whispered as he directed the light of his lantern under a craggy overhang on the river's bank.

"Do you think he found another ride to somewhere else? Maybe somewhere warm?" Alex asked.

"That boy is usually pretty leery of strangers, but he's hitched a ride before to get away from me. I reckon anything's possible this time to get as far away from me as possible."

Alex could hear the pain in Clint's voice. He couldn't believe that he felt a little sorry for his former nemesis.

Ninety minutes later, Alex called off the search. "He's not here. Let's head back to the vehicles."

The two men climbed the bank back to the road when Alex's phone rang.

"Are you coming back home tonight?" Allison asked.

"I'm not sure what to do. The problem is that we don't know where to look. We know that Jared's been around here, but after following every lead and checking every place we can think of, we can't find any trace of him."

"So you didn't find him at Bear Canyon? I thought for sure that's where you'd find him."

"I didn't go to Bear Canyon today. Why do you think he'd be there?"

"I remember how much he talked about it when you and Daniel took him up there. He kept talking about the lake looking like Heaven, plus that's the place he circled a million times on his map."

Alex ran his fingers through his messy hair. "That's got to be it. I forgot all about Bear Canyon because we visited so many other places over the summer while you were in Boston. He loved that lake, and I bet that if he's still up north that I'll find him there!"

"Isn't it freezing up there?" Allison asked.

"It is, and a sleeping bag isn't going to be much protection. Fortunately, Clint had the foresight to bring some camping lanterns, so we should probably hit the road."

"Okay, call me right away if you find him," Allison replied with her voice cracking to hold back the tears. "Be careful, Alex."

"I will. We both will."

Once he ended the call, he turned to Clint. "I've got a solid lead. Let's move your gear to my car. It's got good tires, and where we're headed, we're going to need them."

Chapter 41

T he engine roared as Alex pulled his SUV onto the highway and
started the climb toward Bear Canyon Lake. He looked over at
Clint leaning forward in the passenger seat with his nose a foot from
the windshield.

"You should put on your seatbelt. We could hit a deer or elk up
here."

"I don't care if I get hurt. I'd deserve any pain inflicted on me."

"Why would you say that?" Alex asked.

"I'm a horrible father and my son hates me. I can't get anything
right."

"Jared is a great kid. You can still have a relationship if you're
willing to put forth the effort and change for the better. Nobody's
perfect."

"I bet you've never hit your kids."

Alex nodded. "You're right, I've never hit my kids, but I've made
my share of mistakes now and in the past. I'll continue to make
mistakes, but my kids will always know I love them. They'll know
that I have their best interest at heart even when they don't agree with
or understand my decisions."

Clint leaned back and put on his seatbelt. Alex's mind drifted as
the drive grew quiet. He thought of how distracted and naïve he'd
been with Olivia and how fast kids can veer off the straight path. It
was the same for adults. Alex realized Clint has been off the straight
path for so long that he may not remember what it looks like but
could get back on with some effort and forgiveness. Even the most
lost father's mistakes are redeemable.

Seventy-five minutes later, Alex and Clint pulled off the gravel road onto a dirt area used as a parking lot for the lake. His vehicle was the only one parked in the area, and as far as Alex could tell, he was the only one at the lake. The county planned to close the road for the winter that weekend, and nobody else had a reason to fight the cold in that remote part of the forest.

Alex jumped out of his SUV and the frigid air slapped his face. Each breath formed a unique cloud of crystals until the next one replaced it. He looked at his watch.

"It's after midnight so it's going to get even colder. Let's stick together on the search so that we don't miss anything. We've got to find Jared fast if he's here."

"I'll follow you," Clint replied.

They trekked down to the shoreline and surveyed the area. Ten steps into their search, one lantern went out.

"I guess I didn't fill that one up all the way," Clint said as he shook the lantern.

"That's fine. We can still do this with one lantern."

Alex guessed he knew how a ninety-year-old man felt walking along the water's edge. The single lantern was marginally effective at cutting through the dark, moonless light and the footing was treacherous on the wet, wobbly rocks. Every step was an adventure and a potential broken bone.

"Let's walk the entire perimeter to ensure we cover every potential place to hide," Alex stated.

Two and a half hours after they started, in what would have been a sixty-minute trip during the day, Alex and Clint completed a full loop of the lake. They climbed back into Alex's car and turned on the heater.

They took turns using the one lantern and Alex's superior hat and mittens to search for Jared while the other warmed up in the SUV.

This routine continued until the pre-dawn glow appeared in the sky.

Clint left for his search while Alex kicked off his shoes and warmed his icy feet under the heater after his shift. The shimmering lake outside his windshield reminded him of the day he hiked with Daniel and Jared from their campsite to the lake. Alex could still see the look on Jared's face when he climbed up the small hill above Bear Canyon Lake and got an eagle's eye view of a place he previously only dreamt about. Alex closed his eyes and prayed. He kept his eyes closed until he got too warm and turned down the heat. Straight out of his windshield across a small inlet on the lake was the hill Jared ascended on his first trip to Bear Canyon Lake. Alex pictured the joy on his face.

"That's it!" Alex shouted into the empty vehicle.

Alex jumped out and yelled for Clint to return. The sky lightened enough to ditch the lantern as they started toward the hill. They needed to reach the opposite side since that's the direction Jared came from the campground during the summer. Ten minutes later, they got to the top of the rocky hill and scanned the area but saw no sign of Jared. Clint hopped down the west side while Alex chose the east side. He slid down several large boulders until he reached the bottom. He backed up several steps to get a full view of the hill.

"I thought for sure he'd be here," Alex muttered as he looked up and down and then left and right to find Jared.

Defeated, Alex started toward Clint when something caught his eye between two massive boulders. He craned his neck to get a better look.

"Is that a red jacket?"

Alex darted toward the small clearing between two boulders and noticed a familiar red jacket covering the head of someone curled up in a sleeping bag. He yanked away a poncho tied above him and gently pulled back the hood to get a better look. It was Jared.

"Clint, over here. I found him!"

Alex gasped when he saw Jared's face. It was pale, with a large purple bruise over his left eye. Alex wasn't even sure Jared was alive, so he shook him.

Clint arrived to find Jared looking lifeless between the boulders. He dropped to his knees and helped Alex shake him. Clint kept repeating, "I'm sorry, Jared," as they watched for signs of life.

Jared opened his eyes.

"You're alive. Thank God!" Alex exclaimed.

Clint popped up and shuffled several yards away. He kicked at rocks and punched a tree.

"What's wrong?" Alex yelled.

Clint rushed back to Alex's side with bright red-rimmed eyes. "I can't believe we almost lost him because of me."

Alex grabbed Clint by both shoulders, "You're here now and your son needs you. Let's get Jared out of here."

Clint nodded and Alex turned back to Jared.

He tried to talk, but nothing came out. Jared was alive but in terrible condition, and he needed medical attention.

"Jared, can you stand up?"

Jared shook his head.

Alex helped Jared sit up and then slid his neck under one arm.

"Clint, get under his other arm and we can lift him up and help him to my SUV."

The two men lifted Jared to his feet. His head bobbed on his neck until he noticed Clint.

"Why's he—?"

"I'm here to help, son. I'm sorry about everything. I'll never do that again," Clint interrupted. He pulled off Alex's fur hat and put it on Jared.

Jared rolled his head next to Alex's face on the opposite side.

"It's true Jared. Your dad is here to help."

Jared's head dropped as he lost consciousness again.

"Let's go!" Alex shouted.

They buckled Jared into the front seat and Alex covered him with his coat. He cranked up the heated seats and the blower as high as possible. Alex reversed out of the small lot and spewed gravel as his SUV sped down the dirt road while Clint watched from the backseat. They needed to get Jared to the hospital in Payson as fast as possible.

One hour later, Alex pulled onto the street for the Payson Medical Center and followed the directions for the Emergency entrance around the single-level cluster of medical buildings. He pulled up to the sliding doors, parked, and sent Clint inside to get help. A minute later, Clint arrived with a nurse and they helped Jared out of the SUV and into the wheelchair. The nurse spun Jared around and took him back through the doors while Clint followed close behind, wringing his hands.

Alex found a parking spot and caught up with Clint at Registration. He took a seat in the waiting area and prayed while Clint filled out paperwork.

A short while later, Clint entered the waiting room.

"Only family members are allowed back in the ER. I'll come back and keep you updated on Jared or I'll tell that staff it's okay to share any news with you. Thank you for helping me find my son."

Alex watched Clint hurry back to the ER, and he turned his attention to the TV on the wall next to him. After a minute of watching CNN, Alex pulled out his phone and texted Allison. He shared that they found Jared and that he was in the hospital in Payson but couldn't go back to the ER with him. Alex ended the text to Allison that he'll call her after he spoke to the doctor.

Two hours later, Alex woke from dozing in his chair when he heard his name.

"Alex Garza for Jared Gellar?"

Alex saw a man in surgical scrubs and mask standing in the entrance of the waiting room. When Alex stood, he took off his mask and walked toward him.

"Are you Alex Garza?"

Alex nodded.

"I'm sorry."

Chapter 42

A lex couldn't believe his ears. They were too late. First, he failed Edgar and now Jared. He couldn't save anyone that he tried to help turn their life around.

Visions of Jared's face flashed through his mind when Alex noticed that the doctor was still talking. He said something about toes. Alex rapidly blinked his eyes and shook his head.

"Excuse me, what did you say?"

"I said that I'm sorry, but we couldn't save all of Jared's toes. They all had pretty severe frostbite and unfortunately, we had to remove two of his toes on his left foot. He is also recovering from dehydration and a mild case of hypothermia. He'll make a full recovery from hypothermia but will need physical therapy to help him walk correctly with missing toes. It's a good thing you found him when you did."

Alex exhaled loudly. "Thank you, doctor."

"He'll be moved into a regular room soon and then you can see him."

The doctor left the waiting room and Alex fell back into his chair, battered from the peaks and valleys of his emotions. He dialed Allison's number on his phone and told her the news.

After another hour and a trip to the hospital cafeteria for a late lunch, Alex received word he could see Jared.

Alex followed the nurse down the corridor to Jared's room and he looked out a window as he passed. Clint was sitting by himself on a bench with his face buried in his hands in the hospital courtyard.

"Is that Jared's father?" Alex stopped and asked the nurse.

"Yes, he took the news about the amputation of his son's toes pretty hard. He stormed outside right after we told him."

"Can I go out and check on him?"

"Sure, come check in at the nurse's station when you're ready to see Jared."

Alex went outside and sat next to Clint. Once he was aware someone was next to him, Clint sat up straight and looked ahead. "I can't believe I did that to my son."

Alex returned a quick nod but did not respond.

"He's never going to want to see me again and I don't blame him. What am I going to do?"

"You should get some help. Work on yourself first and then you can work on your relationship with Jared."

Clint continued to look straight ahead.

"Let me take Jared home so we can help him recover and you take that time to concentrate on your recovery."

Alex was getting used to the more balanced Clint, but felt this suggested plan might have pushed him too far. He watched Clint squirm on the cold bench as he pondered the prospect of getting help for himself. Clint jumped up from the bench and Alex did the same. He watched Clint closely as he extended his hand to Alex.

"I'm going to get some help. Take good care of Jared."

Alex shook his hand.

"I will."

"Thank you for helping me."

Alex left the courtyard and after a quiet knock, tip-toed into Jared's room.

Jared sat up in the bed with a blank look on his face. Alex noticed a large bandage over his left foot.

"How are you feeling, buddy?" Alex asked as he took a seat next to Jared.

Jared turned his head and tried to smile but failed. Next, he tried to talk, but nothing came out.

Alex reached over to the water cup next to the bed and handed it to Jared. He took several sips and passed it back to Alex.

Jared swallowed hard and tried to speak again. "Okay, I guess."

"I'm thrilled that you are alright. The doctor says that you'll make a full recovery."

Jared raised his head to see the bandage on his foot.

"Yes, your foot will recover too," Alex answered the question that he knew was on Jared's mind.

"What's going to happen to me? I know Clint helped find me, but I still don't want to live there. What am I going to do now?"

Jared coughed multiple times and motioned for the water again, so Alex hurried to refill his cup and handed it back to him. After a long drink, Jared tried to talk, but Alex put his hand up to stop him.

"You don't have to decide anything right now. Did you forget what today is?" Alex asked with a wry smile.

Jared's forehead wrinkled as he squinted at the blank wall, trying to remember the significance of this date. He reached out and grabbed Alex's shirt and twisted it.

"It's my birthday!"

"Yes, it is! It's November fourth and you are eighteen today, so you can decide where you go tomorrow."

Jared let go of Alex's shirt and his arms dropped by his side. It was the most relaxed Alex had seen Jared in months.

"Can I go—Can I go back with you?" Jared asked in a whisper.

"I think that's a good possibility. I'll work on that and you try to rest."

Jared smiled and his eyes fluttered. "Okay."

Alex patted Jared on the shoulder and let him fall asleep. Once he was in a deep slumber, Alex left the room and called Allison from an empty hospital room a few doors down. He shared all the details of his search and discovery of Jared. His update included the medical report from the doctor, Alex's plan to bring Jared home with him after he's released, and Clint's plan to get treatment for his addiction in the hope that he and Jared would eventually reunite.

Alex thought he'd better check on Jared. When he arrived in the room, Jared was holding a cupcake with a candle and Clint by his side.

Alex backed out slowly and watched them interact. Clint shared details of the search and commented on how he wished he could have seen Bear Canyon Lake in the light. He pulled out of his jacket pocket an old map that Clint claimed was buried at the bottom of his glove box. He opened it and pointed to some of the other places Jared circled as a future destination. Alex noticed a brief smile appear and quickly vanish on Jared's face.

Maybe there is hope for this father, Alex thought.

When Clint left the room, Alex caught up with him so they could discuss the current matter with ADCJ.

"ADCJ is still looking for Jared so I need to let them know we've found him. What should I tell them?" Alex asked.

Clint paused for several seconds and smiled, "Tell them me and Jared were on that fishing trip in the woods. We had a good time, but it got so cold the last night that Jared got frostbite and that's why we are here. That's the story I want to tell."

"Okay, I will. Can I also tell them that I'll take Jared home with me so you can work on getting better yourself?"

Clint nodded and put his hand on Alex's shoulder. "Make the call."

Alex left Linda Flowers a voicemail letting her know that he'd at last gotten a hold of Jared. He shared the story that Clint wanted to tell and followed up with his request to take Jared home instead of back to Buckeye.

"Jared wants to finish up his school year and recover at home with us in Scottsdale. Clint Gellar is okay with it. I think he's going to try to get some help for himself."

Alex ended his message saying that he'd call back tomorrow during regular business hours to catch her live.

The next morning, the night shift doctor told Alex that they'll discharge Jared after changing the dressings on his toes. He'd have to see a doctor in the Phoenix area several times a week but could recover at home. Alex ran to the cafeteria to grab a coffee while waiting for the doctor on the next shift to come and discharge Jared.

On his way back to the room, Alex's phone rang. It was Linda from ADJC.

"Alex, I listened to your plan and I'm okay with it, but there's one hitch. Jared is still legally under the custody of ADJC until a judge releases him. We need his parents to bring him in to get him in front of a judge and do this the right way, so Jared isn't just switching from one problem to another."

"I think Jared could get their cooperation to do that."

Chapter 43

Jared moved back into his old room down the hall from Gaby, Daniel, and Olivia. Other than his new physical therapy sessions three days a week, he resumed his previous routines with the Garza family. Jared went back to Scottsdale North High School to complete his senior year. Olivia drove him to and from school every day, and they also went to the high school ministry events together two nights a week. He checked in regularly with his parents, who had seen an addiction counselor.

One week before school finals in December, Jared surprised Alex and Allison with some good news. Scottsdale Community College accepted his application, and he could attend in the fall once he graduated from high school. Jared would be the first person in his family to attend college. The news elated Alex and Allison, so they planned a quick party for that weekend and invited all their friends, family, and co-workers to celebrate the good news.

During the party, Alex visited all the guests in the house to celebrate Jared's accomplishments. Next, he went outside to talk to everyone huddled under the patio heaters on the back patio. He hugged Mateo and Daniella when he found them enjoying cheese and crackers from the food table. Together, they stood and watched Jared move from guest to guest to receive congratulations.

"You've done an amazing job with that young man," Mateo said while he kept his eye on Jared.

"Thank you, but I didn't really do anything. It was all Jared. I'm so proud of that kid. He's got a bright future now, and I'm not sure I would have guessed this would have happened when we first met him one year ago."

"He couldn't have done it without your guidance and support," Mateo said." I think this was a big moment for you because you didn't just save Jared. You finally saved Edgar. You did it for him, and now someone going down the wrong path return to the right path. All because of you. Edgar would be so proud of you."

Alex tried to respond but couldn't. His lips quivered and then tears flowed.

Mateo wrapped an arm around his shoulder and the brothers stood remembering, grieving, and yet also rejoicing.

Alex found his voice again. "It feels amazing to give someone hanging by a thread, a final thread, the opportunity to redeem themselves and then see them do it. I could never tire of this."

"I hear you, little brother. I feel the same way about ESBB."

Alex nodded. The life he wanted, the one he could live with his whole heart, was within reach. But to have it, there was a final thread in his life that needed to be clipped.

For the next few hours, Alex enjoyed the company of many friends and co-workers. As the number of party-goers thinned out, Allison, Mateo, and Daniella joined Alex at a table of Emerson Churchill co-workers near a heater outside. They took turns telling stories about all the events for the year and laughed at the gaffes of their co-workers.

Mr. Park arrived at the party and joined the group. Once the operations manager finished telling her story, Mr. Park spoke.

"Alex, congratulations on an exceptional year personally and professionally. Very impressive."

He raised his glass and everyone else standing at the high-top table did the same.

"Thank you, Mr. Park."

"You may need to celebrate one more time in the new year."

Alex furrowed his eyebrows. "One more time?"

"I'm recommending you for partner at Emerson Churchill. We'll vote on it after Christmas and the New Year."

"I'm sorry, Mr. Park, but that won't be necessary."

The table grew dead quiet, and Mr. Park tilted his head.

"Excuse me?"

"I will resign my position at the end of the year so I can work full time at ESBB. We are going to put prisons out of business."

Mr. Park scoffed, "What? How do you expect to do that?"

"Education. We will expand Education Stars to juveniles, families of inmates, and inmates long-term after serving their time. We'll turn inmates and potential inmates into engineers, doctors, artists, entrepreneurs, or whatever they choose. Our plan is to force states to close prisons across America because they are no longer needed, and if this lofty dream is possible, ESBB is the organization to do it."

"I thought you wanted to be a partner. Isn't that why you worked so hard all year?" Mr. Park asked with confusion still plastered on his face.

Alex watched Jared walk out of the house onto the back patio.

"It was until I met that young man." Alex motioned to Jared. "He taught me so much about what's truly important in life. Yes, a wonderful career is important, but not the most important thing for me. He reminded me about why I started ESBB in the first place, so I'm going to pursue that dream now."

Mr. Park shook his head and took several steps away from the group, "I think you are making a huge mistake walking away from becoming a partner, but I'll respect your wishes. Best of luck in your new endeavor."

Alex watched Mr. Park leave and then turned to all the open mouths at the table. Soon each co-worker took their turn to shake Alex's hand and wish him luck. Next, Alex turned to Allison. She did not look as happy as Mateo at his surprise revelation.

He pulled her aside and asked, "Are you mad?"

"No, I'm not mad, just a little shocked."

"I know but I've been thinking about this a lot lately. We can make it work financially with some cutbacks. I don't need such a fancy car and we can find other areas to save."

"I know you've been thinking about this so I'm happy for you. Does this mean you won't be working twelve-to-fifteen-hour days anymore?"

"I'll work hard like I always do, but I expect to make a lot more recitals and ball games than I did before," Alex replied.

The stoic expression on Allison's face turned into a bright smile. She moved to her tiptoes and planted a peck on Alex's cheek. "Good! I'm so glad you'll get to pursue your passion and dream." Allison whispered, "and I get my husband back."

The new year brought new experiences, opportunities, and challenges to the Garzas and their house guest. Olivia and Jared joined the youth ministry at church as teachers to junior high students. Jared even made new friends at church with a couple of high school seniors from another school.

The high schoolers also thrived in their academics. Olivia got back to straight A's in all her classes, and Jared received the best grade he could remember. His love for history paid off when he achieved an A on his last report card in May. He graduated from high school and planned to start his freshman year at Scottsdale Community College in August.

Allison made up for Alex's lost income with more gigs at the Scottsdale Center for Performing Arts, while Alex immersed himself in fundraising for ESBB. By April, the non-profit had raised fifty percent more than the same period during the previous year, which covered Alex's new salary within the organization.

To celebrate Jared's high school graduation, they sent out invitations to the biggest guest list ever. They would have catered food under a tent in their back yard and even paid for two hours of live music.

Days after Jared took his last final exam in high school and the night before his big graduation party, Alex noticed Jared was talking to someone in the driveway. Alex squinted and looked closer at the security camera feed on his phone. Jared was standing outside of his father's pickup truck talking to Clint and Becky.

Ten minutes later, Jared waved to the truck as Clint sped away and walked back into the house.

"Was that your parents?"

"Yeah."

"They would have been welcome to come inside to visit with you."

"I know. They were excited to give me a graduation gift before anyone else.

Jared held up a gift card with a red and white bullseye on it and a picture frame. "They wanted to give this to me before the big party so it was a quick visit."

"That's great. What's in the frame?" Alex asked.

Jared looked at the frame for a few seconds and then held it up for Alex to see.

His heart skipped a beat when he recognized it was a glittering mosaic image of Bear Canyon Lake.

"My parents made this for me with broken glass around the house and yard. They put it together to make a scene of Bear Canyon Lake for me—" Jared couldn't finish his sentence. He stared at the frame and wiped his eyes.

"That's a very thoughtful gift. I wasn't expecting that," Alex stated as Jared recovered.

"I was pretty shocked, too. The counseling is helping and they've both been sober for over ten weeks now. They know that they still have a long way to go, but I want to support them the best I can. I told them I plan to major in counseling with an emphasis on substance abuse in college. My mom and dad both said they were proud of me. I've waited a long time to hear that and it felt awesome."

The next day, the tent truck and crew arrived and began setting up. Just as the sun was setting, creating a purple and orange fire in the sky, the first guest arrived. The regular guests of Garza events trickled in, but this celebration called for a national guest list.

The full RIHARP crew from Texas arrived in their vehicles. Rey and Christina pulled up first with their two children. Next, John Nickerson and his wife Stacy arrived. Last, Rick and Felicity Powell, along with their former RIHARP inmate James Edmunds pulled in with Pastor Scott in his enormous SUV.

The Texas RIHARP guests mingled with Linda Flowers and the ADJC staff once the music started and the servers passed around trays full of tasty appetizers.

Two hours later, after the band took a break, Pastor Scott clinked his glass and asked everyone to bow their heads. He prayed for Jared and all the graduates leaving high school and entering a new chapter in their lives.

After Pastor Scott finished his prayer, all the guests dispersed and broke out into smaller conversations. Alex saw John Nickerson by the dessert bar, so he meandered over to him.

"Thank you for inventing Sure Cuffs. We would have never met Jared if it weren't for your technology."

"You're very welcome. It's so rewarding to see all the good that has come from Sure Cuffs."

"Do you have any more exciting innovations you're working on?"

Before John could answer, Alex's phone rang in his pocket.

"It's my father," Alex said after he checked the caller ID. "I have to take this."

John smiled, patted Alex on the shoulder, and rejoined the celebration of another life saved by Sure Cuffs.

The End

Author Notification List

R eceive updates about new releases, discounts and promotions, and exclusive stories, in my occasional email notifications. **Sign up now** at: https://robertgoluba.com/newsletter/

OR

Text **NEW** to **(844) 465-7100** to receive a text notification of each new book I release. Nothing else. Ever.

About Author

Robert Goluba is an author of Christian Suspense. He was born and raised in Central Illinois, where he attended college, served in the Army National Guard, and met his wife. At age thirty, after a self-diagnosed allergy to snow, he moved to sunny Arizona where he now lives with his wonderful wife, two kids, and canine companion.

He's published three novels and a novella in the Dangerous Redemption Christian Suspense Collection, Absolute Command (Prequel), Inviting Danger (Book 1), Last Second Chance (Book 2) and A Final Thread (Book 3) to complete the trilogy. He's also published a collection of inspirational short stories based on Bible parables, called Hope Refreshed.

For more information, visit www.RobertGoluba.com